D1500825

PROTECTING SPARROW (SPECIAL FORCES: OPERATION ALPHA)

PREY SECURITY #4

JANE BLYTHE

Cover designed by Q Designs

Dear Readers,

Welcome to the Special Forces: Operation Alpha Fan-Fiction world!

If you are new to this amazing world, in a nutshell the author wrote a story using one or more of my characters in it. Sometimes that character has a major role in the story, and other times they are only mentioned briefly. This is perfectly legal and allowable because they are going through Aces Press to publish the story.

This book is entirely the work of the author who wrote it. While I might have assisted with brainstorming and other ideas about which of my characters to use, I didn't have any part in the process or writing or editing the story.

I'm proud and excited that so many authors loved my characters enough that they wanted to write them into their own story. Thank you for supporting them, and me!

READ ON!
Xoxo
Susan Stoker

I'd like to thank everyone who played a part in bringing this story to life. Particularly my mom who is always there to share her thoughts and opinions with me. The wonderful Amy Queau of Q Designs who made the stunning cover. And my lovely editor Lisa Edwards for all her encouragement and for all the hard work she puts into polishing my work.

CHAPTER ONE

January 18th

 :48 P.M.

IT WAS every pilot's worst nightmare.

Sometimes it didn't matter how good you were at flying —and Sparrow Oswald was one of the best, a member of the Air Force's elite Nightstalkers—the ability to remain in the air was taken out of your hands.

As she fought with the controls, doing what she could to get the damaged Black Hawk to the ground in a way that didn't kill all of them on board, she thought of her family. She'd been excited to be heading home in the morning for a full month of leave before she deployed again. It had been months since she'd last been home. She'd only met her soon-to-be sister-in-law, Olivia, once in person, and hadn't had a chance yet to actually see and hug her niece, Cleo, who had been missing for a decade before being found late last year.

Now, she was never going to get that chance.

Although she was giving it everything she had, Sparrow already knew that the helicopter had been too badly damaged by the missile that had hit it for her to be able to land safely.

It would be a miracle if any of them survived the impending crash.

Her co-pilot knew it too, although just as she was, he was doing everything he could to try to abate some of the damage and get them down in a way that at least gave them all a shot at surviving.

They were currently above the Goda Mountains of Djibouti, returning from a classified mission, she hadn't been expecting any trouble. It was supposed to be a simple flight back to Camp Lemonnier, where she would spend the night before heading back to New York in the morning.

The excitement about seeing her family that she had been feeling just minutes ago had turned into a deep sense of despair, but she kept it hidden from the seven men on board. Sparrow was tiny, not quite five feet tall, and being a woman in a predominantly man's world meant she had to fight to earn the respect her fellow Nightstalkers were given automatically. One thing she had learned early on when she joined the Air Force was to never let them see you sweat. People were much more likely to think you were capable and competent if you acted like you were capable and competent.

So that was what she was doing right now.

The ground was quickly coming up to meet them. She could smell smoke from the damage the missile had caused. She hadn't known until it was too late that someone was firing at them, and she had no idea who that someone was or why they would be shooting at her helo.

What she did know was that she would do her best to attempt to save these men's lives. They were good men, the SEAL team had been kind and respectful, probably in part because of who her family was. The Oswalds were well known in military circles. Her oldest brother Eagle had been a SEAL, next brother Falcon had been in Delta Force, and younger brother Hawk was an Army Ranger. Besides that, she and her five siblings owned one of the best security and black ops companies in the world, Prey Security.

Not that she threw around her family name to garner respect she hadn't earned. Sparrow wanted to be respected because she was good at what she did, not because of her last name.

Still, as good as she was, she wasn't good enough to get this helicopter down without them all dying.

Accepting this, she yelled to the others, "Brace for impact."

Not a single person hesitated to obey, they all trusted her to do her best, while she felt the same acceptance that none of them were walking away from this alive.

While the others braced, Sparrow continued to fight against gravity, working the controls and doing whatever she could to try to minimize impact.

It didn't work.

They hit the ground with bone-breaking force.

Pain speared through her head as it slammed into something and the world around her disappeared.

It was a groan that roused her.

Sparrow wasn't sure if it was her own or someone else's, and she wondered how she was even still alive.

She should be dead.

They should all be dead.

It was simple physics.

Their altitude when they were hit, the speed with which

they dropped, the fact that they were just tiny people in a piece of metal and the earth was so much bigger, all of it meant she should have died on impact.

Only it seemed she hadn't.

Another groan caught her attention, and this time Sparrow knew it hadn't come from her.

Someone else had survived too.

They were really fighting against the odds today. Could she dare to hope that more of them were alive? Was it too much to pray that all eight of them had survived?

Ignoring the blinding pain in her head, Sparrow turned to see if her co-pilot had survived.

One look at the man confirmed he had not.

His neck had been partially severed, his head hanging off at a weird angle, and even in the dark she could see his eyes staring sightlessly ahead.

He was dead. That meant one—or hopefully more—of the SEALs had made the noises she had heard.

Sparrow unbuckled her harness and reached out to press her hands against what was left of the side of the helicopter to help her stand, and pain rocketed through her. It was focused between her left shoulder and neck, she'd probably broken her collarbone. Before attempting to stand again she took stock of her body, trying to figure out where else she was hurt. Besides the hammering in her head and her collarbone everything else just felt sore and battered.

Sending up a quick prayer of thanks, she was more careful as she stood this time and cradled her injured arm against her chest as she made her way to the back of the helo.

The smell of blood and human waste was strong, and she gagged before leaning over and vomiting up the contents of her stomach.

Feeling no better, she ignored her discomfort and made her way from motionless body to motionless body.

One SEAL was dead, then two, then three, and then four, and she was starting to believe that she had been imagining the groaning or that it really had been coming from her.

Was she the only survivor?

It wasn't until she reached over SEAL number five that she was finally rewarded with the thump of a pulse and ragged breathing.

Relief hit her deep. She didn't want to be the only one left alive. Maybe it was cowardly of her, but the thought of being out here alone until someone could send help—she'd called in the fact that they were hit but it would take a while to get a team to them—was not an appealing one.

"Hold on, Colt," she told the badly injured man as she went to check his last teammate. SEAL number six was alive too, and relief that two others had survived quickly turned to concern over how she would move two huge SEALs on her own.

The smell of gas was heavy in the air, and Sparrow was worried the helo was going to blow, so she didn't have time to come up with a good plan. Instead, she just grabbed the nearest pack, knowing it would have what they needed to survive for at least a few days inside it and a couple of weapons. She put the pack on, slung the weapons over her shoulders, ignored the way the world tilted and swirled around her, and the pain in her collarbone, and grabbed onto Colt.

As soon as she started dragging him toward the helicopter's door he groaned, his eyes fluttering.

"Colt?"

"Sparrow?" the man rasped.

"Yeah, just hold on, sorry, I know this hurts, but I have to get you out," she told him, continuing to make progress pulling the much larger man along with her toward the jagged hole where the side of the helicopter used to be.

5

"Anyone else make it?"

"Just you, me, and Heat." Blood dribbled down her face, and tears of pain streamed down her cheeks. Keeping her balance was hard enough on her own let alone dragging along a man twice her size, but she didn't stop.

Couldn't stop.

"Lemme help …" Colt slurred, but she didn't bother wasting energy telling him he couldn't help right now.

The lower halves of both his legs had been severed. Unless help came quickly he was likely going to bleed to death.

But right now, he was alive, and she would do everything she could to make sure he and Heat remained that way.

Out of the Black Hawk now, she pulled him over the rough and uneven ground until they were what she deemed a safe distance away should the helo explode.

Although her body begged for rest, Sparrow turned and headed back toward the helicopter to get Heat. She swayed as she went, but somehow managed to remain upright.

She was about halfway back when the Black Hawk exploded.

The force sent her sprawling to the ground.

She thought she heard screams, but reality was even if he had been conscious, Heat would have been killed instantly.

She hoped.

She prayed.

The screams were probably her own.

Unconsciousness came calling for her, but she fought against it. Colt was hurt badly, he needed help, she had to get to him … had to help him … had to get them someplace safe until help came … despite her best efforts her eyes closed, and she faded away.

* * *

9:12 P.M.

ETHAN ZIMMERMAN FLEW his plane toward Camp Lemonnier, Africa's only permanent US base. He had headed out as soon as he'd received a call from Eagle Oswald. He knew the Oswald family—as pretty much everyone associated with the military did—and had served with his younger sister Sparrow.

It seemed there was someone with a grudge out to get the Oswald family, and Sparrow specifically had just been threatened.

Eagle hadn't been able to get any information on his sister which meant she was probably out on a mission, but if she was here in Africa then sooner or later, she'd turn up on the base. All he had to do was fly there and wait, warn her as soon as he saw her if her brother hadn't already gotten word to her.

His satellite phone rang and keeping his attention half on flying he answered. "Zimmerman."

"Hey, Ethan, it's Colonel Hackett," the person on the other end announced.

"Colonel," he greeted, wondering why the man was calling and how he'd even gotten this number. It had been several years since he'd retired from the Air Force, and he hadn't kept in contact with anyone.

"Eagle Oswald has been calling in a panic, worried about his sister," the Colonel explained.

"He called me too."

"You still in Airolaf? Still flying medical aid around Africa?"

"Yes. I just left, heading for the base, thought since Sparrow and I were friends I'd come personally to see if I could find her."

"We just got a distress call from her about fifteen minutes ago. Her helicopter was shot. We've lost contact with them, last known location was over the Goda Mountains, right near you. Since we know this could be personal, an attack aimed at Sparrow, and I knew you were in the area, I'm hoping you can help us try to find the helo. We're sending a team, but you're closer, and since we don't know what's going on and can't make contact, the quicker we find them the better."

For a moment Ethan couldn't speak. Sparrow's helo had been shot down? Chances were she and everyone else on board were already dead. But if they weren't …

"On it," he said already altering his course.

"Ethan, this request isn't anything official, it's just me reaching out to an old friend and asking him to fly around over the mountains for a bit, see if he can find anything out of the ordinary."

"Got it." They weren't really friends, but nobody needed to know that.

"Keep in contact."

"Let me know if you find them and if there's anything I can do to help."

"Will do."

When he hung up the phone, Ethan immediately punched in another number and waited for it to be answered. Had Sparrow's helicopter been shot down by someone after her, or was the helo targeted because it belonged to the US military? In these parts, reactions were mixed when it came to the US and its military base. He knew this firsthand because a lot of villages were reluctant to accept the medical supplies he delivered because they believed it was a bribe of sorts from the US. More than once he had had to offer several assurances that he worked for a charity called Medi-Hope that provided medical supplies and medications, they were not in any way affiliated with the military and were actually an international aid agency based out of England.

"Did you speak to her?" Eagle Oswald asked as soon as he answered. No wasting time on pleasantries, not that Ethan had expected it from Eagle. The man was intense and very good at what he did, in part because he was straight as an arrow and didn't beat around the bush. What you saw was what you got from the billionaire security firm owner.

Breaking the news as gently as he could he said, "I just got a call from Colonel Hackett at Camp Lemonnier ..."

"Hold on, let me put you on speaker," Eagle interrupted, obviously sensing this was going to be bad news. "Okay, you're on with me, Raven, her fiancé Max, Falcon, Falcon's girlfriend Hope, Dove, and my fiancée Olivia."

Although he had been friends with Sparrow for years and had met all three of her brothers at various times, and Raven's ex-husband—who was now apparently her fiancé again—pararescueman Max Hathaway, he had no idea who Olivia and Hope were, or even that Eagle and Falcon had met women and fallen in love. One of the reasons he'd moved to Africa was because he needed to get away from the memories that had been trying to swallow him whole. Part of the problem with that though, was he'd lost contact with a lot of people he used to know, the Oswald family included.

"What do you know?" Eagle asked.

"About fifteen minutes ago, Sparrow called in that her helo had been shot, they've since lost contact with her," he explained.

He could hear shocked gasps and knew how hard this must be for Sparrow's family. From what he knew of them they had grown up very unconventionally on an off-the-grid farm. The six siblings were close, and this had to be hard for them, especially after the brief recap Eagle had given him on what had happened over the last few months. Sometimes you had all the money in the world to protect yourself and the skills and training to do it, and it still didn't mean you could stop the inevitable from happening.

This he knew all too well.

"Chances are no one survived the crash," Eagle said slowly. The man didn't even pretend to think that the helo hadn't crashed. If Sparrow hadn't checked back in it was because she couldn't.

"She crashed in the mountains right near where I live, I'm headed there now, and they'll be sending a team out to search as well," Ethan explained. "I'll find her, you have my word on that. If she's alive I'll get her someplace safe, and if she's not then at least you'll know what happened, and I'll bring her body home to you." It wasn't a promise he made lightly. He knew how important it was for closure to be able to bury your loved one in a place where you could go and visit their body. Pretty much the only time he returned to the States these days was to visit his wife's grave.

"If you need anything, just let me know. If you don't have her located within the next twelve hours, I'll pull one of my teams off a mission and send them out. You need us there, and we will get straight on a plane." From the tone of Eagle's voice, Ethan could tell he was considering just getting on a plane and flying straight to Djibouti immediately.

"Just give us a bit of time to search first," he said, knowing it would take a while. The Goda Mountains were a region of almost one thousand square kilometers. Depending on where the helo crashed, it could take them the better part of a couple of days to locate them. But Eagle and his family coming over here wasn't going to speed things up, and having to handle her family—even though they wouldn't be hysterical or demanding—was only going to slow things down.

"I'm trusting you to find my little sister, Ethan," Eagle said gravely.

"And I won't let you down. I promise," he added. Making promises wasn't something that Ethan did lightly. He knew that promises were easily broken even with the best of intentions. The last promise he'd made had been to his wife, Sierra. He had promised her that they would get her well, that he would find a treatment that worked, that he wouldn't let her die.

But she had died.

He'd broken that promise to the woman he loved and that had haunted him ever since.

Still, there wasn't anything else he could say. He would keep looking until he found Sparrow. Whether she was alive or dead, he would bring her home to her family.

"Thank you," Eagle said.

A chorus of other thank-yous echoed from the others, and he muttered a quick you're welcome and hung up.

Uneasiness settled on him. Sparrow was a friend, one who had kept in contact with him sporadically after he'd lost his wife, but the last time he'd seen her he'd felt … something akin to attraction. Sparrow was a beautiful woman, tough and strong, smart and funny, she would be a great catch, but that was just the problem.

He wasn't fishing.

He'd already found love and lost it. There was no way he would put himself through that again and falling in love with someone else felt like a betrayal to Sierra.

It wasn't like Sparrow was looking for love either, and she had never given any indication that she was attracted to him. If he found her alive, he'd send her right back home to her family and would probably never see her again.

Then he'd go back to his small African house where he

lived alone with only the memories of his dead wife for company.

* * *

9:37 P.M.

PAIN SHRIEKED through her collarbone as she dragged the much larger man across the rough ground.

Sparrow knew she couldn't go on much longer. She had already thrown up so many times there was nothing left in her stomach, but still she continued to dry retch. The dizziness was getting worse not better, and the pain was so bad it was all she could do not to scream.

Even if she had survived the crash injury-free, moving the big SEAL would have been difficult. As it was, she wasn't sure she could go on much further.

"Sparrow, stop," Colt murmured.

She did, long enough to wipe a bead of sweat out of her eye anyway. Sweat poured down her, drenching her clothes, something she knew would be a problem when she finally stopped moving. It was January, and it got cold in this area at night, both she and Colt were at genuine risk of hypothermia.

"Can't," she said breathlessly, stretching her back then reaching down again to grab his tactical vest and resume pulling him further from the crash site. "We haven't gone far enough away yet." The burning Black Hawk was a fiery beacon for whoever had shot them down to locate them. It was only her and Colt left alive, and she was the only one who was mobile so it was up to her to get them someplace safe.

"You're ... hurt ..." Colt said haltingly, his voice strained and heavy with pain. "Need ... rest."

"I know you do. I'll get you someplace safe soon," she promised. She was looking for a cave, or a crevice, where she could hole up, something that allowed her to protect them both until help arrived.

Colt's hand grasped hers. "Not me ... you. You ... need rest."

She waved off his concerns. "I'll rest later," she told him but didn't really mean it. She needed to remain alert and watch out for them. Already she had a mental checklist going. First thing was to get somewhere safe before whoever shot them down arrived. Then she'd do what she could for Colt's injuries. She'd already put on pressure bandages laced with clotting agents and tied tourniquets once she'd gotten him away from the helo, but she wanted to see what else she could do. After that, she would backtrack and do what she could to clear away the bloody trail they'd left behind them. Then there was nothing to do but watch and see who arrived first, help or whoever had tried to kill them.

Beginning her trek again, Colt let out an almost inhuman scream as his damaged legs were pulled across the rough ground.

The sound was something Sparrow knew she would never forget, and she prayed he would hurry up and pass out again, for her sake as well as his.

Thankfully, after another agonized scream, Colt did in fact lose consciousness.

Weaving on her feet, Sparrow somehow managed to keep moving, and when she spotted a rocky outcrop that provided shelter and some cover with a few shrubs and more rocks she headed toward it.

There were no more sounds from Colt, and she was glad that he was out of pain for the moment. Her own pain levels were off the charts, but she was awake and in one piece, which meant she had a lot to be grateful for.

When she reached the outcrop, Sparrow almost cried in relief.

Her body begged her for rest, even just a moment to sit and close her eyes, but she resisted temptation.

There was too much to do.

Colt was counting on her.

She did let out a sob of relief when she shrugged out of the heavy pack and immediately the release of pressure on her broken collarbone eased some of her pain.

Opening the pack, she rifled through it, finding the first aid kit. There were more bandages and painkillers, but what she really needed was fluids and blood for a transfusion, and there was none of either.

Sparrow removed the dirty, blood-soaked bandages and used what she had to clean Colt's wounds, thankful that he didn't wake up. She wasn't sure she could do this while he was awake and looking at her. It wasn't that she was queasy per se, but she hated being the cause of another person's pain. It was one of the reasons she'd gravitated toward the Air Force. She was a Nightstalker, the Air Force's elite. It wasn't like she'd never fired at the enemy and killed people, but that was different, that was from a distance. Causing pain up close like she was with Colt right now made her queasy.

When she was finished cleaning and re-bandaging his legs, once again tying tourniquets around both in a probably futile attempt to stop the bleeding, she staggered back to her feet. Leaving his weapons and pack close by in case he woke up and needed them, she could be caught or captured, she wanted Colt to at least have a chance at surviving without her.

Finding a broken branch near their little hideout, Sparrow snagged it and backtracked the way they had come doing her best to wipe away evidence of her footprints and Colt's blood. Although she thought she had done a reasonable job she was sure that if someone was intent on finding them there would still be a trail to follow.

Still, she'd done the best she could in the dark and headed back to Colt, wiping away these sets of footprints as she went.

Her head was spinning dangerously.

The world faded in and out around her.

Doggedly she kept walking.

"You have to get back to Colt," she murmured aloud. It was the only thing keeping her going. Oswalds were nothing if not persistent and determined. They'd had to learn how to be growing up on a farm where they grew all their own food, produced their own material for clothes, and had no electricity or running water. Every day had been a struggle to survive that most people couldn't understand.

Somehow, she managed to make it back to Colt and dropped to her knees beside him to check his pulse. He was still alive, but the bandages were already soaked with blood.

Her hands shook badly but somehow, she managed to grip the end of the tourniquet and tighten it. It wasn't enough, she was too weak to get it as tight as it needed to be, not that it was probably going to make a difference.

As much as she didn't want to admit it, Sparrow knew that Colt was dying. There just wasn't anything she could do for him out here.

Sparrow picked up a weapon. She'd go and do a perimeter check then come and see how Colt was doing. Then she'd alternate between the two until someone came for them.

She just prayed Colt made it that long.

Ignoring her body's pleas for rest, Sparrow shoved to her feet.

And immediately blacked out.

When she came too again her head was resting on something soft. For a moment she couldn't place where she was.

When she went to move something pressed very lightly on her shoulders. "Rest for a moment, Sparrow."

"Colt?"

"Take a moment. You're hurt too," he said, and she realized he must have woken up while she was out and pulled her head into his lap.

"Not as bad as you are." Pressing her good hand to her head as though that could soothe the pain, she sat up slowly. "How are you feeling?"

"Not gonna make it, Sparrow."

"You will," she said firmly.

"No … won't. Body already … shutting down."

"I'll give you another shot of morphine, see if I can get those tourniquets tighter, add more bandages," she rambled, already reaching for the first aid kit.

"Won't … help. Tell my wife I … love her. Her and the kids … my everything. Tell her I'm … sorry. Didn't want it to end this way … wanted to grow old with her."

Colt's breathing was harsh. Even in the dim light she could see his color was bad, and his whole body was shaking badly. The bandages were soaked, and blood puddled beneath his two stumps. Without being able to give him a transfusion and close up those wounds he would bleed out.

Sooner rather than later.

How could she deny him his dying wish?

"I'll tell her. I'll make sure she knows you died a hero," she promised, wiping at the tears that were falling.

"You make sure … you get … yourself … out of … here," he wheezed. He was struggling to breathe, it wasn't going to be long.

"You want another shot of morphine?"

"Yeah."

She prepared the drug, injected it, and then took Colt's hand. She might not be able to save his life, but she could at least make sure he wasn't alone when he died. "I'm right here, Colt," she assured him. She put her free hand on his forehead and gently stroked his hair. She wished there was something she could do, but there wasn't. "I'm sorry."

"Not ... your ... fault."

"I'm the pilot. We crashed. Of course it's my fault."

"No. Nothing you ... could do."

Sparrow didn't agree.

It was her job as the pilot to get her people safely back to the ground. She had failed. Six people were already dead, and she was about to sit helplessly by and watch the seventh die.

* * *

10:04 P.M.

As soon as he saw the flaming wreckage, Ethan knew he'd found them.

It wasn't easy to set his small plane down, but the helicopter had crashed in a valley, and there was just enough space to land. It helped that he had spent the first eight years of his flying career in the Air Force, working hard to become a Nightstalker. He could set a plane or helo down anywhere, and he had regularly flown while being shot at. In comparison to some of the things he'd done, this was a piece of cake.

Despite that, it had been a long time since he'd had to set his plane down in conditions like this. Usually, he flew from the small base where he and three other aid workers lived together, to whatever village they were delivering medical supplies to. That more often than not meant landing on a nearby road. Nowhere near as nice as a landing strip if he was landing at an airport, but better than setting down in a valley filled with rough terrain.

His skills might be a little rusty, but he landed without incident and immediately grabbed his weapon and jumped from the plane. Whether this had something to do with the threat against Sparrow and the Oswald family or the US military, someone had shot the Black Hawk down, and that person had done it for a reason. No doubt they were out here somewhere, moving in, looking for survivors, but he didn't go anywhere without his weapon. Ethan might not be in the military anymore, but he was still in Africa, and it always paid to be prepared.

Now Ethan cautiously approached the fiery wreckage, looking for signs that someone had made it off the helo alive.

Had it exploded on impact?

If it had, then no one had survived.

But if it hadn't caught fire until after it had been on the ground for at least a couple of minutes, then there was a chance someone was still alive.

Ethan couldn't help but hope that if there were survivors that Sparrow was one of them.

Although it seemed impossible that if you were in a tiny piece of metal thousands of feet in the air and you came crashing down to earth you could survive, he had seen a lot of situations he could only call miracles in his time in the military. People beat the odds all the time, and he prayed Sparrow and the others were among them.

Until he saw eight bodies, he would hold out hope that there were survivors.

Approaching carefully, he got as close to the burning wreckage as possible, but he wasn't interested in trying to see inside it, he was looking for signs that someone had walked away. All eight people on board were highly trained. They knew they'd been shot down, knew whoever had done the shooting would be coming to check out their handiwork, so they had to get away.

He'd worked his way halfway around the helo when he saw them.

Footprints.

Someone might be alive, but they wouldn't be uninjured, no one was that lucky, so Ethan quickly grabbed the survival kit he always carried, which included a well-stocked first aid kit. Then he started walking.

In the dark it was difficult to find signs of the trail, and he didn't want to use a flashlight because he didn't want to draw attention to himself when the shooters showed up. So, he moved carefully, checking every few yards or so for signs he was heading the right way.

It ended up being the lack of signs that someone had recently walked along it that had him finding what he hoped was the correct path. He would bet his plane on the fact that someone had cleaned away all evidence that they had been here.

Although he wanted to hurry, find any survivors, provide whatever aid he could, and call into base that he'd found them, he resisted the urge, relied on his training, and continued moving slowly and cautiously.

The further he went the more he started to notice other things. Marks that looked like drag marks in the dirt, dislodged stones, and branches of shrubs that looked disturbed. Then he saw what looked like blood. Whoever had been cleaning up was doing a worse job the further they got from the wreckage.

Injured?

It would make sense if one of the injured had carried another injured person through the valley, then they had gone back to try to eliminate the trail so no one could find them. Only it looked more like someone had been dragged along not carried.

The SEALs wouldn't have had to drag anyone, they would have carried them, and Sparrow's co-pilot was a man, again he would have had the upper body strength to carry someone.

It had to be Sparrow.

She had to be alive. Alive but injured, if the fact that she had started missing puddles of blood and obvious drag marks were anything to go by.

Picking up speed now, he knew where she had gone to seek safety as soon as he saw the overhanging rocks. As he crept closer, not sure if he was the first to stumble upon whoever was hiding in there and knowing that they were no doubt expecting trouble, the large puddles of blood confirmed he was in the right place.

No bullets came flying at his head as he moved through the opening, and when he looked inside, he saw Sparrow on her knees, crying softly, holding the hand of an obviously dead SEAL.

Knowing Sparrow would be armed and wouldn't hesitate to defend herself, injured and grieving or not, he called out her name, hoping that familiar word would be enough to calm and reassure her.

"Sparrow."

Her head whipped around, and she raised a weapon only to lower it almost immediately when she recognized him. Ethan's heart cracked at the raw pain and despair on her face. There were signs of physical pain, and her face was streaked with blood, but it was the guilt and grief that hit him hard. He was a pilot too, he knew the responsibility you felt for those who stepped inside your bird. Having been hit and crashing, Sparrow would be feeling the deaths of the others hard.

"Ethan? Ethan Zimmerman?"

"It's me. How you doing, wisp?" he asked, using the nickname he knew she had hated when they were training. Sparrow was a tiny wisp of a thing, and the first time someone had called her that she'd used her smaller size to knock them down to the ground, twisting their arm behind their back till they were begging her to let go. She'd earned herself a punishment but also the respect of all the guys, and although the name stuck no one ever doubted again that she was a tough little thing.

Ethan may or may not have been the guy she cut down to size.

Okay he was, and while he regretted embarrassing her, a firm friendship had ended up growing between them.

A cross between a sob, a laugh, and a growl came out of her. "I hate that name, Ethan."

He shot her a grin. "I know." Then he sobered. "How're you going, honey?"

"They shot us down."

"I know."

Her brow furrowed and she winced. "How did you know? Why are you here?"

"Eagle called me."

"My brother?"

"There's a chance that your helo was shot down because someone was after you," he broke the news as gently as he could.

Sparrow gasped. "After me?"

"Someone is after your family."

"I know ... Raven told us ... they were trying to take her and Cleo to whoever it was. Oh ... is this ... this is my fault." Her gaze flew to the dead SEAL, and one hand lifted to cover her mouth.

"We don't know that, wisp," he told her. He was about to

move closer, check her out to see how badly she was hurt and what other injuries she had that he couldn't see, but he caught sight of lights moving in the distance in the opposite direction from where he'd just come. Checking her out would have to wait. "We gotta go, wisp."

"What? Why?"

"We got company."

"We can't leave Colt." She turned her stricken gaze onto him, pleading with him, but this was something he couldn't give her.

"They probably won't look here, they'll be heading for the plane. A team is already on the way here, your friend won't get left behind." He had to wonder if the SEAL meant something more to her than just someone who had happened to be on the helo who she had obviously tried and failed to save.

"His wife … he wanted me to tell her he loved her," she whispered.

"And you will, wisp, you will," he promised. Ethan couldn't deny he felt something hearing that the SEAL was married. Relief maybe? That was stupid, he and Sparrow were just friends. Friends who lived on different continents and who would probably never see each other again once they got out of here. "But right now, we gotta run."

Since it was clear that Sparrow was in no condition to run on her own, Ethan crossed to her, snatched her up, and took off at a dead run. For a man who no longer made promises he'd made several in the last hour, first to Eagle Oswald and now to the woman he carried over his shoulders.

A woman he hadn't thought of in years but who now almost made him want to have a life again.

* * *

10:52 P.M.

. . .

LEAVING COLT BEHIND FELT WRONG.

Logically, Sparrow understood what Ethan had said. Colt was dead, whoever was coming would be heading for the helo. They'd have no reason to know he was there or even think he was around, and she and Ethan had to get out of here before they arrived. Still, her heart hurt knowing Colt was all alone now.

Ethan was running, the jolting movement sending arrows of pain through her skull and the nausea in her stomach quickly became so overpowering there wasn't any energy left to worry about anything except trying not to throw up down Ethan's back.

It had been a long time since she'd seen or heard from Ethan. She'd always thought of him as a good friend, even if their first interaction hadn't gone too well. Unfortunately, the nickname wisp had stuck, but fortunately the friendship had stuck as well. She'd felt awful for him losing his wife, she'd met Sierra quite a few times and the woman was a lovely person. Sometimes life wasn't fair, and it definitely wasn't fair that Ethan had lost the love of his life when they were only twenty-seven.

That was four years ago now, and although she had tried to keep in contact with Ethan, the last time she'd seen him was a couple of years ago at a barbecue with a bunch of their friends. That day she'd thought she felt something brewing between them as they talked and reminisced, but she'd known he was still grieving, and she wasn't sure if he was ready to move on with someone else so she hadn't mentioned it.

Shortly after Ethan had packed up his life and moved to Africa.

Now he was suddenly here. Of all the people her family

could have reached out to it was a guy she was insanely attracted to but was pretty sure she could never have.

Ethan suddenly threw open a door and dumped her in the seat of a small plane. She cried out as the movement jostled her broken collarbone and pounding head, causing Ethan to hesitate for a moment before slamming the door closed and rounding the plane.

As soon as he was in his seat, he had the engine running, and a moment later they were taking off.

Sparrow rested her head back against the seat and tried to breathe deeply. In through her nose and out through her mouth until the pain and nausea subsided enough that she could crack her eyes open and angle her head so she could see Ethan's profile. "There's really a chance someone knew I was on that helicopter and shot it down because of that?"

"According to what your brother told me, yes. This relative who's after your family knows you're in Africa and threatened you."

She had already been feeling guilty that the helo had gone down on her watch, killing everyone on board but her, now knowing the attack might have been aimed at her because a relative was after her and her siblings she felt so much worse. Why was someone related to her ... wait, what?

"What do you mean a relative is after us?" Last time she'd spoken to her family, right around Christmas, they'd known that someone was after them and that their parents' murders weren't random. They were all supposed to die that night, but no one had mentioned anything about it being a relative who arranged the hit.

"That's what Eagle said. Apparently, Falcon and Hope were told it was a relative."

"Who's Hope? Oh wait, the woman who helped Raven and Cleo? Falcon and Alpha team were going in to rescue her, I guess that means they succeeded." She was pleased to hear that. The woman had shown Raven kindness knowing she could be punished in retaliation. There was no way her family would have left her behind.

"Since Hope was there with the rest of your family when I called to tell them about the crash, I'm thinking your brother did more than just rescue her."

Her mouth fell open in shock.

Positive she must have misheard.

That or the concussion was playing mind games with her.

"What did you just say?"

"Eagle introduced her as Falcon's girlfriend on the phone."

"Falcon's *girlfriend*?" If there was ever a word she never expected to hear in a sentence with her brother's name it was that. As far as she knew, Falcon had no plans to get involved with anyone, he barely even allowed his own siblings to get close to him let alone a stranger. She couldn't help a pang of hurt. She had nothing against Hope Delancey, but she missed her brother, and she was still angry and hurt that he had cut them out of his life for two years. She was jealous that he'd allowed Hope in when he continued to shut her out.

"I hear ya, from what I know of your brother I'm shocked to hear he's dating someone, but I'm happy for him."

Sparrow was too, but still she couldn't help the jealousy that he apparently had no use for her in his life, and yet he had no problem meeting a woman. It just seemed like the icing on the cake of a really bad day.

"Close your eyes and rest for a bit. Once I get you to my place, I'll be able to take a look at your injuries."

"Your place?" She had assumed he was flying her back to base.

"If the helo was shot down because someone was after you then they'll be expecting you to go back to the base, and someone had to have sold you out or they couldn't have known you were going to be on that helo, so I don't think you're safe there."

What he said made sense, and she was officially on leave as of midnight. Maybe it was a good idea to spend the night at Ethan's and then fly back home in the morning. Home, where there was apparently a new member of the family to meet.

Sparrow relaxed into her seat and let her eyes fall closed.

She must have dozed off because she woke with a horrifying sense of déjà vu.

"Were we just hit?" she asked, bolting upright in her seat.

"Yes," Ethan said tightly.

"Because of me? Ethan, I'm so sorry, you should have left me behind." Panic clawed at her. She couldn't take another death on her shoulders. If there was any justice, this time she would be the one to die and Ethan would walk away in one piece.

"Put your belt on," Ethan ordered.

She reached for it, wincing when pain ripped through her shoulder.

"You okay?"

"Think my collarbone is broken," she replied through gritted teeth as she snagged the seatbelt and somehow managed to get it buckled.

Ethan whistled. "And yet you dragged the SEAL over a mile. Good job, wisp."

The nickname made her lips curve into a smile despite the fact that she was about to crash land for the second time tonight. "Focus on getting us down, Ethan."

"Yes, ma'am," he said with a grin. "They didn't get a good shot at us like they did at your helo, we're going to go down hard, but we'll make it to the hangar."

"We're close to your place?"

"Yep, just up ahead."

She desperately wanted to do something to help but with the way her head was spinning, and the pain coursing through her body, Sparrow knew she would be more liability than assistance.

So, all she could do was sit and watch as Ethan wrestled with his plane as the ground came rushing up to meet them. The landing was rough. They hit hard and skidded more than rolled along until eventually they came to a stop.

They were both breathing hard, both shocked to be alive, and as Ethan turned to face her, his blue eyes sparkling in the dull light inside the plane, she had to battle the urge to kiss him.

Adrenalin overload, she assured herself.

"That's how it's done, wisp. You need a few more lessons while you're here?" Ethan teased.

"Still as humble as ever I see, blondie," she teased back. Ethan had always hated when she'd countered his wisp with a blondie, although she'd always thought his blond locks were rather sexy.

"Hey, no need to be humble when you're as awesome as I am." Sparrow laughed and then winced, and Ethan immediately grew serious. "Come on, I need to check you out."

"And we need to call the base and my family, tell them I'm okay and where to find Colt's body."

"Already done, did that while you were taking a little nap."

"Thanks." It was a relief to know her siblings wouldn't be worrying about her. "How do you think they …" she trailed off when she caught sight of what was in the back of the plane. The boxes of cargo had been thrown about, and some of them had broken open, spilling out their contents. Her gaze snapped to Ethan's unable to believe what she was seeing. Surely he wasn't … no. That was crazy. Ethan would never do that. "Ethan, why are there drugs in your plane?"

CHAPTER TWO

January 19th

 2:22 A.M.

"Why are there drugs on my plane? Is that what you just said?" Ethan demanded, turning to see what Sparrow had been staring at with such a look of horror on her face and saw it.

Drugs.

There really were drugs on his plane.

There had to be several kilograms of cocaine there, packed in amongst the medical supplies.

Cocaine.

Here.

On *his* plane.

Immediately, he looked back to Sparrow. "I didn't put

them there. I swear. I didn't even know." It seemed important that she know he wasn't a drug smuggler. That he had no idea someone was using his plane to traffic drugs.

She reached out a hand to cover his. It was the first time a woman had touched him since Sierra's death, usually, he made it clear physical contact wasn't allowed. Since he'd moved here, the only women he'd seen were those in the villages they delivered supplies to, who had no desire to touch him, and fellow aid worker Esme, who had quickly picked up on his reluctance to be touched.

A woman's touch was something he had grown to fear. There was only one woman he wanted to be touching him, and she was gone. But Sparrow's touch didn't fill him with panic, it didn't make him want to recoil, it didn't bring up memories of Sierra and the usual punch of grief to the gut.

Sparrow's touch made him feel good.

It was soothing.

Healing.

"I believe you, Ethan," she said softly.

He wasn't sure he would if he was her, but he wasn't going to look a gift horse in the mouth. "Thank you."

"You don't need to thank me, Ethan. I know what kind of man you are, and I know you would never be involved in drug trafficking, but someone who has access to your plane is."

Until Sparrow said the words, he hadn't even thought about that.

The number of people with access to his plane was limited. The doctor, Oliver Gabler, nurse Esmerelda Takeda, and Evan Kikkert, the coordinator, working with the charity's main offices in England to make sure everything ran smoothly on their end. The four of them lived on a small compound. There was the hangar where he kept his plane, four tiny houses, an office, and a warehouse where they stored the supplies once they were brought in and prepared them to go out to each village. They also provided a clinic for walk-ins, but none of those people would have enough access to load drugs onto the plane.

He was about to explain all that to Sparrow, but her dark eyelashes fluttered against her pale cheeks, and he realized that priority number one right now was treating her.

Since he no longer trusted any of his colleagues instead of waking Dr. Gabler and asking the man to take a look at Sparrow, Ethan decided he'd do it himself. Then once he had her settled, he'd decide what to do with the drugs. He didn't want to leave them here because whoever had hidden them would come back for them, but he also didn't want to move them because they might lose their chance to figure out who was using the charity as a front to traffic drugs. Moving the drugs also tipped his hand, the smuggler would assume he was the one to find them and could come after him, putting Sparrow in more danger.

For now, though, he focused on Sparrow. "You stay there, I'll come around to get you."

"I can walk," Sparrow said, but her voice had lost any substance, and she sounded about ready to crash. Actually, he was surprised she was still conscious and as lucid as she was given the amount of blood on her head and the killer headache that had to accompany it.

"Sure you can, wisp, but I'm here to take care of you." As he climbed out of the plane and rounded it to Sparrow's side, he thought of the last time he'd cared for a woman. When it was clear she wasn't going to recover, Sierra had decided that she wanted to die at home, so they had set everything up, and he had cared for her in those final weeks. Then there were all the times he'd held her hair back while she threw up, cooled her sweat-dotted brow with a cold cloth, and fed her plain broth when she was too weak to do it herself. Chemo and radiation were brutal on a body, and in the end neither had been enough to save the woman he loved.

Now he scooped up another woman into his arms, cradling her against his chest as he carried her to his house. Sierra had been tall, five-ten to his six-two, but Sparrow was tiny, not even five feet tall, carrying her felt like carrying a child, only Sparrow was one hundred percent woman.

He was all too aware of that as she rested her head on his shoulder. Her breath was warm against his neck, and she placed one of her hands above his heart, which started beating way too fast.

Sparrow didn't seem to notice, and he was able to easily balance her to open his front door. His house was one room with a primitive kitchen up one end, the sink had a pump, and the stove ran off his generator. There was a square kitchen table with four chairs, and a battered sofa under the window by the door. His place had no bathroom—he used an outhouse and the outdoor shower—and just the one bedroom, which was where he headed now.

In the bedroom, he placed Sparrow right on top of the covers and went to start removing her clothes but stopped short.

Sierra had been his high school sweetheart and the only woman he'd ever been with. It had been four years since she died, but he'd never even been tempted by another woman.

Until now.

The attraction he felt for Sparrow Oswald bothered him on many levels. It felt like a betrayal to Sierra to even think about another woman, and Sparrow had never given him any indication that she was attracted to him. At the moment he wasn't sure which bothered him more.

"Sparrow, I have to take your clothes off so I can check you for injuries," he told her. The last thing he wanted was for her to feel like he was somehow taking advantage of the situation.

She gave a small moan that could have been an acknowledgment or not, but since this had to be done, he stripped off her boots and socks, then her blood-soaked pants and top with the utmost professionalism. He left on her panties—white cotton ones with a sweet little bow that were simple but surprisingly sexy—and a simple white cotton bra with a matching bow between her small but perky and round breasts.

Bruises were forming everywhere, but as he methodically made his way from her feet up to her neck, probing each muscle, joint, and bone carefully, he found that the only likely serious injuries she had were the broken collarbone and the concussion. That she had managed to drag a man twice her size over a mile from the crash scene, injured and in pain, and attempted to save his life left him in awe of the tiny wisp of a woman. Sparrow had guts and determination galore, she was beautiful in a way she rarely tried to draw attention to, and every one of her muscles was toned to perfection. Ethan knew Sparrow was ultra-competitive and was always up to trying to outdo the guys.

Walking into his kitchen, he filled a bowl with warm water, grabbed a washcloth and returned to the bed, where he perched on the edge of the mattress and looked down at the passed-out woman. It looked weird seeing a woman in his bed, weird but not wrong, and that freaked him out.

He still loved Sierra. He couldn't imagine ever feeling what he had for his wife for another woman, and yet part of him liked seeing Sparrow lying against his sheets, her warm, soft body against his hip. Taking the cloth, he began to clean her face, wiping away the blood that stained her smooth skin. The cut would probably need stitches, and he was definitely out of practice giving those.

When Ethan gently took hold of her chin and angled her face his way her eyes fluttered open.

Their gazes met, and he could have sworn he *felt* it. Felt a connection between them, but it wasn't a connection he wanted or had any interest in exploring.

Still, almost against his will, his thumb swept across her lips before he moved it away so he wouldn't do something they would both wind up regretting.

Maybe he needed to rethink the whole celibacy thing. Maybe if he had sex with a woman who meant nothing to him then it wouldn't really be cheating because it would be just sex.

Ethan didn't know if that was the answer, but he did know one thing. The woman in his bed didn't mean nothing to him, therefore there would be no sex between them.

As he set the washcloth aside and retrieved supplies to stitch her wound, Ethan felt a pang of regret that there would be no sex with Sparrow.

* * *

2:26 P.M.

FOR ONCE IT wasn't the pounding in her head that woke her it was the lack of pain.

Sparrow blinked and opened her eyes, wincing as the sunlight streaming through the windows seemed to go right through her skull. Okay, maybe she wasn't pain free, but it had diminished to the point where she no longer wanted to just chop her head right off.

"How're you feeling?"

She turned her head to see Ethan lounging in a battered but comfortable-looking armchair by the window. He had a book in his hands, but he put it down when he saw she was awake. Every time she had woken during the night, he had been right there, helping her shift into a more comfortable position on the bed, giving her painkillers if she needed them, and bringing her glasses of water so she didn't become dehydrated.

He had taken really good care of her, and it had been such a long time since anyone had taken care of her. Not since her parents had died. She'd been twelve then, and that night was forever etched into her mind. The months afterward had been hard. Eagle was already in the military, Raven was recovering from life-threatening injuries, and Falcon was angry and bitter and turning in on himself, which meant it had been up to her to try to hold the family—what was left of it anyway—together.

Sparrow had followed in her big brothers' footsteps to join the military where being a woman, and a tiny one at that, had meant she spent most of her time proving her strength, which didn't play into the being vulnerable and allowing people to take care of her role. She'd never been in love before, she'd had a few hookups, but between deployments and spending most of her time with guys she worked with, there weren't a lot of opportunities to meet guys.

As awful as she had felt all night, and as awful as she still felt, it had been nice having someone there to watch over her. It was too bad that Ethan was still in love with his wife. She liked him, respected him, was attracted to him, they had a lot in common, they'd been friends for a long time, and she could actually see herself falling for him.

"I'm feeling a little better," she answered as she sat up slowly in deference to the mild dizziness she was still experiencing. "What time is it?"

"After two," Ethan replied, coming to sit on the bed beside her.

"After two?" she echoed, shocked. That meant she had been asleep for over twelve hours. "In the afternoon?"

Ethan grinned at her, and the sexy smile wasn't helping her growing attraction to the sweet man who had come running to help her and then taken care of her. "You think we get bright sunlight at two in the morning, wisp? Guess you haven't been in Africa all that long after all."

She smiled back, it tugged on the stitches, but the small discomfort was worth it. She wasn't going to be here long, but she'd enjoy Ethan's company while she was. "No, smart Alec, it just doesn't feel like I was asleep for that long."

"Well, you were, your body needed it. You ready to get up?"

"More than." She was already starting to get antsy having been stuck in the same place for so long. Sparrow lived her life always on the go. Even when she was deployed somewhere for a length of time she worked out in the gym, sparred, and made sure she kept busy.

"Hungry?"

Sparrow curled up her nose at the idea of eating. While her stomach had definitely settled down some, she was still a little queasy. Still, she knew she had to eat, she was recovering from a concussion, her body needed fuel. Slowly she nodded. "I'll try a little something."

"What about some fruit? It should be pretty easy on your system," Ethan suggested.

"I guess."

"Such enthusiasm."

She fought a smile and rolled her eyes at Ethan's teasing then winced. "Don't try to make me laugh, blondie."

"Wouldn't dream of it, wisp," he shot back with a grin.

"I'm going to go to the bathroom first." She looked around then grimaced. "Can I assume you only have an outhouse?"

"Sorry the accommodations aren't up to your standards, sweetheart," Ethan teased.

Sparrow debated the childishness of it but poked her tongue out at him anyway. "You know I grew up using an outhouse, I just outgrew those roughing it days."

"I thought you loved camping."

"So long as there's a real toilet," she said with a grin. "But since there isn't I guess I'll have to make do."

"Yep, you will," Ethan agreed cheerfully, then he grew serious. "You okay to make it out there on your own? I don't want you getting dizzy, passing out or falling, and hurting yourself worse."

"I'll call out if I need you," she promised. She would too, she might be embarrassed by having to ask a friend—especially one she was attracted to—to help her go to the bathroom but she wasn't stupid. Being a little embarrassed was better than causing herself more injuries, especially given what they'd found in Ethan's plane last night. "Once I get back, we need to talk."

"Yeah, we do," Ethan agreed gravely. He took her elbow and helped her stand, keeping a hold of her until he was sure she was steady enough to remain on her feet. Then he pointed to a set of folded clothes on the dresser. "They'll be too big, but they'll do for now. You need help getting dressed?"

Sparrow was comfortable enough in her body not to be embarrassed that she was standing before him in her underwear, and confident enough in the fact that Ethan was a good guy and wouldn't take advantage of her not to feel concerned. "I might need some help," she admitted.

With a simple nod he sat her down again, lifting first one foot and then the other to get them in the borrowed pants. He helped her stand and then pulled them up, his fingers brushing against her legs as he did. Although she felt a tingle burn through her, his face was all business as he reached for the shirt, carefully helped her get her bad arm in first, and then the other and buttoned her up.

His apparent disinterest in her would have been a blow to her ego, but she suspected it had more to do with the fact that he was still hung up on his wife than anything else. Ethan was a good man, the gentle and easy way he'd helped her dress told her he'd done it many times before. He'd cared for his wife until the very end, just thinking about how hard that must have been had her eyes misting.

"You okay?" Ethan asked. "Your arm bothering you? Your head? Do you need more painkillers?"

If he thought she looked teary because she was in pain, she wasn't going to correct him. Bringing up his dead wife right now wasn't a good idea. "I'm fine."

Ethan took her elbow again and guided her out of the bedroom and to the front door of his tiny little house. When he opened the front door, he pointed her in the direction of the outhouse.

Alone when he went back inside to prepare her something to eat, Sparrow took a moment to look around. The compound was fenced in, there was the hangar, a couple of other smaller buildings, and one larger one. There was no one hanging around that she could see as she walked the dozen or so yards to the outhouse, but she was very aware that someone who lived here was involved in smuggling drugs. What would they do if they knew their secret had been discovered? As much as she wanted to get out of here, go back home and spend time with her family, she wasn't going to leave Ethan to deal with this on his own.

Sparrow did her business, washed her hands in the wooden water dish, and then made her way back to Ethan's place. By the time she got inside and over to the table where he was cutting up fruit, she felt like she'd just run a marathon.

"You okay?" Ethan asked, eyeing her shrewdly.

Seeing no point in lying, she nodded but added, "Been a long time since I had a concussion, I forgot how much it wipes you out."

"You can go back to bed once you've eaten."

"After we discuss your problem," she said. "We should call the base, let them know what we found." If a drug smuggler was working around this area, they should make sure it was reported to the proper authorities.

Ethan grimaced as he set a bowl of fruit salad in front of her. "I'm going to be suspect number one. They'll never believe it wasn't me. The drugs were on my plane. I'm the only pilot here. Logic says it's me."

"Not necessarily. Every person here has access to the plane. How many full-time aid workers are here?" The last thing she wanted was for Ethan to get blamed, but she also couldn't pretend they hadn't seen those drugs, and she knew he wouldn't do that either. She'd give it a day or so, see what she and Ethan could find out. She was hurt so no one would blink an eye if she said she was going to recuperate for a few days before heading home, which gave the two of them time to investigate before they reported what they'd found.

"There are four of us."

"You're the one who knows them. Tell me about them. Which one do you think could be the drug smuggler?"

"None of them," Ethan answered immediately.

"Now that we have that out of your system, let's be more objective. Run through each person's background with me. I'll be your sounding board. Chances are that there will be signs there once you know what you're looking for. So, you talk, and I'll listen." She picked up a piece of strawberry and popped it into her mouth. Although she'd been worried about feeling nauseous the sweet fruit with the tiny hint of tart was delicious and immediately gave her a little burst of energy.

Ethan started talking, and she listened to every word he said, asking questions when she needed more information on something. As they talked things out, bouncing ideas off one another, Sparrow noticed how well they worked together. They were a good team, good enough that they just might be able to figure out which of Ethan's colleagues was trafficking drugs before she left, so they could turn the person in.

She wished there was a chance for them to see if they could be a good team in other areas too.

* * *

4:04 P.M.

"You sure you don't want to rest for a while first?" Ethan asked as Sparrow laced up her boots.

"No, I want to do this. We have to figure out who's trafficking the drugs before ..." Sparrow trailed off and looked up at him, eyes wide. "Before they realize that we found the drugs. What did you do with them?"

"I thought about hiding them," he admitted. Once he'd gotten Sparrow settled, he'd even gone looking for a shovel thinking he'd pack up the boxes of drugs and bury them. It had seemed like a good plan, and it was sure to reveal who the smuggler was, but it would also paint a giant target on him as it would be obvious that he was the one who found and took the drugs. If it was just him, he might not have worried about it, but it wouldn't be just him. As soon as they realized Sparrow had been with him, she would be a target too.

"You *hid* them?" Sparrow asked incredulously.

"No. I said I *thought* about it. It would have tipped the smuggler's hand, they would have had to reveal themselves, but it also would have put us both in danger."

Sparrow bristled. "I can handle danger."

"Normally sure, but right now you're injured. So, I packaged the boxes back up. No one will know that they were broken. No one knows we know, so we can ask our questions without raising suspicion." Having Sparrow here was the perfect opportunity to ask those questions. It would have looked off if he had randomly started nosing around about his colleagues' lives, but Sparrow was new, it made sense she might try to get to know them.

"Not a bad plan," Sparrow said with a smirk. "I give you a B."

"Only a B?" he asked. Ethan picked up a sling and gently grasped her elbow as he slipped it on, positioning it so it would take the pressure off her broken collarbone.

"Only a B," she echoed, but her voice had gone breathy, and her eyes were fixed on his lips like she was thinking about ... kissing him?

That was crazy, and positive he was imagining things, Ethan quickly stepped back. "Guess I got some work to do if I want to raise that grade."

Her smile was warm, and there was no hint in her eyes if he'd read her correctly—further confirming his assumption that he hadn't—and she laughed. "You think you *can* get that grade up, blondie?"

"You know I did graduate high school with a 4.0 GPA," he teased. Actually, he'd basically gotten perfect grades all the way through school, and his parents had had grand plans of him becoming a brain surgeon or rocket scientist. They'd been disappointed when he had joined the military right after graduating.

"I know, I know, you're very smart." Sparrow's eyes twinkled because he knew she had also graduated with a 4.0 GPA. After being homeschooled until she was twelve, she had taken to formal education like a duck to water and had quicky learned to make friends, play sports, and still managed to get great grades.

When Sparrow stood, he reached out and took her hand —purely to help her stay steady because he knew she was still dizzy—and led her to the door. No one was about, it wasn't a clinic day so there were no patients, and since no one had come knocking on his door with questions about his damaged plane, no one knew about that either.

"Let's go play cops and robbers," he said as he led her toward the communal living area.

"I always thought I'd make a good cop."

"Yeah?" he asked somewhat dubiously. Somehow, he couldn't picture Sparrow as a cop. She was a little too outspoken, he couldn't see her dealing with criminals. She'd get too annoyed with them.

"Hey!" She playfully nudged his shoulder. "I'd be a great cop."

"If you say so."

When they stepped inside the room, three heads snapped in their direction, and three mouths dropped open when they saw he wasn't alone.

"Who's this?" Esme asked, her voice a tad bit shrill.

"How did she get here? Who is she?" Dr. Oliver Gabler asked, his eyes narrowed suspiciously like he suspected Sparrow was up to no good.

They'd decided to be honest about who Sparrow was and how she ended up here, hoping that knowing she was with the military might spook the smuggler enough that they slipped up.

"This is Sparrow Oswald," he said as he guided her to the

table and helped her sit. "She's an old military friend of mine." It was clear from the expressions of his three colleagues that they were all familiar with the Oswald name, not surprising in the least given how well-known and respected Prey Security was.

"What is she doing here?" Evan Kikkert asked. Of the three full-time workers here, he was probably closest with Evan. They were the same age, they got along well, talked sports, threw a ball around when they had time, and the man had an interest in flying. Ethan had even given him a few lessons.

"Someone is after Prey, shot down her helicopter. We have mutual friends, and since they knew I was in the area they asked me to see if I could find the wreckage. Since someone sold her out, I thought she'd be safer here while she recuperated, then she's going home," he explained.

"Why didn't you call me last night?" Oliver asked, bounding out of his seat to hurry over and grab his medical bag. "Let me take a look at you."

Sparrow smiled sweetly at him when he crouched before her chair. "I hope we didn't offend you by not calling you last night. I was just a little freaked out, and I didn't want to be around anyone I didn't already know."

She hit just the right amount of appeasement and self-deprecation to have the older man eating out of her hand. "It's no worries, dear, I'm not offended, just a little thrown and concerned. Let me take a look at you."

While the doctor checked her vitals, she got the man talking. The doctor was the one Ethan knew the least, but what he did know was that the man had grown up in Africa, making him—at least in Ethan's mind—the most likely candidate to be the smuggler.

"What made you decide to work here in Djibouti?" Sparrow asked.

"I grew up just across the border in Ethiopia. My parents were missionaries. When I got my medical degree there was never any question that I would come back here to work," Oliver replied. Ethan hadn't known that the man had lived in Ethiopia for his entire childhood. Had he made connections while he was there? Is that how he'd become mixed up in trafficking drugs?

"How long have you been working here?" Sparrow asked.

"Going on twenty years."

"Wow. I think that's amazing. Instead of taking a comfortable job and making a lot of money, you came here and dedicated your life to ensuring these people get access to the things we take for granted back home." Sparrow smiled at the man, and he practically beamed back at her. Ethan had to rethink his whole Sparrow wouldn't make a good cop position because she was working Dr. Oliver like a pro.

"It was an easy choice to make," Dr. Gabler replied.

"What about the rest of you?" Sparrow turned her attention to the others. "This can be a dangerous place for a woman. What made you decide to come here?" she asked Esme. "Ethan said you were a nurse."

"I am," Esme replied shortly. The woman was the newest one here. Oliver had been here for years, Evan had arrived around two years ago, but Esme had been here not quite six months. The previous nurse had been a sweet, grandmotherly woman in her seventies who had gone home only because her daughter had been in a bad car accident and needed full-time care.

When it was clear that Esme wasn't going to elaborate, Sparrow didn't bat an eye, just smiled, nodded, and turned to Evan. "I'm not quite sure what you do. Ethan said something about coordinating things?"

"My family runs the charity," Evan explained. "I got into some trouble a while back. My family thought I needed to get my head on straight, realize how good I had it, so I got sent out here. I didn't like it at the time but being here it ... changes you."

Ethan hadn't known that. He'd thought he and Evan were friends, they spent most of their time together. He'd known that Evan's family had founded the charity almost seventy years ago, but not that Evan had been exiled out here because he'd gotten into some trouble.

In just five minutes Sparrow's sweet smile and non-threatening persona had gotten more out of their suspects than he could have on his own. Oliver had spent most of his life in Africa. He could have any number of connections to anyone, including one of the warlords who might be looking to get into trafficking drugs. Evan had been sent here against his will because of some sort of trouble. Had it had something to do with drugs? And Esme, who was usually bubbly and perky and would talk your ear off was sitting there almost sullenly. Did she suspect they knew about the drugs?

* * *

4:33 P.M.

"You look good, all things considering. The stitches were almost as good as I would have done," Dr. Gabler admitted, somewhat reluctantly. "But if you get worse you let me know immediately."

"Of course," Sparrow said, nodding agreeably. All it had taken was a compliment, and the man had been putty in her hands. That would teach Ethan to think she wouldn't make a good cop. Casting a glance at Ethan, she gave a discreet nod. It was time to mention that they'd been shot at and see the others' reactions. They had no idea if it was the same person who shot down her Black Hawk that had shot at Ethan's plane, but it was a logical conclusion. That or whoever was involved in trafficking the drugs had seen Ethan fly off and was worried he'd found the drugs and was either keeping them for himself or was turning them in to the authorities.

"So," Ethan said slowly as the other three all turned their attention to him. "When I was bringing Sparrow back here someone shot at my plane."

Esme's eyes widened in shock. "Someone shot at you?"

"Shot *at* you, or shot you?" Evan asked.

"Shot us," Ethan confirmed.

"You crash-landed?" Dr. Gabler asked. "Are you injured as well? You should have called me last night."

Not being consulted was obviously a dint to the man's ego, but that only meant he was likely to tip his hand if he was involved because he was flustered. "Ethan got us down like a pro," she said.

"How bad is the damage?" Evan asked. "Is the plane still operational? Fixable? Do I need to ask for a new plane to be sent in?"

Sparrow tried to gauge the man's expression to figure out if his concern was really just what he needed to do to get the plane issue sorted or if he was trying to cover by pretending he cared only about the plane as he tried to figure out if they knew anything. She couldn't tell though. According to what Ethan had told her, Evan was his closest friend out here, but Ethan hadn't known that Evan was out here because he'd been exiled by his family. She would need to figure out a way to dig up dirt on the man, and find out if he had ties to the drug world.

"I might be able to fix it. Want to come take a look with me?" Ethan asked.

"Yeah, I think I better. We have a delivery scheduled for next week, and we're going to need the plane operational by then," Evan said with a sigh like the whole thing was one big bother.

"If there's anything my family can do to help, please let me know," Sparrow said. "Ethan's plane got shot helping me so if we can get you parts quicker, or loan you a plane, just let me know."

"That's very generous," Evan said with a polite nod. She couldn't tell if he meant it or was trying to be dismissive because he didn't want Prey sniffing anywhere around here.

"Why don't you go lie down for a while," Ethan suggested, resting a hand lightly on her shoulder. "Esme can walk you back to my place."

"Oh, I was going to go with you and Evan, see if I could help," Esme immediately protested. The woman seemed awfully anxious all of a sudden to get to the plane. From what Ethan had said she didn't have any mechanical knowledge or a lot of interest in flying.

"Maybe Dr. Gabler can walk me," she suggested. She wanted a moment alone with the man to find out more about what kind of connections he might have here.

"I have to pop into town," Dr. Gabler said. "But I can see you to Ethan's place if it's necessary," he added as though duty dictated that he must, but he also cast a glance at his watch like he had someplace to be.

"No, I'm sure I'll be fine," she said sweetly.

"All right, I won't be long," Ethan assured her.

"No problem." The five of them all got up and dispersed. It took Sparrow a little while to get back to Ethan's house because she was still wobbly on her feet, but the dizziness was receding, and the fruit had helped settle her stomach. Sparrow rated herself at maybe seventy-five percent, a definite improvement over last night. She needed to be sharp, aware, because they were here with a drug smuggler, and there was no telling what the person would do if they felt like they were backed into a corner.

As she reached Ethan's place, she got that feeling. The one that said someone was watching her. Esme? Dr. Gabler? Evan? She didn't know, but it had to be one of them because the only other people here were a couple of guards who manned the gates to the small compound.

They didn't know what to make of her, that was for sure. The injuries confirmed her story, but she still wondered if they would try to check her out. She'd have to reach out to a few friends back at the base and ask them to let her know if anyone called and asked about her.

Taking a discreet look around as she opened the door and stepped inside, she couldn't see anyone, but the feeling of being watched continued until she closed the door behind her. Sagging onto the sofa, she took a moment to gather her strength before she found Ethan's satellite phone and called her brother.

"Yes?" Eagle's demanding voice came down the line, and Sparrow couldn't help but smile. Her oldest brother was big on being in control, he liked to have his way, and he assumed that everybody should follow his commands without question.

"It's Sparrow."

"Are you all right? Ethan said you were hurt but alive. When are you flying home?" His voice had softened as soon as he knew it was her, and she smiled again. She and her siblings were close, growing up they had quite literally been all each other had. Just them and their parents on their off-the-grid farm. Even as adults they'd remained close, and she got that familiar ache in her chest as she thought of how easily Falcon had ignored them for two long years where they didn't even know what had happened to him.

"Concussion and a broken collarbone, and I can't come home right away."

"Why not?"

"I don't want to say too much because Ethan and I need to keep it quiet for a couple of days, but I need you to look into the three people who work here with him." She rattled off the three names. If anyone could find anything to point to which of the three aid workers was in bed with a drug trafficker, it was Prey.

"I'll get Olivia on this right away," Eagle told her. Olivia was Eagle's fiancée and was pregnant with their first child. She had been friends with Falcon first, he'd gotten her into a mess she couldn't get out of, and despite a rocky start to their relationship Eagle had saved her life, and the two were now happy and in love. Olivia was also a computer genius who had joined Raven's tech team, temporarily taking the lead as Raven helped her daughter Cleo adjust to regular life now that she was back with the family.

"Thanks, I appreciate it."

Eagle paused for a moment before asking, "Are you two in trouble?"

"No."

"In danger?"

"No. At least I don't think so. Not yet anyway."

"Very reassuring, Sparrow," Eagle said dryly. "Do I need to send out a team?"

"No. That will tip our hand. So far no one knows anything but Ethan and I, and we want to keep it that way for the moment. It's just for a couple of days, then I'm going to be coming home. Just don't want to leave him to deal with this on his own."

"That's very nice of you."

From the tone of her brother's voice, she could tell he was trying to figure out if there was something more going on here than what she'd said, but there wasn't, and there wasn't going to be. She might be interested in Ethan, but it wasn't reciprocated. At least it wasn't reciprocated in any meaningful way.

Ignoring his hinting, Sparrow asked instead, "Is everyone else safe?"

"We have bodyguards on Raven, Dove, Olivia, Hope, and Cleo. Falcon and I are being careful, we were able to get word to Hawk so he knows too, but it was you we were worried about. You were the one who was threatened. You need to be careful out there. If your helo was shot down because of you, they probably know by now that you didn't go back to Camp Lemonnier, which means they'll be looking for you. If they look closely enough, they should be able to find you at the aid camp if they can connect you to Ethan. You need to be watching your back."

To be honest, it wasn't someone after her family that she felt was the biggest threat facing her at the moment, it was the drug traffickers. She only had a couple of days here with Ethan, and unless they figured out who the smuggler was, he wasn't safe when she left. Whether they were together or not she didn't want to leave Africa knowing that Ethan had a great big bullseye painted on his back. A bullseye he only got because he had dropped everything and risked his life to come running to her rescue.

CHAPTER THREE

January 20th

3 :56 P.M.

"YOU COULD HAVE STAYED BEHIND," Ethan told Sparrow as they both piled into his truck.

"I could have," she agreed cheerfully. Despite the fact that they'd spent the majority of the day arguing, she was still in a great mood. It wasn't really an *argument*, more of a disagreement, and he loved that she didn't care that he didn't think she was right and wasn't afraid to tell her. While he loved Sierra with everything he was and would have gladly grown old with her by his side, she had a habit of sulking. Any time they didn't agree, she would stick her bottom lip out and pout, while Sparrow just talked it through with a smile.

Not that he should be making comparisons between the two.

Sierra was the love of his life and Sparrow was an old friend he was grateful to have by his side helping him with this, but he knew was leaving in just a couple of days.

"Thought you would have wanted a break from me by now," he said as he turned on the engine.

"What? Because you're wrong about who the drug smuggler is but won't admit it?" she teased, her blue eyes twinkling as she grinned at him.

"You're the one who's wrong," he shot back, but he found himself grinning too. Things were so easy with Sparrow. She was calm and easy-going, it took a lot to make her angry. His love with Sierra had been young love, the real thing, but there had been an immaturity to it, a naivete that came with getting together in high school. Back then, he'd thought that everything would be easy, that they would just sail through life, he'd been unprepared for the challenges that came with his job and constantly being away from home. If he had it in him to fall in love a second time, he could see it being with someone like Sparrow. The kind of love that would grow with a woman like that would be more mature, have more knowledge about the ups and downs of life, but still be as passionate and fiery as what he'd had with Sierra.

"You say that and yet here we are following Dr. Oliver Gabler into the village to see where he goes every day at five," she said, her smile turning smug.

"I'm taking you to the village to follow him because I want to be thorough. I think the smuggler is Evan. He never told me he hadn't wanted to come and that his family had sent him here because he'd gotten into trouble. I bet anything that when we hear back from Prey, we're going to find out that Evan had a drug problem." She'd told him when he returned to his place yesterday evening that she'd called her brother, and he thought it would be a waste not to utilize their resources.

"You could be right, but I still think it's Dr. Gabler. You have to admit it is suspicious that he goes to the village at the same time *every* day."

He'd never thought about it before but now that he had, Ethan agreed. While he still thought Evan was the most likely candidate, there was something odd about the doctor's constant visits to the village. When Sparrow had suggested they follow him to see where he went, Ethan had quickly agreed. Better to eliminate a suspect right off the bat so they could focus their attention on the others.

The village was small and only a few miles from the aid agency's compound. Ethan made the occasional trip out there, but the whole point of taking this job and moving to Djibouti was to escape from life. He wanted the solitude—craved it—and out here he got it. It was like unplugging his life and creating a whole new one. One that carried virtually no reminders of the one he'd left behind.

It was the only way he could survive the loss of his wife.

"How many people live in the village?" Sparrow asked.

"Couple of thousand. There are a few stores and a marketplace too."

"So, it could take us a while to find where Dr. Gabler went."

"It might," he agreed. They'd had to wait until after Oliver left, there was only one road to the village, and this wasn't like back in the States. There would probably be zero other cars on the road so they couldn't follow the man, they had to hope they could find him when they got there. If Oliver knew that they were following him, there was no way he would lead them to wherever it was he went each day.

"Do you come here regularly?"

"Maybe a couple of times a month."

"So, no one will think it's odd seeing you walking around?"

"Don't see why they should, and if anyone mentions it to Oliver, I'll just say you wanted to visit an African village."

"I *do* want to visit a village," Sparrow added. "We're not allowed to leave the base, and when I do it's only for a mission. I've traveled the world a bit but never spent time here that wasn't just for work. I'd love to go on a safari one day."

When he'd picked Africa, it had been purely because it was about as far away from his old life as he could get. His time here had been healing, the only memories of Sierra were in his head, and he was doing something good here, delivering medical supplies to people who otherwise wouldn't get access to them. Never once had he really thought about the magnificence of the continent beyond the disconnect from his old life that it offered. Now that he saw Sparrow's enthusiasm for this beautiful continent, he found a desire to experience it for himself.

"I've never been on a safari, but it does sound like fun. Maybe when we get this mess sorted out, we should go together."

Sparrow's eyes widened as she turned her attention from the road to stare at him.

Damn. Did she think he'd just invited her on a date?

That wasn't how he'd meant it, he'd just thought that it was something they both wanted to do, and he thought he'd have fun with her.

"Just as friends," he rushed to add, hoping he hadn't hurt her feelings.

"Yeah, maybe," Sparrow said without much enthusiasm. She turned her attention back to the road, and the rest of the drive passed in uncomfortable silence.

"Here we are," he announced as he pulled up at the edge of the village.

"No sign of Dr. Gabler's car," Sparrow noted.

"This is where the few shops are, and the market takes place once a week over there." He pointed to a spot under a few trees just to their right.

"So, he didn't come to visit any of the shops, he came to visit someone who lives here. He ever mentioned any friends?"

"Nope. Not that we usually discuss much other than work."

They both got out of the car and started walking. Ethan waved to a couple of people he knew, and they stopped so Sparrow could buy strings of brightly colored beads, then they started walking through the village. It would be much easier to just ask if anyone had seen Oliver and get directions to where he was, but that tipped their hand. They were going to have to do it the hard way, wandering through the village and hoping they caught sight of him.

Neither of them spoke as they walked around, they were both looking for the doctor, and he could tell Sparrow was also absorbing what life was like for most of the people of Djibouti. Everyone they walked past watched them with interest, especially the kids, some of whom trailed along behind them whispering and poking each other.

Collecting a following wasn't ideal, drawing more attention to him than he'd like, but they definitely had a foolproof story if Oliver did happen to see them, all they had to say was that Sparrow had wanted to visit the village. It wasn't even a lie, he suspected even if they weren't trying to find a drug trafficker she would have wanted to visit before leaving.

Leaving.

Sparrow was leaving in a day or two, and knowing it left him feeling ... lonely.

It didn't make sense, he hadn't thought of Sparrow Oswald in the couple of years since he'd last seen her. He made it a point to think as little as possible about his old life, it was too painful. And thinking of a beautiful woman he was attracted to was the last thing he wanted to be doing. Being alone was precisely why he'd come here, but now the thought of Sparrow leaving made him feel *too* alone, *too* isolated.

"Uh, Ethan, do you see what I see up ahead?" Sparrow asked, elbowing him lightly in the side.

Turning his attention away from thoughts of the pretty black-haired beauty at his side, he said, "No, what?"

"Men. With guns. Heading this way."

* * *

5:12 P.M.

"Guns?" Ethan echoed, turning to see what had snagged her attention.

According to what Ethan had told her, two warlords were vying for control of the area, and it made sense that one of them was responsible for the drugs they'd found in Ethan's plane. Sparrow would have to do some more research into both of the warlords, find out as much about them as she could, so they could figure out which one of them was smuggling drugs.

No one else seemed to give much attention to the men with guns, at least not outwardly, but she did notice that people started collecting their kids, ushering them indoors. With the street suddenly a lot quieter than it had been a moment ago, the two of them stood out even more than they had.

Their white skin, and Ethan's blond hair, were beacons telling anyone looking for them that they'd found the right people.

"This way." Ethan grabbed her hand and pulled her between two houses. They hurried down the narrow street and into the next one over.

"Think they're looking for us?" she asked, looking around to see if anyone else was here. She didn't know enough about the warlords to know how many soldiers they had, or whether they were likely to flood the village with armed men if they thought that she and Ethan were trying to get in the way of their trafficking.

"Possible. It's not unusual for either of the warlords to have men wandering around, some of them have families here, and others come to make purchases at the market or the few shops. There has also been the odd time we've received emergency calls because there have been clashes between the rival warlords and villagers have gotten caught in the crosshairs."

"So could be nothing to do with us."

"Could be. If Oliver does suspect that we know about the drugs, and he came here to meet with his contact then they absolutely could be after us. We don't know who else in the village could be involved so someone could have tipped them off that we were here."

"Guess we'll just have to wait and see." At least they were both armed, although she didn't want to have to shoot anyone—nor did she think the Air Force would be pleased to have one of their elite pilots involved in a shootout in an African village—she would if she had to.

"Best thing we can do is make it look like we are just here for you to look around," Ethan said as they strolled down the street.

He was still holding her hand, so she curled her fingers

around his and tried to make it look like there was something romantic between them. When Ethan had offered for the two of them to go on a safari together, she'd thought for a moment that he was opening a door to let her in. It wasn't like she expected him to jump right into a relationship, especially given that the two of them had jobs that would make any kind of relationship difficult, but she had thought he was at least giving her a chance.

The way he had quickly backtracked made it clear she was wrong.

Even now she could feel the stiffness in his body, and although she was holding his hand, he had basically released his grip on hers. If she let go, his hand would drop so quickly you'd have thought she'd burned him.

Had she?

Not in a physical sense of course, her hand was the same temperature as everyone else's, but maybe he felt this heat between them too. To be honest, she had no idea, he was really good at hiding his feelings. She knew he missed his wife, but he never mentioned her, and she was sure by the looks he gave her when he thought she wasn't looking that he was attracted to her.

Attracted to her but wasn't going to do anything about it.

If they ever ended up having anything between them, it would be just sex, nothing more, and Sparrow wasn't sure that was what she wanted. It wasn't that she'd never had meaningless sex before because she had, and even the boyfriends she'd had she had always known it would never last, but somehow the thought of empty, meaningless sex with Ethan made her feel cold.

So cold in fact that she shivered, and Ethan immediately tugged his hand free. She would have missed the contact, but he wrapped his arm around her shoulders and pulled her closer. The movement tugged on her broken collarbone, but the pain faded as warmth spread through her, and she willed Ethan to feel it too.

"You feeling okay?" he asked, his voice low and concerned, and she sighed. He wasn't feeling anything but friendly concern.

"Fine," she replied.

"You want to turn around and head back to the car?"

"Not yet, we haven't got what we came for." She couldn't keep the drugs a secret forever. She had a couple of days grace because she could claim the concussion messed with her head, but sooner rather than later she had to report what she knew. It was only the fact that she didn't want Ethan to get into trouble that had held her off so far. He was right when he'd said they would zero in on him, his plane his drugs, that would be the conclusion, and they might not even look into the others, meaning the real drug smuggler would go free.

"We can come back tomorrow."

"Not if someone did tell Dr. Gabler we were here. Once we can explain as you showing me around, but we come back tomorrow and we look suspicious, effectively ruining any chance we have to link Dr. Gabler to the drugs."

"*If* he's the trafficker."

"If he's not then we can eliminate him as a suspect," she reminded him.

"How long until you have to report the drugs?"

She caught the desperation in his tone. Nothing sucked more than being blamed for something you didn't do. "There's no set time, but people will probably start to get suspicious of why I'm still here within another day or two. If we can find something definitive that points to one of them before then, we can report that."

"Thank you. I know you don't have to be doing this. You

could have called this in and left me to deal with the consequences. I appreciate that you stuck around."

Sparrow stopped and turned to face him. "Ethan, you came looking for me just because my brother asked you to, even though we haven't spoken in years. You came for me knowing my helo had been shot down, likely because someone is after me specifically, but either way, you knew you were walking into a dangerous situation. You didn't hesitate to be there for me, no way I'm walking away until we sort this out."

He looked at her for a moment, then blinked slowly. "I don't know what to say."

"Thank you tends to work pretty well," she teased.

He laughed, and his eyes twinkled with gratefulness, mirth, and something else. Something she was hesitant to name because she knew when it came to Ethan Zimmerman, she had the propensity to let herself get hurt. Badly hurt.

Before he could say anything, she saw a couple of men approaching. "Ethan, more men with guns at your three o'clock. Two of them, and not the same ones as last time."

Without turning to look, he took her hand again, and they darted between the nearest houses, heading for the next street over. Two groups of armed men wandering around meant there were likely more. Whether or not the men were after her and Ethan remained to be seen, but she certainly wasn't going to wait until it was too late to find out.

"More up ahead," Ethan murmured, and she saw a group of three men this time passing by the street they'd just left.

"Following us?"

"Not sure, but they're looking at us," he replied.

"What should we do?" They were outnumbered. There were at least seven armed men in the village to their two, that didn't bode well for her and Ethan.

"Nothing until we know for sure they're after us."

"If they are, we should try to take them in alive. At least one of them," she added. "That way we can find out what they know, and if they are involved with the drug trafficking then we'll be able to find which of your colleagues is in on it."

"Sounds like a plan. They're coming."

Sparrow's hand hovered over her weapon. The men looked at them curiously, but they didn't have their weapons up and pointed at them. It looked more like they were trying to feel things out, see if she and Ethan were up to something.

A distraction.

They needed a distraction. Something for the men to discount them as any sort of threat.

Without thinking, Sparrow curled her good arm around Ethan's neck and pulled him down, pressing her lips to his in a kiss she knew she wouldn't soon forget, fake or not.

* * *

5:33 P.M.

SOMETHING SHIFTED INSIDE HIM.

Sparrow's soft lips pressed against his and Ethan was too shocked to do anything, like the sensible thing that would be to gently push her away and let her down nicely, telling her he still loved his wife and didn't want to move on.

Only he couldn't do that because Sparrow had kissed him to make the armed soldiers think they were just here to walk around, she was trying to make them look as non-threatening as possible.

Yeah.

That was why he didn't stop the kiss.

Insert eye roll there.

Ethan knew that it had nothing to do with where they

were, the soldiers with weapons who may or may not be after them, or the fact they were here to potentially trap a drug trafficker using his plane to move the product. The reason he didn't end the kiss was simple.

He didn't want to.

Sparrow shifted, moving closer, her breasts crushed against him, soft and supple and he found himself wanting to take them in his hands, tease her nipples until they stood at attention, then close his lips around the hard little peak and flick it with his tongue until she was writhing beneath him, begging for more.

Only then would he move down her body, trailing a line of kisses as he went, to settle between her legs. Then he'd put his hands and mouth to good use, stroking and sucking, until she could think of nothing else but what he was doing to her. She'd come on his fingers and tongue, and then he'd bury himself inside her and make her come again before he allowed himself his own release.

When Sparrow's lips parted and she made a soft, little, needy sigh, he very nearly threw everything to the wind— their location, the potential danger, the fact that he didn't want to be feeling this way about a woman—and took her then and there, the consequences be damned.

She tasted like fire. He knew that was weird, fire didn't have a taste, and if you tried to imagine what it would taste like he suspected you'd think of smoke. But that wasn't at all what it was like. Sparrow tasted like heat, fiery desire, and explosive passion. Sierra's kisses had been sweet like sugar, but then her personality had been very different from Sparrow's. Sierra had been quiet, almost shy, she had a big heart, and she loved to help others. She taught preschool and was amazing with small children. Sparrow was a warrior, strong and fierce, she protected those she loved, she stood by her friends, and he knew without a doubt that she would fight beside him if the soldiers attacked.

Sparrow shook up everything he knew about his future and everything he thought he knew about what he wanted in life.

Panic bubbled inside him, and he quickly stepped back.

He was breathing heavily.

She was breathing heavily.

They stared at each other for a long moment before he finally said, "They're gone. Guess we fooled them into thinking we were making out for real."

A flicker of what he thought could be disappointment flared in her eyes, but it was quickly gone. "Yeah, guess we did."

Everything felt awkward now, while just moments before they had shared what could quite possibly be the best kiss of his life, now they felt miles apart. That wasn't what he wanted. Not wanting another relationship didn't mean he wanted to hurt someone he liked and considered a friend. But Ethan wasn't sure how to fix the sudden distance he had created.

He wanted to, though.

Panic was again bubbling inside him only this time it wasn't because he felt too close to Sparrow, too close to doing something he shouldn't. Now it was because he felt too far away from her.

Silence dragged between them, and he was about to blurt out something—probably something that would wind up making things worse even though that wasn't his intention—when her attention shifted to something over his shoulder.

"Ethan, it's Dr. Gabler," she whispered.

"Where?"

"He just came out of that house." She pointed to the one

on the corner of the street they had turned down to evade the soldiers.

"Let's follow him." As he turned to hurry after Oliver, he snagged Sparrow's hand and tugged her along with him. The ruse they were lovers seemed to have worked well so far, may as well keep it up. If anything, if Oliver was involved, he would think the reason Ethan had gone after Sparrow and the reason he hadn't told anyone she was there right away was because there was something between them.

Sparrow tried to pull her hand free even as she followed him. "Ethan, you don't …"

"I want to," he said gruffly, hating that it was true, but it was. Nothing had changed, he still wasn't looking to find love again, but he wasn't ready to let Sparrow go just yet. It didn't feel fair because he had nothing to offer her, but for this moment he needed to be selfish and maintain the connection to her.

They hurried down the street and turned the corner just in time to see Oliver stopping outside another house. They quickly crossed the street, he was headed for an old truck parked there, intending for them to hide behind it and see who Oliver was talking to, but just as they were in the middle of the street the doctor turned.

"Busted," Sparrow muttered.

Because there was nothing to do but act casual and pretend they had nothing to hide, Ethan lifted a hand and waved to Oliver. "We'll have to head over."

"Stick to our story, you're showing me around, and we made out a little. If he is working with the soldiers then they could have reported that we were, uh, kissing," Sparrow finished a little uncomfortably.

They were going to have to talk about the kiss. He didn't want things to be awkward between them even if they weren't going to see each other again after she left.

Oliver waved back and watched as they walked down the street toward him. "What are you two doing here?" he asked when they reached him.

"Showing Sparrow around," Ethan answered smoothly. "She was feeling better and was bored. Thought I'd show her the local village."

The doctor eyed them suspiciously. "Thought you were in the Air Force, stationed at Camp Lemonnier. Surely you've been to African villages before."

Sparrow pasted on an easy smile. "Never visited a village under these circumstances before."

Oliver cocked his head, then shook it slowly. "No, I don't think so. Something else is going on. You were asking all those questions yesterday, I thought you were being polite, but now I think you had an ulterior motive. You followed me here. Why?"

"Why do you come here every day at the same time?" Sparrow countered.

A long sigh whooshed between his lips then he closed his eyes. "My family lives here."

"Your parents?" Ethan asked. As far as he was aware, the man wasn't married and didn't have any children.

"No. My wife."

"Wife?" Ethan echoed. "I didn't know you were married."

"My parents didn't approve. They might have come here to be missionaries, but they looked down on the natives as they called them. Didn't want me to marry one, wanted me to marry a nice, wealthy white woman. But I fell in love with Precious before I went back to the States for medical school. When I moved back over here my parents were thrilled, thinking I was following in their footsteps, but I didn't come back for them, or even the people here, I came for Precious. We were married, and we have four beautiful children, the oldest is nearly twenty and just had her first child. The baby is sick, that's why I was sneaking supplies. That's why you're here right?" he asked Sparrow. "Because of the missing supplies. I knew it was wrong, but I couldn't stand by and let my grandson die."

As far as Ethan knew, no one had noticed any missing supplies. He and Evan didn't have a lot to do with using them, just packed and unpacked the planes, and Esme hadn't mentioned anything. While those medical supplies were supposed to help as many remote villages as they could, Ethan could understand Oliver's choices.

Family was everything.

There wasn't anything he wouldn't have done if it would have given Sierra a chance at life. Should the doctor be punished? Perhaps. Was Ethan going to report him to the aid agency? Absolutely not. How could he? It would make him a hypocrite when he would have done the same thing in Oliver's shoes.

"I come every day to visit my grandson, see what I can do for him," Oliver explained. "If the cost of helping my family is losing my job then it's a price I'm willing to pay."

"You're not going to lose your job," Sparrow said kindly.

"Really?" Oliver asked, sounding taken aback.

"Really," Ethan confirmed. Oliver Gabler wasn't the drug smuggler, he was just a man doing the best he could for his family.

"And I'm really not here because of missing medical supplies," Sparrow told him.

"So, I confessed for nothing?" Oliver grimaced.

"Yep," Sparrow agreed cheerfully. "But we'd love to meet your wife, kids, and little grandson."

The doctor smiled warmly now. "I would love to introduce you."

As the three of them headed into the house they were standing in front of, Ethan couldn't help but be impressed with Sparrow. It was like there wasn't a single situation she could be placed in where she didn't know exactly what to do. She put people at ease, was calm under pressure, cared, and kissed like a goddess. It was like she was the perfect woman.

No wonder she confused him.

CHAPTER FOUR

January 21st

 1:46 A.M.

SPARROW WANDERED RESTLESSLY around Ethan's house. Since it was small, just one room and the bedroom, there wasn't really enough space to pace properly.

She felt frustrated.

And she didn't mean she was annoyed they hadn't found the smuggler.

She was sexually frustrated. That kiss they'd shared yesterday had turned her on more than some of the guys she'd dated touching more intimate parts of her body. She couldn't even lie and say she'd kissed him to maintain their cover. As far as she had been concerned that was just a convenient excuse.

But Ethan had regretted it.

Oh, he'd kissed her back, and she knew he had been turned on too. There was no way he could deny it, she'd felt his length growing hard and pressing against her, but he had regretted it nonetheless.

He'd all but jumped away from her, not what a woman wanted to see after just sharing the best kiss she'd ever had with a man she was insanely attracted to.

Things between them had been awkward ever since. They'd met Dr. Gabler's family, then driven back out here, eaten dinner with all of his colleagues, before they'd gone to his place, and she'd made the excuse that she was tired so she could retreat to the bedroom. Of course, gentleman that he was, Ethan had been sleeping on the couch so she could have the bed, just one of the many things she liked about him.

The satellite phone rang, and she wandered over to it and picked it up, glad for the distraction. "Hello?"

"Hey, Sparrow, it's Olivia."

"Hey, Liv." Although she'd only met her soon-to-be sister-in-law in person once the two of them had been exchanging emails since Olivia and Eagle got together and they'd grown close. Sparrow liked Olivia, and she'd been looking forward to spending time with her, helping to shop for baby things for the new little one joining their family in just a few short months.

"How are you feeling? Eagle said you have a concussion and a broken collarbone. I'm so glad those were the only injuries you ended up with, you could easily have been killed."

Too easily. She'd had nightmares last night about the crash and the men who hadn't survived. "I was lucky," she agreed. "Please tell me you have something for me." The more time she spent around Ethan, the harder it would be to leave. She needed to help him sort out this mess, clear his name, and then get home to her family. If nothing else, maybe the few days she'd spent with him had shown her that maybe she was more ready to find love than she'd thought she was. When she did get back home, she would make an effort to meet some guys.

"As a matter of fact, I do have something for you," Olivia said, and Sparrow could hear the smile in her voice.

"Well, don't keep me in suspense."

Olivia laughed. "I used the program Raven developed when she was searching for Cleo and programmed in as many keywords as I could think of that might get a hit."

"And you did get a hit?" Computers were not her thing at all. She could use them of course, for simple things like email and scrolling through social media, but programming was outside of her skill set.

"I did. There are two warlords in the area, and when I looked into them, I found one of them is quickly becoming one of the biggest drug traffickers in all of Africa. He's even started expanding into Asia and both North and South America. His name is Omega Chidubem, and I was able to hack into an online dark web forum he's using to communicate with his smugglers. I found a bunch of messages over the last several months all signed by someone who calls themselves E."

"Evan or Esmerelda?"

"Or Ethan," Olivia added.

"Ethan is not involved in trafficking drugs," she said indignantly. She knew it with as much certainty as she had that both of them had enjoyed that kiss and wished it could happen again.

"Not saying he is," Olivia soothed, "just pointing it out. If we turn in the information now it still puts Ethan on the hot seat."

"You really don't think Ethan is involved?" She knew she

didn't, but Sparrow also knew that maybe she wasn't objective when it came to the sexy pilot. She'd had a crush on him for a long time now and the fact he'd come to save her, at risk to his own life, only added to that.

"Definitely not. If he was, no way would he have agreed so quickly to go looking for you when Eagle called. Now there's no way to prove that the E is either of your suspects, but at least it's a start. I'll keep digging, see what else I can find, but, Sparrow, there's one more thing. Omega has ties to Le Entregar, looks like he was providing them with drugs to get the women who worked in some of their brothels hooked to keep them more compliant. That means he and his men could have been the ones who shot down your helicopter. Even if he doesn't know that you found the drugs, he could be connected to whoever is after our family and therefore still be a threat to you."

"Okay, that's good to know. I think we're reasonably safe here, and hopefully, we find something soon to prove it's either Evan or Esme." She'd already called home yesterday when they returned to let her family know that Oliver Gabler was out as a suspect. "I really need you to keep looking into those two and tell me everything you can about them."

"On it. Be careful."

"I will. Thanks, Liv."

Once she hung up and set the phone down the restlessness she felt grew. She was sick of just sitting around. Dr. Gabler and Esmerelda were working in the clinic, Evan was helping Ethan with the plane, which meant that everyone should be occupied. Maybe it was time she did a little snooping of her own.

Strolling out of Ethan's place, she headed to the outhouse first to take care of business, but then instead of going back to Ethan's, she headed further away toward what she knew was Evan's house. She'd start there, take a careful little look through his things, see if she could find anything to indicate he was involved, and then she'd move on to Esme's place. If she was quick, she could take a look at both houses before the clinic closed at one for a half-hour lunch break.

Grateful for the fact that there were no locks to these little houses, and that they were small enough it wouldn't take her long to search, Sparrow slipped through the front door to Evan's house. While the layout was the same as Ethan's, and the basic fixtures were also the same, Evan's house looked and felt nothing like Ethan's.

Where Ethan's was reasonably tidy, Evan's was a mess. It looked like an explosion of paper and trash had gone off in here, only to have everything picked up by a tornado and thrown around and around until things were everywhere.

Most of the litter appeared to be sheets of paper, empty chip bags, and candy wrappers. There was also an assortment of soda cans and she stepped on one, making it crunch beneath her boot, the sound loud in the empty house as she crossed to where there was a stack of papers so high it reached to her knees.

Sparrow picked up the top sheet and was surprised to find it was music. It had obviously been drawn up by Evan, the black lines drawn in pen, the musical notes in pencil. Beneath were words, most of which had been scratched out. She picked up another sheet of paper and another to find each one had music written on it.

Evan hadn't mentioned anything about being a musician, but it was clear he had to be. Did that have something to do with why his family had insisted on sending him over here?

It was an interesting idea, although if he had been a musician, he must have been using a different name because surely that would have been one of the first things to pop up on Olivia's search.

She was wondering how to fit music into the conversation at dinner tonight when she was grabbed from behind.

Although she was recovering well from the concussion her reflexes were still slow, her mind still not quite as sharp as it used to be—as it *should* be—and it took her precious seconds to process that whoever had grabbed her meant her harm.

Training eventually kicked in, and she kicked at the knee of the person holding her. A grunt of pain confirmed she hit her target, but her attacker was bigger and stronger than her and didn't loosen their grip.

Still, she had spent her life learning how to take down people bigger and stronger than herself, and she was about to execute a maneuver that would give her the upper hand, when her assailant grabbed her injured arm and yanked it from the sling, causing pain to shoot through her body.

That was all the man needed to shove her face-first against the wall, her injured arm in their grasp so they could use pain to control her, a knee pressed into the small of her back leaving her pinned in place and helpless.

12:25 P.M.

A PRICKLING in his gut had Ethan setting down the spanner and walking to the hangar door.

Nothing looked out of place. The four little houses stood silent. The communal room was similarly quiet, and the small clinic had the usual couple of dozen people hanging around outside it, but everyone appeared to be standing around quietly talking amongst themselves while they waited their turn to be seen by Dr. Gabler.

Nothing discernible should have caught his attention and yet the feeling in his gut didn't diminish.

Something felt wrong and yet he had no idea what.

Deciding he was just on edge from having to sleep on the couch while a gorgeous woman he was having trouble containing his attraction to slept in his bed in the next room, he turned to face the plane again but didn't move. All night he'd been painfully hard but hadn't wanted to do anything about it while Sparrow was right there. Instead, he'd tossed and turned, getting little sleep, and this morning he felt cranky and sexually frustrated.

He and Evan were working to see what repairs they could make to the plane with the supplies they had on hand before they called the agency to ask for whatever they didn't have. While he worked, his thoughts circled continuously around Sparrow and whether or not one-time sex with her counted as cheating on Sierra or not.

Realistically, Ethan knew that Sierra was dead, their marriage ended with her life, and he was free to sleep with anyone he wanted. But in his heart, it wasn't that simple. He still loved her and sleeping with another woman felt like a betrayal.

One he wasn't sure he could make, no matter how badly he wanted Sparrow.

"What's up?" Evan asked, coming to join him in the open hangar doorway. "Something wrong."

"No, nothing," he answered honestly. At least he hoped he was answering honestly, but that sixth sense warning that something was off was still pinging like crazy.

"Then let's get back to work."

Evan returned to the plane, but Ethan found he couldn't move. He needed to check on Sparrow, that was what his gut was trying to tell him. His gut had saved his life before, and in the military, he had learned to trust it implicitly, but it had been years since he'd retired, and now he feared his gut was out of practice.

"I need to go check on Sparrow," he announced. He'd rather have her think he was crazy than ignore his internal warning system if something really was wrong.

"Why?"

Ethan shrugged. "She's still recovering from a concussion, she's been alone all morning, I just want to make sure she's okay."

Only it was more than that, he acknowledged as he hurried toward his place. What he felt for Sparrow wasn't the same as his love for Sierra had been, but the last thing he wanted was to lose another woman who was important to him. Maybe he shouldn't have left her alone. She should be monitored at all times while she was recovering, and he should have insisted she hang out with him where he could keep an eye on her no matter that she'd seemed much better.

"Sparrow?" he called out as he entered his house only to find it empty.

Was she taking a nap?

Or had she passed out?

He ran into the bedroom only to find it empty, the bed neatly made.

Where was she?

Running back outside, he looked around, wondering where she would have gone and not told him.

To the communal rooms?

He headed there next, but once again, he found the space mockingly empty.

She couldn't have just disappeared into thin air, she had to be around here somewhere.

The outhouse?

Ethan was heading over there, worried she'd been feeling sick and maybe passed out in there—because he was sure she wouldn't go anywhere without telling him first, not that there was really anywhere to go—when he saw a small girl come skipping out the outhouse door to meet her mother.

So, Sparrow wasn't there.

That only left the other buildings on the property. Would she go over to the clinic to see if she could help out if she got bored? She might have, he could see Sparrow not enjoying just sitting around taking it easy. If she wasn't there then the only other options were the others' houses, but surely she wouldn't go and search their houses on her own looking for evidence of drug smuggling.

No.

Sparrow wouldn't do that.

Ethan sighed and closed his eyes, scrubbing a hand down his face. Yeah, she would. She wanted to find out who had used his plane to traffic drugs almost as much as he did. He could see her getting bored and snooping alone.

Evan's house was closer, so he headed there first. As he reached for the door handle, he was all ready to rip Sparrow a new one for being so reckless, especially when, whether she liked it or not, she was still recovering physically and psychologically from being shot out of the sky. He'd heard her having nightmares last night and had wanted badly to go to her, comfort her, but he'd refrained because he'd known how it would end. The two of them naked and in bed together.

That fled his mind when he opened the door to find Sparrow shoved up against the wall, her injured arm twisted up behind her back, and a large man pinning her in place.

Rage—red hot and furious—surged through him and he didn't even think.

Just acted.

Sparrow was in trouble. His world tunneled until that was all he could think about.

He launched at the other man. Sparrow's assailant was black, dressed like one of the villagers, and thankfully unarmed. He must have come in with the rest of the people to go to the clinic but then followed her when she came in here to snoop.

A well-placed fist to the side of the man's head had him crumpling to the floor.

Sparrow gasped and turned to face him, her shirt was rumpled, and it looked like the man had had his hand inside it.

A second wave of rage came over him, and he delivered a swift kick to the man's unprotected ribs before turning back to Sparrow.

She was breathing hard.

He was too.

Just like after their kiss yesterday only this time for a very different reason.

"You okay?" he asked as Sparrow gingerly moved her arm, cradling it against her chest.

"Yeah, he got the drop on me, concussion dulled my reflexes. I almost had him, but he got my arm, twisted it, and pain distracted me." She said it like she'd done something wrong, but even with her training it would be easy for a larger person to get the advantage, especially when there was an injury to exploit.

"Did he say anything to you?" Was this a random thing, the case of a man seeing an attractive woman alone and vulnerable and taking advantage, or was it one of the trafficker's soldiers trying to get information out of Sparrow because they suspected she knew about the drugs?

"Didn't get a chance to say much," Sparrow replied. "Olivia called, said she found messages in a dark web forum from one of the warlords in the area who's a known trafficker. The messages were signed E. It has to be Evan or Esme. I just wanted to try to find something to prove which one. He came in just before you, grabbed me, shoved me up against the wall, felt me up a little, then you came in." She offered up a weak smile, and her blue eyes shone with gratitude and something more. There was something genuine in them. Whatever it was she felt for him, he suspected it ran deeper than just physical attraction.

Which meant it was even more important he keep some distance between them.

Only his body didn't seem to agree. His heart thudded almost painfully in his chest, and he had to curl his fingers into fists to keep from reaching for her, pulling her into his arms, holding her until he could draw a full breath and his fear receded.

If he hadn't come in, then the man would no doubt have raped Sparrow. Women weren't valued around here. They were considered things to be used for a man's pleasure and at his whims.

After that, the man might have killed her or tortured her for information or depending on who he was and if he worked for someone, he might have snatched her, taken her away to be sold.

The thought of something happening to Sparrow almost paralyzed him.

His feelings for her obviously ran deeper than physical attraction as well. No way this level of deep protective rage could be swirling inside him at the sight of her in danger if it was just physical.

He liked her.

More than he should.

More than he wanted to.

And he wasn't sure how much longer he could go on denying it, and yet he didn't know if there was room in his heart for another woman.

Would letting Sparrow in mean he had to let some of his love for Sierra out?

CHAPTER FIVE

January 22nd

3 :16 A.M.

"Mmm," Sparrow moaned in delight as Ethan slipped a finger inside her, curling it so it hit that hidden spot. "More, I need more."

"I got you, babe."

Another finger slid inside her, stretching her, filling her, but it wasn't enough.

"More," she whispered on a breathy sigh.

"Here you go."

His thumb found her throbbing little bundle of nerves, working it until she was writhing beneath him.

But still, she couldn't quite get there.

Pleasure was shimmering tantalizingly out of reach.

Her hips came off the bed seeking more, and she shifted uncomfortably, so close she could feel it and yet not quite close enough.

"More, Ethan, more," she begged. "More, please, more."

She woke with a start, her unsatisfied body humming its displeasure that dream Ethan hadn't been able to make her come.

Sparrow groaned in frustration. It was hell being this close to Ethan and yet not being able to touch him, kiss him, not even talk to him about what she was feeling because she knew he didn't feel the same way and she didn't want to make things even more awkward than they already were.

Her whole body was pulsing with a heavy need, it flowed through her blood, tingled in her tightened nipples, and throbbed almost painfully between her legs.

"This is ridiculous." Sparrow huffed as she threw back the covers. They were two consenting adults, if nothing else, the attraction went both ways, and from the way Ethan was careful not to touch her, not even get close enough that he might accidentally brush against her, she knew that he was walking around as turned on as she was.

At least they could put themselves out of their misery. One night of hot, no holds barred, no strings attached sex was exactly what they both needed right now. And she could do that. She'd live in the moment just until the sun rose and deal with the broken heart in the morning when she had no choice but to remember that a relationship with Ethan was never going to be on the table.

She was reaching for the doorknob when she froze.

What was she thinking?

Maybe she could do a night of hot, no holds barred, no strings attached sex with another guy but not with Ethan.

With Ethan there were already strings whether either of them liked it or not.

With a frustrated groan, she turned and went back to the bed, sliding beneath the covers. She squirmed uncomfortably, the desire flowing through her was growing not diminishing. She was never going to get any sleep like this.

Somewhat uncertainly, Sparrow moved her hand between her legs. It wasn't like she had never touched herself before because she definitely had. She spent a lot of time on military bases with a bunch of guys she wasn't allowed to date, but she'd never done it with the man she wished was touching her just on the other side of the wall.

It felt wrong.

Silly even.

And definitely childish.

People had no strings attached sex all the time, and she was sure if she pressed him Ethan would agree.

But that was just it. She didn't *want* Ethan to agree only because she pressed him to, or because their chemistry was off the charts, or because the sexual tension hovering between them consumed him.

She wanted him to touch her only because it was what he wanted. Because he acknowledged there was more than attraction between them, and that while things might be hard given their work and living situations, he was at least willing to give them a shot.

Her fingertip brushed tentatively across her begging little bud and then pressed a little harder, swirling the pad of her finger through her wetness before bringing it back to her bud. It still felt weird doing this with Ethan next door, but she was desperate here.

The explosion caught her totally off guard.

Red and orange flared outside the window as whatever the bomb had hit was blown up in a fiery ball of flames.

The force of it sent the small house rocking, the furniture

moved along with it, and she rolled off the bed, hitting the floor hard.

Pain spiked in her collarbone, spiraling out through her shoulder and down her arm, but she quickly pushed the pain away. There was no time for daydreaming—or night dreaming—about Ethan, and no time to worry about the broken bone. Someone had just fired a missile or something at the aid compound.

"Sparrow?" The bedroom door was flung open, Ethan's figure silhouetted in the doorway as he scanned the room. When he located her, he hurried to her side, dropping to one knee beside her. "You okay?"

She sucked in a breath and willed the pain to recede. "Yeah. Just fell off the bed when the explosion hit. Do you know what was hit?"

Ethan's large hand gripped her good shoulder, and he helped her sit. "No, I came to check on you first."

"Think this is because of the drugs?" She allowed Ethan to gently cup her bad elbow and help her to her feet.

"Maybe. Not the first time an aid agency has been hit though. Sometimes they come for the food, sometimes the medical supplies, sometimes they just come because they can and they want to cause problems, prove they're in charge."

Too bad they couldn't know which option it was before they went out there.

There was always the chance that this was about her. That whoever was after their family and had shot down her helo had somehow tracked her to here and was hellbent on doing whatever it took to get her.

If that was the case, the last thing she would do was allow anyone else to be hurt because of her.

"Ethan, if this is because …"

"Don't even go there," he warned, thrusting a pair of sweats at her. "Put these on."

"You don't even know what I was going to say," she said, sitting on the edge of the bed and gingerly leaning forward to slip one foot into the sweatpants.

"Sure I do. You were going to say that if whoever fired at the compound did it because they know you're here, and that they're here to get you, that you'd surrender to them if it meant no one else got hurt or killed because of you."

"Huh," she said, casting a quick glance up at him. "Guess you did know what I was going to say after all."

"You're not hard to read, wisp."

She hoped she was at least hard enough to read that he had no idea what she'd been doing in here when the explosion hit. It would be totally embarrassing if he knew that she had been about to get herself off to fantasies of him.

"So, what's the plan?" she asked as she shoved her feet into her boots which he set before her.

"We go out quietly, see what we can see, and pray it's not an army on the way because there's no way the two of us, Oliver, Evan, and Esme can hold off an army." Ethan paused, then passed her a black sweatshirt. "You should call the base. If it is one of the warlord's armies coming in we don't want them to get the drugs, or get their hands on you and Esme."

They both knew what would happen to her and Esme if they were taken captive. They would be brutally raped and then eventually killed or sold. If whoever was after her family was behind the assault, she might wind up facing worse, but she would gladly sacrifice herself to spare Esme and the others.

"If we call in the base then we have to tell them about the drugs. You know that means they might take you into custody until they sort this mess out," she warned.

"At least everyone would be alive."

"All right, if you're sure."

"I'm sure."

Taking the satellite phone, she quickly called in what had happened to Camp Lemonnier, asking that they send out a team to help.

"You going to be okay with a weapon?" Ethan asked once she hung up.

She narrowed her eyes at him. "You really have to ask that, Zimmerman?"

Ethan flashed her a grin. "Just checking."

He passed her a weapon, and after checking it the two of them walked side by side through the house. Just as they reached the front door a second explosion hit, rocking the world beneath them.

Sparrow reached for the door. They needed to find out what was going on and how bad it was. She hoped that Oliver, Evan, and Esme had implemented whatever emergency protocols they had, so she and Ethan could focus on neutralizing the threat.

"Sparrow, be careful, don't play the martyr, okay? Give us a chance to get this under control before you do something that you can't take back," Ethan warned.

Because he looked so serious and sincere, Sparrow nodded. "I won't do anything reckless. We'll work this as a team."

"A team," Ethan echoed, and he sounded almost wistful.

She wished they had time to talk, but a third explosion lit up the night and the two of them slipped outside, ready to face this threat side by side.

* * *

4:02 A.M.

WITH SPARROW BY HIS SIDE, the two of them crept outside.

Three explosions meant someone was determined to get to the compound. Or it seemed like they were determined to destroy the compound.

If it was whoever was after Sparrow and her family, Ethan suspected they would have moved in with more stealth, wanting to take her alive, but then again, they had been willing to shoot down her helicopter, knowing it would more than likely kill her. Maybe they'd decided trying to take the Oswalds alive wasn't working too well and they may as well just start taking them out one by one.

Sure that this had to do with the drugs and not Sparrow, Ethan kept a close watch on her as they moved across the open space, just in case she did try to do something stupid. She'd promised to do this together, but he also knew the guilt she was carrying around over the death of the SEAL team, and if she thought he or one of the others were going to be hurt, she still might give herself up.

"What's your emergency plan?" Sparrow whispered as she surveyed the damage to the compound just as he was doing.

"Everyone goes to the underground bunker, it's set up to withstand basically any attack, and there are enough supplies for them to be there a couple of days."

"Think everyone made it?"

Ethan looked around, thankfully two of the missiles had hit empty space, but one had taken out the back half of the hangar where his plane was stationed. The bunker was by the communal building so chances were that when the explosions wakened everyone the others would have immediately executed emergency protocols and gone to the bunker. "Yeah, I think so."

"They won't be waiting for you before securing themselves, will they?"

"They'll close and bar the door, they'll only open it if the person on the other side says the code. It's cabbage patch by the way."

"Cabbage patch?" Sparrow snorted.

He smirked. "Mrs. McDonald, who was the nurse here for almost forty years, had a thing for those Cabbage Patch dolls."

"Cute. I never had one of those, I was too old by the time we moved to the city, but Dove had one and I always liked it, just thought I was too old for a doll."

Ethan had never thought about how weird the Oswalds upbringing must have been. Living only on an off-the-grid farm, no contact with anyone outside their family, none of the things most kids took for granted. A desire to show her some of the things she had missed out on filled him, but he shoved it away, now definitely wasn't the time or the place to be even thinking about Sparrow and how she made him feel.

"Looks like they're firing from the west," Sparrow said, already focused back on what was happening.

"Coming in from the gate."

"Are the guards here overnight?"

"Yeah, there's a night shift." Although how much good that would do them he didn't know, the guards certainly hadn't done anything earlier when that man had assaulted Sparrow. The man had been taken in by the local police although Ethan doubted anything would come of it. The man hadn't said anything about who he was, why he was there, or why he'd gone after Sparrow. She had claimed she'd seen him sneaking around and gone into Evan's house to see what he was doing to keep their cover, but given the raid on the compound tonight he assumed that Evan knew they were onto him.

"How trained are your guards?"

"Not trained enough to take on an army."

Sparrow nodded. "We need to figure out how many men

are here. We should make our way to the fence and circle around from there. If there aren't too many, we can take them out, otherwise we'll just have to hold them off for as long as we can."

"And if there's too many we head to my plane and fly out," Ethan added because he wasn't dying tonight, and neither was Sparrow.

"I don't like it, but I agree."

Thankful she wasn't fighting him on it the two of them started moving, watching each other's backs as they made their way to the wire fence surrounding the property. Things were quiet, and he hoped that meant that whoever was here was backing off. Maybe it was just someone trying to make a statement. Although they were here to help, not everybody saw it that way. It wasn't uncommon for places such as this one to be targeted.

The sound of gunfire started when they were closer to the gates.

Looked like there were at least a dozen men on the other side of the fence, all well-armed.

"At least there haven't been any more explosions," Sparrow whispered.

"Probably means they already used what they had. Guards will probably surrender any moment." The guards likely wouldn't be killed by whoever was attacking them, if anything, they might be recruited. Unless the guards were already in on the drug trafficking. It wasn't hard to buy people off in this part of the world. People were struggling, often starving, with usually no access to medical care. The possibility of actually making money had led to a lot of people working for one of the warlords.

As if his words made it happen, they could see the gates open from where they were hiding.

"How many do you see?" Sparrow asked.

"A dozen, maybe two dozen. How long till your people get here?" He didn't think they could hold the soldiers off long enough, not with just the two of them. He was confident that the bunker would keep the others safe in the meantime because he had worked on it himself while he was here, reinforcing everything and making it virtually impenetrable.

"Not quickly enough. We can take out some of them but not without them knowing where we are and returning fire. We could try splitting up? You stay here. I'll circle around to the other side, get them from both angles."

"We're not splitting up," he said quickly. He wanted them together, where they could watch each other's backs. "And they'll spread out as soon as they come through the gate. Our best bet is to try to make it to the hangar."

"What about the bunker?"

"It's closer to the gate, they'll see us, but if we backtrack to the hangar and get into my plane we might make it there before we're spotted."

Sparrow hesitated for a moment before nodding. "Yeah okay." It was clear in the bright moonlight that she wasn't pleased about getting in a plane knowing they could be shot at so soon after being shot out of the sky, but she also knew it was their best bet. Even if this wasn't to do with whoever was after her, it was likely the traffickers knew she was onto them in which case they were kind of here for her anyway.

Together they moved stealthily through the night, Ethan anxious to get to his plane. That was where he felt at home, up in the sky. While his plane wasn't equipped with weapons like the ones he'd flown in his time in the military, it would do the job he needed it to do. Get Sparrow to safety.

His own safety was of secondary concern.

They were almost to the hangar when they were suddenly bathed in bright light.

Accompanying shouts said they'd been spotted.

"Go, get the plane ready. I'll hold them off and jump in at the last moment," Sparrow said.

His every protective instinct screamed at him not to leave her behind. What would he do if he got safely out of here, but she didn't? It would destroy what was left of him and take away the only pieces Sierra hadn't taken with her when she died.

Still, he knew she was right.

It was their only chance.

Hating it, he allowed Sparrow to lay down covering fire while he ran to his plane, jumped in, and started it up.

Gunfire continued to sound as he drove the plane slowly toward the open hangar doors. They were lucky the front part where his plane was hadn't been destroyed in the explosion. Usually, the plane was kept to the back of the hangar, but because he and Evan had been working on it yesterday, it was toward the front.

This would be close. He'd need to stop beside Sparrow so she could jump on board and then take off quickly under heavy fire.

Sparrow didn't turn as he approached, her concentration was on firing at the approaching soldiers, but he knew she was aware of him because as soon as he was close enough, she turned and scrambled into the plane, immediately leaning out the door so she could keep firing.

Ethan did what he had been trained to do, he let Sparrow keep covering fire going while he got them up into the air. They'd managed to get the plane workable, but he wasn't sure how long they would last in the air, especially if they were hit.

It wasn't until Sparrow finally sagged into her seat that he let out his first real breath since the first explosion had gone off.

"We made it," Sparrow sighed.

"Yeah, we did," he agreed.

"We make a good team." She said the words, but didn't look at him and he couldn't help but wonder if she was hinting that they might make a good team in other areas as well. "Where are we going? The base?"

"We didn't finish fixing the plane, not sure how long we can stay airborne and don't want to risk going that far. Let's go to the village. I can put it down just outside it, I know of a place where I can hide the plane for a few hours, then we'll go to Oliver's family's house. No one would think to look for us there."

"Makes sense," Sparrow agreed.

A few minutes later, he landed the plane and taxied it into an abandoned hangar. "This was the old compound, they moved to the newer one about a decade ago, but I knew this was out here. Should keep the plane safe for a while."

"Boxes are gone, whoever was smuggling the drugs obviously took them."

"I'm not surprised."

They both got out of the plane and started walking toward the village. Neither of them spoke. He didn't know what Sparrow was thinking about, but he was preparing himself for the possibility he would be arrested. Just because Sparrow believed he was innocent didn't mean anyone else would. While he had to hope he would eventually be cleared there was no telling how long that would take. And there was always the chance he wouldn't be cleared.

"Ethan." Sparrow nudged his side as they walked through the village. "Do you see what I see?"

"What?" he asked, looking around to see what had caught her attention. When he followed her line of sight and saw what she was looking at, he gasped.

* * *

4:53 A.M.

"IT'S EVAN," Sparrow whispered.

"What's he doing here?" Ethan asked what she could only assume was a rhetorical question given there was only one logical reason she could think of why the man was here in the village instead of back at the compound that had just been attacked by armed soldiers.

"My guess is hiding out here, so he doesn't get caught up in the shootout," she said.

Ethan took her elbow and pulled her over so they were between two houses but still had a clear view of Evan. The other man was standing outside a house but making no move to head inside.

"We don't know that for sure," Ethan cautioned.

"Okay, so is it normal for him to sneak out of the compound without telling anyone to come down to the village and be standing around at five in the morning?" It seemed pretty obvious as far as she was concerned. They were down to only two suspects, Evan and Esme, one of those suspects conveniently happened to be away from the compound right as it was attacked. As far as she was concerned, two plus two definitely equaled four.

"No, as far as I know it's not normal. If he was leaving, he should have told someone, and we're supposed to stay in the compound overnight for our own safety. I guess since Evan's family runs the charity that maybe the rules don't apply to him. Maybe he's here to meet a woman," Ethan suggested.

"I guess that's possible," she somewhat grudgingly acknowledged. Men liked sex and Evan had been here for a few years, it made sense he would want to get his needs attended to at some point. It was even possible he had one woman, in particular, he came to see. After all, Dr. Gabler had a whole family at the village nobody knew about, so it was plausible Evan had a girlfriend—or at least a mutually beneficial arrangement with a woman—here.

Still, the timing was too big a coincidence to ignore.

"There's a truck pulling up," Ethan said.

Half a dozen men were hanging out the sides of the open-backed vehicle, the canvas sides were rolled and attached to the roof, and the men made sure their weapons were on show so anyone who was out and about could see them. Did these men work for the same person who had ordered the attack on the compound?

Logic said it was likely.

What were the chances that the compound was hit by armed men and in the closest village one of the people who worked at the compound was met by a bunch of similarly armed men?

"They're stopping right beside Evan," she said. "This has to be enough proof to show that he is the trafficker."

"I wish we could get close enough to hear what they're saying."

"You not convinced?" After she'd been attacked yesterday, she'd reported what she'd found to Olivia who had managed to dig deep and find that when he was a teenager, Evan had changed his name, wanting to get away from his family and the life they tried to force onto him. His career had ended when he'd gotten addicted to drugs, performed a few shows high, and said things he shouldn't have while on stage. Only after his wife had left him taking their two kids with her and gaining full custody, had Evan gone back to his family and tried to get them to help him get his kids back. His family had refused, instead sending him to rehab and then over here to prove he was worthy of being a father. Already a drug addict, it wasn't a stretch to think the man might have been angry at his wife and family, and for losing the career he'd chosen, and decided to stick it to the world.

"I am, but I want something we can use that he can't try to wriggle out of."

Betrayal was evident in Ethan's voice. He'd already told her that Evan had been the one he was closest to out of his colleagues, and she suspected that Ethan even thought of the man as a friend even if he hadn't used the word to describe Evan. Moving to Africa had been as much about wanting to escape all memories of Sierra as much as it had wanting to make sure everyone had access to the things his wife had no doubt taken for granted during her struggle with cancer. Ethan had wanted to cut contact with everyone, keep his grief to himself, and she doubted the plan had been for him to make a friend while he was here. But it was clear from the expression on his face as he looked at Evan that he had made a friend.

A friend who had ended up using the thing Ethan loved the most against him.

Flying was all Ethan had left, and if he was anything like her, it was what gave him peace. There was nothing like cruising above the earth. Up in the air you felt free. How much more would she need that feeling of freedom if she had lost the person she loved the most?

"Let me get closer," she suggested. "Evan already thinks I'm here because of the drugs, we can use that to our advantage. As far as he knows you don't know anything, if he thought you did, I suspect you'd already be dead. He probably thinks I was in his house yesterday looking for proof—"

"Which you were," Ethan interrupted. Although he'd saved her and clearly cared that she'd almost been raped and either killed or kidnapped, he'd also ranted and raved at her once they got back to his house, asking what she was thinking going in there alone. He'd told her she should have waited so they could go together, but she'd pointed out that Evan would have been home by then.

"Okay, which I was," she acknowledged, "it's not a coincidence that the compound was attacked tonight. He probably thinks we're both back with the others in the bunker. If he sees me, it will throw him, that's how we'll get him to confess."

"You're not going over there on your own."

She bristled at his tone. That wasn't Ethan's decision to make. She was used to making life and death decisions. When she was flying, she was the one in charge, the one who made the final call. Sometimes she was given orders by her superiors, and she followed them, but because things were unpredictable, weather could change, the amount of fire they were taking could change, all in an instant, she usually had final say. She didn't do well with people who weren't in her chain of command telling her what to do.

"It's our best option and you know it. You're just going all macho alpha on me. Well, I have three brothers, and I don't let them boss me around, I won't let you do it either. I know how to take care of myself."

"Sparrow," Ethan said gently, reaching out to grasp her hand. "I didn't mean to upset you or imply I don't think you couldn't take down all of those men unarmed, but I don't want you to get hurt."

She softened. "That's sweet—kind of—but you know this is our best bet at getting something he can't wiggle out of. I don't want you to go to prison while this mess gets sorted out."

"I don't want that either, but it's better than you winding up dead."

"I have no intention of getting myself killed. You stay here, I'll pretend that I followed him here from the compound and that I don't know about the attack." The idea of Ethan sitting in a cell while an investigation was conducted didn't sit well with her. He might not have thought about her over the last few years, but she'd thought of him several times. Wanted to reach out, but how did you know what was an appropriate amount of time after a man lost his wife to contact him? It wasn't like she had intended to offer herself up for sex or marriage, just hang out, be friends, see where things went. Things might not be going anywhere between them, but she would make sure that his name was in the clear. "I got this, Ethan, have a little faith in me."

"I have faith in you, wisp, never doubt that."

The sincerity of his words struck her. She could swear it was real admiration, real affection in his eyes, mixed with a heavy dose of real fear.

Was Ethan really that worried about her being hurt?

With a small smile on her lips, Sparrow turned to face Evan Kikkert who was talking to the driver of the truck, and darted quickly back into the street so he didn't know that she wasn't alone. Then she strolled closer, her grin turning into a grimace when six weapons shifted to hold her in their sights. If Ethan really did care about her then he was about to have a heart attack.

* * *

5:04 A.M.

He was about to have a heart attack.

Ethan's entire being rebelled at the idea of allowing Sparrow to walk alone toward what could very well be the end of her life.

If she could read his thoughts, she'd be sassing him right

now about the word allow, but he didn't mean it in the way she would hear it. The way he meant it was about him not her. It wasn't about any failings on her part it was about his failings. You watched your teammate's back, that was the way it worked, and for right now Sparrow was his teammate, and he wasn't there to watch her back. Which made him feel sick.

Sparrow was … he wasn't even sure he could think of a way to describe the spunky wisp of a woman that was adequate enough. She was powerful despite her small size, and pure determination. She was funny, sassy, and kind, and she hadn't given up on him once. In fact, she was walking into an ambush on purpose because of him.

Which again was why he hated it so much.

While she hadn't outright said that she wanted him, she had skirted around the issue several times, hinting that she'd like to see if there could be anything between them. There couldn't be, and yet he hadn't come right out and said that either. That she hadn't made him feel like he was using her for his own purposes and then when he was done, he'd cut her loose and walk away without glancing back.

He would walk away—he had to—but he had a feeling there would be a *lot* of looking back once Sparrow left Djibouti.

As he watched from the shadows and safety the two buildings provided him, Sparrow strolled toward Evan like she didn't have a care in the world. She didn't look intimidated even though she was outmanned and outgunned, and it was that exact air of confidence that he could see had the soldiers hesitating.

Still, they had their weapons pointed at her as she continued walking until she was standing right beside Evan.

Since it was quiet, still early, although he was sure many

of the villagers were awake and deciding to remain indoors where it was safe, he could hear Sparrow when she spoke.

"Fancy meeting you here," she said to Evan.

The man he'd considered a friend—his only friend—fidgeted and hovered from foot to foot. Nervous energy was radiating off him, Ethan could feel it all the way over here. "I, uh, had some … business to attend to," Evan replied.

"Business?"

"Not *business* business," Evan rushed to confirm.

"I don't know what that means," Sparrow said smoothly. She hadn't spared a single glance at the soldiers, and that seemed to be working in her favor. They weren't sure yet what kind of threat she presented so they seemed to be going with the wait-and-see approach.

"Umm, it means …" Evan looked around as though searching for someone who could offer an appropriate response. Then he obviously decided he should go on the offensive. "What are *you* doing here?"

Sparrow shrugged disinterestedly. "Saw you leaving while I was going to the outhouse. Wondered where you'd be going at such an early hour, so I thought I'd follow along. Wanted to make sure you were safe, didn't know you had your own army," she said with a nod at the truck. "Should have gone back to bed, gotten some more beauty sleep."

"You were watching me," Evan growled, "you weren't just "going to the bathroom" were you?" He made air quotes for going to the bathroom, and it was evident that Evan believed Sparrow was in Djibouti specifically because of him.

"I've been watching everybody," Sparrow replied.

"No, you were sent to watch me." He grabbed her and roughly shoved her up against the side of the truck. Although he couldn't see her expression in the dark, Ethan knew the movement would have jarred her broken collarbone.

Rage filled him just like it had yesterday when he'd

walked into Evan's cabin to find a man with his hands on Sparrow. There was something about knowing she was in trouble that got to him in a personal way. He'd joined the military because he hadn't wanted anyone to live in danger and to do his part to make the world a safer place. But that was a generalized feeling, what he felt right now was anything but general. It was specific. *Very* specific. It was an almost overwhelming need to put himself between the petite black-haired beauty and anything that threatened her.

But he didn't.

He trusted Sparrow to know what she was doing.

And what she was doing was standing calmly while Evan ranted at her.

"My family sent you, didn't they?" Evan growled. "They sent you to check up on me because they didn't believe I'd turned my life around."

"Doesn't seem like you've turned your life around if the company you keep is anything to go by," Sparrow said.

"They're not my company, I just had to come, you don't know anything," Evan spat.

"I know someone is smuggling drugs, using the planes from Medi-Hope to do it. I know that you had a drug problem. One that cost you your career, your wife, your kids, and got you banished all the way out here to remote Africa. I don't think it's a big leap to believe you might have gotten yourself mixed up in drug trafficking," Sparrow said.

Ethan moved toward her before he even realized what he was doing. She'd just played her hand, and if the men in the truck were the trafficker's soldiers, she was about to get herself shot.

"I didn't mean for it to happen," Evan wailed. "I thought I was clean, I thought I could stay clean. I wanted to, I wanted to get my kids back."

That was as much of an admission that they were likely to

get, and Ethan was about to move in, positive that between the two of them they could get things under control. But before he could do so all hell broke loose.

He didn't even know who fired the first shot, all he knew was that gunfire pierced the night, and his heart about beat itself out of his chest because Sparrow was dead center in the middle of the chaos.

There was nothing he could do but start eliminating threats and pray that Sparrow didn't wind up one of the fatalities.

Shots appeared to be coming from all around him.

More soldiers?

Just when he was sure that it was too late, that neither he nor Sparrow would be living until sunrise and was preparing himself to be reunited with his wife, everything suddenly went silent.

Deadly silent.

That kind of eerie, almost unnatural silence.

"On your knees, hands where I can see them."

The order seemed to come out of nowhere, but the accent wasn't African, it was American.

Not hesitating to comply, Ethan set down his weapon, got down on his knees, and put his hands on his head. "I'm Ethan Zimmerman," he said as a man stepped out of the shadows and grabbed his wrists, binding his hands behind his back. "I'm former Air Force, used to be a Nightstalker, now I work for Medi-Hope. I picked up Sparrow Oswald a few days ago after her Black Hawk was shot down. She's been staying with me while she recovers. We called in an attack on the aid compound and were able to escape in my plane. We came here to hide out, but we saw our drug trafficking suspect and Sparrow just got a confession out of him. She was surrounded by armed soldiers."

Anxious energy hummed through his veins, and he had to

fight the urge to break the zip ties binding his wrists, remove the men blocking his path to Sparrow, and run to find out if she was hurt.

A second man stepped up, huffing a chuckle. "Why am I not surprised to hear an Oswald is at the center of another mess."

"Your story checks out," the first man said, giving him a onceover before moving behind him again to cut the ties.

"Is she alive?" Ethan demanded already snatching up his weapon and bypassing the two men to head toward the truck where Sparrow had been.

"Not sure," the second man replied.

"Who are you guys?" he asked.

"SEALs. We were heading to the compound when we saw your plane. Wanted to be sure it was you and Sparrow on it, so a few of us parachuted down, followed you here to the town," the first man explained.

Ethan nodded, his focus already on searching for Sparrow. As he approached the truck, he saw Evan Kikkert was dead, his lifeless body riddled with bullets. Similarly, the six soldiers were also dead, their bodies strewn about in and around the truck.

But no sign of Sparrow.

"Where is she?" he demanded as though one of the SEALs were personally responsible for the missing Sparrow.

"She's down here," came a soft voice.

"Sparrow?"

"I'm under the truck," she replied.

Ethan dropped to his knees and reached under the truck, snagging Sparrow's arm and carefully pulling her out, trying not to jostle her too badly. When he had her free, he dragged her into his arms, uncaring that they had an audience who were watching them with unconcealed interest.

"Thank you," he said as he buried his face in her hair.

Because Sparrow had stood by him, they had put a dint in a drug trafficking ring and stopped Medi-Hope from being used to smuggle drugs, and he wouldn't be facing prison time. He had a lot to be grateful to Sparrow for, but maybe the biggest one was the chains binding him to his grief had loosened, giving him the opportunity to wriggle free from them if he wanted to.

Now he had to decide if he did want to.

CHAPTER SIX

January 23rd

:27 P.M.

IT WAS WEIRD, but stepping back inside Ethan's tiny house felt like coming home. Sparrow had become accustomed to the place over the last several days, and it felt good to be back here, especially after all the action of the last thirty-six hours.

Out here it was quiet, peaceful, the surrounding mountains seemed to form a protective little cocoon around them. She could see why Ethan liked it here. It felt like being removed from the rest of the world. Things here were quieter, slower, a more relaxed pace of life, even though the conditions could be hard and it was missing all the modern conveniences they were used to back home.

If you wanted to escape your life, this was definitely the place to come.

As they stepped inside Ethan's house, it felt like the temperature went up a couple of hundred degrees. It was the first time they had been alone together since yesterday morning. After the SEALs had timed their entry perfectly, saving her life, and probably Ethan's too, she and Ethan had both been taken to Camp Lemonnier where they had given statements about the last few day's events. She'd been questioned for hours, asked the same thing over and over again until she thought she would lose her mind if she had to say it all one more time. But finally it was over. Evan Kikkert was dead, as were the soldiers he'd been meeting with. A couple of the soldiers attacking the base had been taken alive and would be questioned about the trafficking ring as well as the attack.

It was over now, meaning she would be flying home in the morning.

She could have spent tonight on the base, but she'd wanted these last hours to be spent with Ethan. This was the last chance she would have to see him, and she wanted to make the most of it.

Sparrow had made a decision while she was lying under that truck listening to gunfire going on around her, and that was that she was going for it with Ethan. The worst he could do was turn her down, and if he did that was his choice, one she would respect, and she'd sleep in the bed, he'd sleep on the couch, and in the morning they'd say their goodbyes.

But she was hoping that wasn't how the evening turned out.

When Ethan closed the door behind them, she turned to face him, taking a step closer but still giving him plenty of space. She didn't want to spook him, and she knew he was pretty close to being spooked. Someone had retrieved his plane, and it had been fixed on base, so Ethan had flown them both out here and would fly them back to Camp Lemonnier in the morning where she would take a flight back home.

The compound was a mess, but Dr. Gabler had decided to stay, as had Ethan, although Esme would be leaving, and Medi-Hope would be sending out people to rebuild and get things up and running again as quickly as possible. The positive was that the bunker had done its job, protecting Oliver and Esme until help arrived.

Heat flared in Ethan's eyes, and his gaze dropped to her lips before moving back up to her eyes.

Relief filled her. He wanted her too, she knew it without a shadow of a doubt, but would he give in to it or were his feelings for his wife still too strong?

Taking a tentative step toward him, she waited to see what he would do.

Hope soared when he took a step toward her.

They continued their dance. She'd take a step, then he would, then her, then him, until they closed the distance separating them. The heat pouring off Ethan's body had her insides clenching in delightful anticipation.

That anticipation dimmed when he dropped his head into his hands, raking his fingers through his hair.

He couldn't do this.

She should have expected it. After all, he had come out here to get away from everyone, and from the looks of things, remained celibate for the last three years. Why would she think he would be willing to break his marriage vows—which clearly still meant something to him—for her?

Sparrow took a step back. She wasn't angry with him, just disappointed, she'd really thought there could have been something good between them, but she respected him for standing by his convictions, and envied him finding a love so great not even death could come between it.

"It's okay, Ethan," she said gently. "I understand. I'm just going to go to bed, I'm tired and we have to leave early in the morning."

She had turned and was three steps toward the bedroom when a hand suddenly circled her wrist, stopping her.

He didn't speak, but he spun her around and crushed his mouth to hers, kissing her hungrily, like he wanted to devour her. Which was fine by her because she was more than ready to be devoured.

Ethan pulled her toward the couch, his fingers fumbling with the hem of her sweater. Looked like he couldn't wait to get to the bedroom. That or he was trying to keep some emotional distance between them by doing her on the couch rather than the bed.

Still, right now Sparrow was too turned on to care. Her own fingers had gone straight to his belt buckle, and she was near frantic to get it undone, have him spilling out into her hands. As soon as she shoved his jeans down his hips enough that she could get to him, she reached into his boxes and wrapped her fingers around his impressive length.

Ethan moaned into her mouth as he dropped onto the couch, pulling her down so she straddled his lap. While she traced her fingertips over his quivering length, he slipped a hand inside her pants and dragged a finger through her wet folds.

A moan escaped her lips, and when he shoved her sweater up, baring her breasts, and closed his lips around one hard little nipple, her body shuddered in response. His tongue flicked, and he suckled first one breast and then the other. His fingers were like magic as they stroked deep inside her, while his thumb kept up a steady pace and pressure on her little bud.

Between his attention to her center and her breasts, her stroking of his length became almost mindless as the orgasm that had eluded her in sleep was now tantalizingly within reach.

When Ethan suddenly pulled away, she mewed a protest before struggling to school her features, thinking he couldn't go through with it. The words to tell him it was okay, that she understood, were on the tip of her tongue when Ethan said, "Condom, want to be inside you when I come."

That plan was a-okay with her. "I hope you don't think this was presumptuous of me,"

she said as she reached into her pocket to pull out a condom.

Ethan shot her a sexy smirk. "Not presumptuous at all."

His hands spanned her waist, and he lifted her setting her on her feet in front of him so he could shove her pants and panties far enough down her legs that he could get access to her core.

Instead of lifting her back onto his lap, Ethan turned her around, his tip nudging at her entrance. Again, she knew he was trying—either consciously or subconsciously—to keep distance between them, and she couldn't say that it didn't hurt, but when she sunk down slowly, taking him inside her an inch at a time, her disappointment faded as pleasure began to take its place.

One of his hands lifted to claim her breasts as she moved slowly, lifting her hips until just his tip remained inside her then sinking down again until he was buried deep.

They quickly found a rhythm that worked.

Ethan attended to both breasts until both her nipples were hard little peaks while his other hand worked the little hard peak between her legs. The angle had him hitting that spot inside her with every thrust. Her breasts were heavy, the throbbing between her legs grew until it felt like it would consume her.

Then he gave the bundle of nerves between her legs a hard tweak between his thumb and forefinger, and it was the last push she needed to fly apart. Ecstasy sparked through each one of her nerve endings, making her feel like her entire body had transcended onto another plane of existence where the only thing that existed was pleasure.

She cried out her release, panting as Ethan gripped both hips now, thrusting into her with an intensity that showed his own desperation. His urgent thrusts continued to spur on her pleasure until she was almost sobbing with the intensity of what he was making her feel.

He came with a soft moan but didn't stop moving, his thrusts becoming harder and faster, and set off a second explosion inside her. She hadn't even known she could come twice one right after the other, and certainly not from penetration alone, but Ethan did things to her that no other man ever had.

That was why her heart shattered when she felt a drop of wetness on her neck.

She'd known it was coming, known he wasn't over his wife, and yet she'd allowed herself hope.

Hope which his tears of regret had just destroyed.

* * *

7:00 P.M.

ETHAN DIDN'T EVEN REALIZE he was crying until Sparrow jerked in his hold, trying to escape him as though he'd hurt her.

He might have been a little rough near the end, but he

was pretty sure he hadn't caused her pain, he'd felt her come a second time. It took him a moment to realize she wasn't trying to flee physical pain but emotional pain.

A few tears had escaped, but they weren't what Sparrow thought they were. At least not completely.

"It's okay, Ethan. I understand," Sparrow said softly.

She'd said those same words to him earlier only she'd been wrong then too.

He had wanted sex with her so badly his body had literally ached to feel her, touch her, taste her, but it was like his mind was fighting a war. His body wanted Sparrow, there was no doubt about it, but his heart was stuck on a woman he could never have again because she was gone.

Hence his brain's dilemma.

Did it listen to the body or the heart?

Even after amazing sex with Sparrow he wasn't sure.

Realizing he was still holding onto her hips in what had to be a bruising grip, Ethan slowly unclenched his fingers, almost reluctant to let her go because he knew once he did, she would be gone forever.

There was no going back.

Although he'd thought about sex with Sparrow the entire flight back from Camp Lemonnier, this wasn't how he'd expected it to play out. He'd thought if it happened, he would take her to bed, seduce her slowly, make love to her even if they weren't *in love*, it would still be slow and special. Instead, he'd ravaged her like a horny teenager, he'd kept almost all intimacy out of it, including not allowing her—or himself—to look one another in the eye while their bodies were joined together.

It hadn't been a conscious decision, just his brain's instinctual response to protect itself from more pain. If he allowed himself to care about Sparrow, it would mean it hurt if he lost her.

As he released his hold on her, and she quickly sprang away, he knew he'd lost her anyway. And it did hurt. Despite his best efforts to maintain distance between them it hadn't worked. Sparrow had barged her way through his defenses, and now he felt like he was damned if he did and damned if he didn't.

"I'm sorry," Sparrow said, refusing to look at him as she pulled her pants up and her sweater down, covering her body like she was ashamed for him to see her.

But he was the one who should be—and was—ashamed.

He was the one who had messed everything up.

He wanted to fix it, but he didn't know how.

Truth was, he had nothing to offer Sparrow. He wasn't moving back to the States, Sierra had taken most of his heart with her when she died so he couldn't offer her love or marriage or kids. This was it, the only thing he had to give her was distant sex and a remote compound in Africa where he hid from the world. That was no kind of life for anyone. Especially not someone as vivacious as Sparrow. She needed people, action, fun and love, and someone who could give her everything she'd missed out on as a child.

Sparrow was almost to the bedroom when he realized he still hadn't said anything.

"Wait."

She stopped but didn't turn around.

"You don't have to be sorry, this was my fault not yours."

He felt rather than saw her wince, and he realized how his words had sounded. He had made it abundantly clear that he regretted them having sex. Which he kind of did but mostly didn't. And it was the mostly didn't that scared him the most.

"No, I'm the one that initiated it. I knew you didn't want to sleep with me, and I pushed for it anyway. Guess it was the adrenalin rush of the last few days." She gave an awkward shrug but still didn't turn around to face him.

His stupidity and terror at the thought of letting go of Sierra had humiliated Sparrow and he hated it.

"If I didn't want to have sex with you, I wouldn't have," he said, hoping it sounded reassuring but pretty sure it didn't.

"Right," she agreed, sounding like she didn't believe him.

Could he blame her?

He had bungled things with her from the beginning. They definitely should not have had sex tonight, he knew that with absolute certainty. He shouldn't have given into the need she stirred up in him, he should have resisted temptation. But it was hard to resist temptation when it was wrapped up in a four-foot-eleven, blue-eyed, black-haired, package of solid muscle.

Ethan had feelings for Sparrow. There was no doubt in his mind about that. The problem was whether or not he could move on and if he wanted to. He was aware that he was his own worst enemy, clinging to his memories of Sierra because he was afraid if he let anyone else in it meant letting her go. If he didn't remember her who would? They hadn't had any children, her parents had died not long after he had left on his first deployment, she had a sister, but her sister had her own family. It had always been just the two of them. If he didn't hold on to her then she would cease to exist, he was all that was keeping her alive. If he made room in his heart for someone else there might not be enough space to hold both, and it would be Sierra who would be moved out.

How did he explain all of that to Sparrow though?

That it wasn't her, that she was slowly breathing life back into him simply by being there, that it was all him. His fears, his uncertainty, his issues.

Not her.

Never her.

"I *did* want to have sex with you," he said. It was the timing that was wrong, he should have sorted himself out first, decided what he could and couldn't give, and then if he wanted Sparrow in his life he should have gone after her and told her that. Instead, he'd let his hormones dictate his actions and hurt the one person who had helped him the most.

"Can we not talk about this?" she asked.

Ethan sighed. The more he talked the worse he seemed to make it. Anything he said to her right now would only be interpreted as him trying to make it up to her for ruining what should have been something special.

What did it matter anyway?

Sparrow would be leaving in a little over twelve hours. All they had to do was get through tonight, which should be easy enough, they'd eaten before they left the base so they could both claim they were tired and go to sleep. Then tomorrow they'd eat and get in the plane, and he'd return her back to Camp Lemonnier where she would go home to her family, and no doubt do her best never to think about him again.

It would be a long time before he stopped thinking about her.

"Yeah, we can not talk about it," he agreed.

She gave a single nod and then fled to the bedroom, slamming the door behind her. There had been a wobble in her voice when she'd asked him not to talk about what they'd done, she'd been trying to hold back her tears.

He'd hurt her.

Actually hurt her.

Because she cared about him.

Her actions had all but screamed it at him over and over again in the few days she'd been here.

He should have accepted her offer of friendship, kept in

contact with her when she went home, let things develop slowly, see if they went anywhere. That way he wouldn't have felt this enormous pressure to make a spur-of-the-moment decision on whether or not he could move on. Instead, he had hurt the one woman—the one person—on earth who could heal the gaping wound in his heart.

Standing, Ethan removed the condom, rightened his boxers and pulled his pants up, then headed outside. His little house had an even littler porch, with a wooden swing he had built himself in the long hours he had with nothing to do. Now he sat in the swing, as he had so many nights before, and stared up at the stars.

Was Sierra up there somewhere, looking down at him and shaking her head at the way he'd handled things tonight? Or was she up there weeping her own tears because the man who had promised to love her forever had slept with another woman?

Their marriage vows might have had the words till death do us part in them but their commitment to one another had been eternal. They had promised to love each other for forever, and he had broken that promise. He was breaking it right now because tonight his thoughts weren't only for the pretty blonde who had been the love of his life, they were also about the gorgeous woman tucked away in his bedroom.

Ethan might be trying to stop two women from sharing his heart, but it was happening whether he wanted it to or not.

CHAPTER SEVEN

January 24th

:21 A.M.

SHE COULDN'T BE MORE ready to get out of here.

Last night had been the most humiliating night of her life. Something she thought she would never be able to say again after a truly humiliating day when she was in high school. She'd been twelve when her parents died, and they all moved to the city. Since Eagle was eighteen, he became their legal guardian, but he was away in the military, so he hired a full-time au pair. She, Falcon, Hawk, and Dove had all gone to school for the first time. Even though she was definitely weird to the other kids, she took an instant liking to sports, and because she was good, she'd been accepted despite her oddities.

Still, she'd been shy and hesitant when it came to boys. She was fine with being friends with them and was usually surrounded by a bunch of jocks who laughed with her and teased her and felt more like brothers than anything else. Until one particular boy when she was fourteen.

Ironically, he looked a lot like Ethan, tall, with blond hair and blue eyes. She'd been enamored with him, daydreamed about him, and wondered what it would be like to kiss him. Then one day she found herself alone with him, she was sure he liked her back, that he wanted to kiss her, so she'd leaned in and touched her lips to his. He'd immediately pushed her away, wiped off his mouth, and asked her what she was doing. She'd been so embarrassed she'd spent the next four years avoiding him.

This was worse though.

That had just been puppy love, but with Ethan she thought she could actually fall in love with him for real. She'd been willing to sacrifice anything to help him clear his name, even her career if it came down to it.

Now as they walked side by side to the hangar, she felt like there was an insurmountable distance between them. It was clear he had regretted what they'd shared the second he got off, going so far as crying as he no doubt felt like he had betrayed his deceased wife by having sex with her.

That was much worse than a guy wiping off his mouth after a kiss.

Falling in love seemed so easy when other people did it. They found someone they liked, who liked them back, they enjoyed each other's company, the sexual chemistry sparked between them, they both fell hard and fast as they got to know one another, and then they were in love.

Why couldn't she find that?

Why did it have to be so hard?

Why did the one guy she really liked have to be dead set against falling in love?

Because she was distracted, Sparrow didn't even realize something was wrong until it was too late. Ethan also must have been lost in thought because he obviously noticed the threat at the same moment she did, dropping her bags and reaching for his weapon just as she reached for hers.

"Drop your weapons," a voice ordered in a heavy African accent.

Since they were surrounded by a dozen men, Sparrow saw no other option but to do what they had been told. She let her weapon fall through her fingers, landing with a soft clunk on the concrete floor.

Ethan released his much more slowly as though he was debating whether or not they could take the men, but logic said they couldn't. Not only were there more of them but the soldiers were surrounding them. The two of them might get off a few shots, maybe even kill a couple of the men, but all they would get for their trouble would be being shot or killed themselves.

All twelve guns remained pointed directly at them until Ethan finally let go of his weapon and it joined hers on the floor.

"On your knees, hands on head," one of the men ordered. It was clear he was the one in charge. He was the only one not pointing a gun at them, although he was dressed in the same fatigues as the others.

Again, there didn't seem to be anything they could do except do as they were ordered. Not if they wanted to live.

Sparrow got to her knees, wincing at the pain in her collarbone as she placed her hands on her head as instructed. Ethan knelt as well, but she could see the fury burning brightly in his eyes, and she prayed he didn't do anything stupid. She might be mortified by pushing him to have sex with her last night when she'd known he was still hung up on his wife, but she still cared about him and didn't want anything to happen to him.

"Easy," she murmured.

He didn't say anything, but he gave the tiniest of nods, indicating he heard her and wouldn't do anything to get himself killed.

Two of the soldiers approached, one roughly grabbed her hands and yanked them behind her back, sending pain firing through her broken bone, but she sucked her bottom lip into her mouth and clamped her teeth down on it, refusing to let out a cry of pain that would show a weakness that could be exploited.

Once her hands were secured, she was gagged, picked up, and carried to the back of a truck that had been waiting for them in the hangar and thrown inside. Ethan was thrown in alongside her, similarly bound, and then both were tied up at the ankles. She knew it was coming, but when her tied wrists were bound to her tied ankles, leaving her hogtied the pain in her collarbone was excruciating.

Ethan was hogtied as well, and then the man leaned over and placed a heavy piece of material over her eyes, blindfolding her. Her last image of Ethan was of the fiercely protective glower he was giving the men abducting them.

Then there was nothing but blackness.

The slamming of a door indicated they had been locked in the back of the truck, and a moment later an engine started and they were moving.

Kidnapped.

They'd just been kidnapped.

Dr. Gabler was staying in the village with his wife, having come clean to Medi-Hope about what he'd done to try to save his grandson's life. Esme had already left, Evan was dead, and she and Ethan had been alone out here, so no one would know they were gone until they didn't show up on base.

That was at least an hour away. By the time anyone realized something was wrong she and Ethan would be long gone.

They could be anywhere by then.

Were these the warlord's soldiers come to get revenge on them for outing their smuggling operation? Was it whoever had shot down her helicopter to get to her? Was it the rival warlord hoping to gain some sort of notoriety by capitalizing on the failures of their competition?

Someone else entirely?

The truck bounced over a rock or a rut in the ground or something, and since they had just been thrown in here, Sparrow went sailing up into the air, then landed hard. Pain roared through her injured joint. Restrained as she was, she couldn't even do anything to brace herself or try to make her landing easier each time she was tossed up into the air.

Then she felt Ethan come up behind her. He was hogtied just as she was so there wasn't a lot he could do for her, but he used his larger body to move them both until she was pressed up against the side of the truck, with him at her back. This position helped to brace her a little against the rough terrain, and although they were both still bounced and jostled about, at least the pain in her collarbone wasn't so bad she thought she was going to pass out.

Since they couldn't communicate, they were both gagged and blindfolded. The best Sparrow could do was curl her fingers so she could brush them against Ethan's stomach in a gesture she hoped communicated her thanks for him being thoughtful enough to try to help her, knowing she would be in pain. She knew that he cared about her, and she was trying not to take his rejection personally, knowing he would have rejected any woman who had been in her place last night, they just wanted different things.

Ethan nudged the side of her face, she assumed it was his way of acknowledging her thanks, and she tangled her fingers in his shirt, needing to feel a connection to him.

She had no idea where they were going.

No idea what would happen to them when they got there.

And no idea how they were going to get themselves out of this mess.

When she didn't make her flight home, she hoped Camp Lemonnier would send someone to look for them, and she knew for a fact that Prey would go all out looking for her, but she also knew there were no guarantees in life. Even with Prey's vast resources, and the US military, she and Ethan might never be seen again.

Time blurred, there was nothing but the bouncing of the truck, pain, and the solid presence of Ethan at her back.

* * *

2:33 P.M.

THERE WAS no way to tell time in here.

Ethan knew they had been driving for hours, but there was no way to tell which direction they were heading. They'd turned so many times that without his eyes he couldn't keep them straight.

His muscles ached from being hogtied so long, he'd lost feeling in his limbs hours ago, and it was getting harder and harder to keep Sparrow braced against the side of the truck. Not that he was giving up, he knew she had to be in horrible pain with her broken collarbone, tied up as she was and getting thrown around back here, and he was going to do whatever he could to try to ease her suffering.

He wished he had tried something back at the hangar. At least then they wouldn't be helplessly tied up and unable to do anything about where they were being taken. Back then they had at least stood a chance at being able to do something, however unlikely it was, they could have taken out the dozen men surrounding them, but now they were completely at their abductor's mercy.

Finally, the truck pulled to a stop. He could hear what sounded like a gate being opened and then voices talking before they started driving again.

This time they wound around several times as they drove up a hill. A driveway?

After only a couple of minutes driving, they stopped again, and this time he could hear the doors open and the men getting out. Light flooded over them when the door to the back of the truck was opened, and Ethan almost wished they were still driving. At least then they were alone, he had a feeling that whatever was coming next would be a lot worse.

He had expected that they would be untied here and now, but instead, he felt hands close around the ropes binding his ankles and wrists together, and then he was dragged out. Joints weren't designed to be twisted into this awkward position, and the added pressure on them as he was carried by two men was excruciating.

Ethan would gladly have endured it though if it meant Sparrow being spared. Her muffled cries as she was no doubt transported the same way he was only served as fuel to the fire burning inside him. He didn't care what the odds were, he would kill these men for causing her pain.

They were carried inside, he could tell because the gentle breeze disappeared, and then they were going down a flight of stairs. The men carrying him groaned, and he was at least partly mollified knowing that carrying a man of his size like this wasn't easy, and they were likely in pain—albeit a lot less pain than he was—as well.

"Put him in there," a disembodied voice ordered, and he was set down on a cool stone floor.

The marginal relief of pressure on his limbs was overshadowed by fear for Sparrow. Were they taking her somewhere else? Had they already separated them? Their best bet at escaping was to be together, but it wasn't like they had any control over that.

"She goes in the one next to his," the same voice ordered, and Ethan relaxed a little. Sparrow was still here.

His blindfold and gag were removed, and then the ropes binding him, and immediately his limbs felt like they had caught fire as blood flow slowly returned. He blinked in the light, his eyes having grown accustomed to the dark, and found himself in a dungeon of some sort. The wall and floor were stone, there were no windows, metal bars made up three of the four walls, and when he looked over, he saw Sparrow in the cell beside his. She, too, had been cut free of her bonds, her eyes scrunched as she tried to look around her.

"You two have caused me a lot of problems," a different voice said, and a man dressed in an expensive-looking suit moved closer to their cells. Omega Chidubem. Ethan had seen photos of the warlord before and seeing him here answered at least one of their questions. They'd been taken by the warlord as payback for interfering with his trafficking business.

If he was waiting for an apology from either of them, he would be waiting a long time.

When neither of them responded, Omega sneered at them. "You may think you can be silent now, but we will see if you can keep your mouths shut when I am removing your skin while you are still alive."

If he thought the threat would provoke either of them into speaking, then again, he was mistaken. While they may scream under torture, neither of them would give this man what he wanted.

With a huff that seemed like something a petulant toddler would give rather than a drug trafficker, Omega turned and flaunted out of the room, the rest of his men trailing after him leaving him and Sparrow alone.

Immediately, Ethan crawled over to the metal bars separating him from Sparrow. "Are you all right?"

"Yeah." Pain was written all over her, in the tight lines around her mouth, shadowed in her eyes, in the stiff way she clutched the wrist of her bad arm, and the way her body sagged against the ground.

Ignoring his own pain, Ethan slipped an arm between the bars. "Come here."

She finally looked over at him, sorrow marring her features, but she gritted her teeth and used her good arm to drag herself awkwardly across the floor until she reached him. "I'm sorry. If you hadn't come after me that night, you would never have found the drugs, and you wouldn't be here right now."

"But Evan would still be using my plane to smuggle drugs."

"He would, and he might be dead now, but Omega Chidubem isn't, and while his operation has taken a hit he can rebuild."

That was true, but they'd still done the right thing, done what they could, and Omega Chidubem bringing them here just might be his undoing. Prey was powerful and well connected. They had limitless resources and would scour the globe to find Sparrow. When they did, Ethan had a feeling Omega would regret his decision to come after them.

"Where are you hurting the worst?" he asked.

"Shoulders," Sparrow replied.

"Turn around, rest your back against the bars," he instructed. Once she had, he put his hands on her shoulders and began to very gently massage, careful not to put any pressure on the broken collarbone. His fingers worked the tight muscles in her shoulders and the back of her neck, and slowly he felt her begin to relax.

"That feels really good," Sparrow said on a sigh.

"I wish I could do more."

"You're here, and you helped me in the truck. If it hadn't been for you, I would have ended up passing out. Thanks for being there. I mean, I wish you weren't here, I wish you were someplace safe, but at the same time I'm glad you are here. Sorry." She shifted around to face him and shot him a weak smile.

Although it sounded bad, and he definitely wished she was somewhere where she was safe and sound, he was also glad she was here. So far together they had made a great team, and Omega was underestimating both them and Sparrow's family. "I'm kind of glad you're here too."

Sparrow's smile grew watery, and she quickly lifted a hand to swipe at a stray tear that had escaped. His heart clenched at her tears. He wanted to be able to take her in his arms, kiss them away, apologize for how things had gone last night, and tell her that he was sorry he couldn't give her what she wanted.

But he couldn't do any of that.

All he could do was settle a hand on her knee and offer her what support he could. It felt woefully inadequate.

"I'm not crying," Sparrow said.

Fighting a smile he nodded his agreement. "Course you're not."

"If I am it doesn't mean I'm not tough."

"Course it doesn't, wisp. You're the toughest little woman around."

"Did you just call me a little woman?" She shot him a glare, but the corners of her mouth were twitching. "I guess it really is true that blondes aren't very smart because I can't think of any good reason you would risk my wrath by calling me that."

"Risking your wrath, huh? Well, I don't want to do that. You might have to tickle me into submission with feathers and unicorn fluff."

"Hey," she exclaimed. "You know I can beat your butt, blondie. You need a reminder you come here into my cage and call me a little woman, see what that gets you."

"Hey now, little wisp, I'm only teasing, don't go getting your panties into a knot."

"My panties are just fine, and none of your concern," she said primly before giggling. "Thanks, Ethan, I needed something to break the tension."

"You're welcome." He was glad that the tension between them seemed to have eased as well. He didn't know how to make things go back to the way they'd been before, when she'd been just his tough-as-nails, little wisp of a friend, but he'd take this small step and hope their friendship was repairable.

"I guess I really am glad you're here." Sparrow lifted a hand to cover a yawn, reminding him of the seriousness of their situation.

"Why don't you sleep for a bit," he suggested. They should make the most of this reprieve because things were going to get worse quickly when Omega returned.

"Just for a bit, then you sleep." Sparrow shifted again so

her back was against the bars, then she took hold of his hand and linked their fingers.

"Agreed," he said. While he wanted to insist she needed sleep more, he knew they were stronger together, and that meant both of them working together to survive this. He moved so his back was against the same bars Sparrow's was, keeping hold of her hand. A few minutes passed, and he thought she had drifted off to sleep when she spoke.

"Crying doesn't really make me weak, does it?" she asked quietly.

"Wisp, you are without a doubt the toughest woman I know. Crying only makes you human."

"Thanks, Ethan."

She turned again until her forehead just rested on his shoulder between the bars. As she drifted off to sleep, her fingers curled around his with the same tenacity she did everything else even as she slept, he wondered how one small woman could make such a big impact on his life.

Sparrow might be worried about being weak, but as his thumb brushed across her knuckles, he knew that the only thing keeping him going was her strength.

CHAPTER EIGHT

January 25th

 0:52 A.M.

"How much longer do you think they're just going to leave us in here?" Sparrow asked, pacing around the narrow cell. It was about ten feet long but only about five feet wide. When she stretched out, she could just fit without having to bend her body.

"I don't know," Ethan replied.

"How long do you think we've been here?" It felt like they'd been here for days, but she suspected that was just her mind playing tricks on her. It was more likely they'd been here for well under a day.

"My guess would be somewhere around eighteen hours."

Sparrow made a face. "That's too specific to be a guess. A guess is something like, less than a day, more than a day."

"Okay, then my guess is less than a day."

When she turned to roll her eyes at him, she saw him smirking at her. He was so sexy when he gave her that look, it was like he was smoldering and making her catch fire too. Right now, he was sitting in the corner of his cage, down the back on the side closest to her. One leg was stretched out, the other bent, one arm propped on his knee. He looked relaxed, carefree like they were hanging out at the park or a barbecue or something. He certainly didn't look like someone currently being held captive by a dangerous drug trafficker.

"Think he's really going to have our skin peeled off while we're still alive?" she asked with a shudder.

"I don't know."

"Do you know anything?" she demanded, although she enjoyed bantering with him and he'd been a good sport answering variations of the same questions for hours now as she paced around her cell.

"I know we're not going to have to worry about how we're going to escape because if you keep pacing like that, you're going to wear a hole in the floor."

"I wish it was that easy." They'd talked for hours about a whole variety of plans, but so far, they didn't have anything that would actually work. They'd both been blindfolded as they'd been brought in here, so they had no idea where they were, the layout of the grounds, number of buildings, how many guards there were, or anything else they'd need if they were planning a real escape.

"I think I hear someone coming," Ethan announced, moving smoothly to his feet and walking until he was at the door of his cage. "You go wait down the back of your cell. As far away from the door as you can get."

"Now is not the time to play at being chivalrous," she chastised, joining him at the front of their cells.

"I'm not playing, wisp, I *am* chivalrous," he said with a wink.

"Okay, fine, you're a super-sensitive guy who is always the perfect gentleman, you hold out chairs, open doors, and tip your hat to ladies, it's still not the time to be chivalrous. We're in this together, and they're either coming for both of us or they already know which of us they want first. Don't do anything that's going to get you hurt."

"I feel the same way about you, don't do anything that's going to get you hurt. You keep quiet, and I'll try to keep their attention on me."

Sparrow reached through the bars to swat at Ethan. "That's what I meant. Don't go trying to be chivalrous. Chances are they know who I am, who my family is, which makes me a better target whether you like it or not. Either he knows and is involved with whoever is after my family in which case he could probably make back way more money than we cost him by handing me over. Or he knows that if he hurts me and offers Prey a ransom to get me back, he can also make more money than we cost him by losing him that shipment of drugs. Either way, he has to know that he gets more mileage from using me than he does out of using you."

From the tightening of his jaw, she knew Ethan knew she was right, he just didn't like it. Whether he liked it or not it was the truth, and she had come to terms with that. While he might not actually peel their skin off, Omega would hurt them, and she was sure he intended to start with her first.

Two armed men entered the dungeon area—besides the cages she and Ethan were in, there were another dozen or so —and like she had predicted, immediately headed for the door to her cell.

She shot Ethan a look that said keep his mouth shut. Even

though they were coming for her first, it didn't mean they weren't coming for him next. If all they wanted was her, they would have killed Ethan back at the hangar and not bothered to bring him along. That they had brought him meant they had plans for him too.

Without bothering to utter a word, one of the guards gestured at her with his weapon, and she stepped out of the gate, allowing them to flank her as they led her out of the dungeon. Her courage faltered a little as she left Ethan behind. She really did feel stronger when he was there, which was crazy because while she had a family she adored, she'd always been on her own. She'd never had a really serious boyfriend who was always there to watch her back, and even though she always had a co-pilot on board with her it wasn't the same as operating as part of a team. When she was with Ethan, she had that feeling of not being alone, of having someone there who would always watch out for you, she liked it and now that it was gone, she missed it.

She was taken through a maze of dark and dingy hallways, and then up a flight of stairs to a large, mostly empty room. There was a couch against one wall, a large fireplace against another, and big picture windows in a third. In the middle of the room was a wooden table with a large plastic sheet beneath.

Well, that didn't look good.

Or take a lot of imagination to figure out why you'd need a rug of plastic under a table.

Her instincts screamed at her to fight back, but she was unarmed, and there were probably dozens of guards here. Even if she got away from these two more would come, and she wouldn't achieve her real goal which was to get herself and Ethan out of here.

So, when they shoved her onto the table, she didn't fight back as they secured her legs to one end of the table, then yanked her arms apart and secured them as well. Her broken collarbone screamed at having to endure more abuse, but there was nothing she could do about it, so she had no choice but to suck it up and deal.

Once she was trussed up, the other door to the room opened, and Omega came strolling through it. He was dressed again in a nice suit, and grinned almost maniacally. It was obvious he was looking forward to this, and she intended to ruin it for him as best she could. She might not be able to get away from him yet, but she could make sure he didn't have the fun he wanted from hurting her.

"Good morning, Ms. Oswald. How have you been enjoying my accommodations?" he asked as he circled the table slowly.

"To be honest, I've had better."

For a moment he looked taken aback by her blasé statement, but then his grin widened. "I'm sorry to hear that. I'm sure I can make some changes to your circumstances since you seem to find them unpalatable."

He stopped at the bottom of the table by her feet, took his time untying her shoelaces, and then remove both her boots and her socks. Sparrow had ridiculously sensitive feet, something her siblings had loved when they were kids because they could hold her down and tickle her until she cried with laughter. Now when Omega ran a fingertip down the sole of her foot her toes instinctively curled, and her foot tried to move away from the tickly sensation.

"I have a deal to offer you, Ms. Oswald," Omega said.

"Oh yeah? A deal?"

"Someone has offered me a large sum of money if I hand you over to them."

She shrugged like that was old news because it was.

"They won't be as kind to you as I have been. They've

been waiting a very long time to get their hands on you. They don't have to get their hands on you though."

"No?"

"No. You come to work for me. I send you out of here, you go back home to your family unscathed, and all you have to do is allow me access to Prey's contacts so I can move my product with less hassle. Easy."

"So, I become a drug trafficker in exchange for what, my life?"

"It is as simple as that." Omega nodded. "This man, he has plans on how he intends to inflict pain on you, before he kills you. I assure you it will not be a quick or a pleasant death. I have heard the details of just what he intends to do. This way you get to keep your life, to me it is an easy decision to make."

She bet it was because this man had no morals. "Who is he?"

Omega tutted. "You should already know the answer to that. At least now, it should be obvious."

"How is it obvious?" All they knew about him was that he was apparently somehow related to them and that he had intended for all of them to be killed along with their parents that night.

"The trifecta, my dear. Human trafficking, now drug trafficking. What's left?"

"Weapons?"

"That wasn't so hard to figure out, was it?"

"So, he's a weapons trafficker," she said more to herself than to Omega. If she survived and made it out of here alive then she would get Prey searching all know weapons traffickers.

"Do we have a deal?" Omega asked.

"Do you really think I'd agree to help you traffic drugs?"

"In exchange for your life and to spare yourself pain then I would think it was a good trade."

"I'd rather suffer and die than help you sell drugs," she said firmly, meeting the man's eye.

"That is a shame. Still perhaps you need a little motivation to change your mind." Omega walked over to the large, antique-looking desk by the window, opened one of the drawers, and retrieved a whip. When he walked back over he stood by her feet. "I cannot persuade you to do this the easy way?"

Bracing herself for the pain that was to come, Sparrow shook her head.

The crack of the whip in the air had her already cringing.

Fire burned along her feet as the leather made contact with the sensitive skin on the soles.

She managed to hold in her scream through the first hit, and the second and third, by the fourth she was whimpering, by the seventh she finally gave Omega what he wanted; her screams of pain.

* * *

1:19 P.M.

What was taking so long?

What were they doing to her?

Ethan had taken up pacing around his cell after Sparrow had been dragged away. For hours he'd watched her pace, tried to remain the calm one because he felt like that was what Sparrow needed. He'd kept his fear—not for himself but for her—under wraps as best as he could and tried to distract her from her own fear with teasing and banter. It had seemed to work and knowing he was helping her helped him too.

With Sparrow gone, he couldn't seem to keep his emotions under wraps anymore. He was pacing the small cell just as Sparrow had been earlier.

This time alone left him with nothing to do but think.

And think.

And think.

About Sparrow, about this thing between them, about Sierra, about the past, about his future and what it looked like.

Sparrow was the best thing to happen to him in a long time, and it was like fate had thrown her in his path. Even after he'd made a complete disaster of their lovemaking and thought it was too late to salvage any sort of relationship between them, fate had stepped in again, forcing them together.

That wasn't all fate seemed to be trying to force.

Here, trapped with Sparrow, not sure what was happening to her or how badly she was being hurt, he couldn't not admit—at least to himself—that he had feelings for her. Real feelings. Feelings that went beyond mere attraction and friendship. Feelings he didn't think were going to go anywhere even if the source was removed.

He could let Sparrow walk away, knowing that she would likely end up meeting someone—probably someone better than him who could give her what she deserved—and having her own happily ever after while he was left alone.

Or he could do something.

Ethan just didn't know what that something would be.

A door opened somewhere nearby, and he stalked to the front of his cage and strained to look down in the direction Sparrow had been taken. A moment later, he saw her being led back, stumbling, and being mostly dragged along by the same two men who had taken her.

Her face was pale, and it looked like she was being carried more than walking on her own.

How badly was she hurt?

"Sparrow?" The word came out a low growl, and he wasn't the only one who heard the danger in his tone because both the guards cast him wary glances.

"I'm okay," she said, but her voice was heavy with pain and panting with exertion.

"You're not. What did they do?" Ethan contemplated taking a swing at the men as they walked past and stopped outside his cell to open Sparrow's. It wouldn't change anything, Sparrow would still be hurting, and they'd both still be trapped, and he'd probably earn himself a beating, but even if he was punished, hitting the men who hurt Sparrow would make him feel better, release a little of the anger threatening to choke him.

"Hit me," she said briefly. When one of the men opened the door to her cage, and the other pushed her in, she stumbled and immediately fell, hitting the ground hard.

Ethan did growl then and reached between the bars to grab one of the men, dragging him closer. He managed to get an arm between the bars and wrap it around the man's throat, strangling him.

The man startled, his hands curling around Ethan's arm as he tried to dislodge it.

The other man yelled and began to hammer his fists on Ethan's arm, and when that didn't work, he swung at his head, connecting with Ethan's jaw. Pain rattled through his skull, but he welcomed it as though it could even out the scales of pain and take some of Sparrow's.

"Ethan! Stop! Let him go!" Sparrow yelled.

He didn't want to.

He wanted to squeeze the life out of this man.

But logic finally caught up with him. They didn't have to hurt him as punishment for killing one of the guards, they could hurt Sparrow instead, and he had already caused her enough pain.

Ethan released the man and stepped away from the door.

The guard he'd been strangling stumbled out of reach, dragging in breath after breath as he rubbed at his neck. If looks could kill Ethan would be dead. But when he lifted his weapon and aimed it the other guard shook his head.

"Omega wants them both alive for now," he reminded his friend.

With a furious glare, the guard turned and stormed away, his friend on his heels.

As soon as they were gone, he crossed to the bars separating him from Sparrow and dropped to his knees. "How badly are you hurt?"

She looked up at him, her eyes wide, clouded with pain, her bad arm clutched against her chest as she sat on the floor. "He used a whip on my feet."

Ethan swore viciously.

That would have been agony.

The soles of your feet were a ridiculously sensitive part of your body, and the cruel torture would have rendered Sparrow virtually immobile. No way would she be able to walk out of here.

He swore again, and then again because it felt good.

"Let me see," he ordered, harsher than he should have, and he practically felt Sparrow's retreat.

He had to calm down. It wasn't her fault she'd been hurt, and she needed some empathy right now, not someone yelling at her.

"Please," he added, calmer this time.

Slowly Sparrow inched across the floor until she could

stick her feet between the bars. Gently Ethan lifted one, resting her heel in the palm of his hand as he surveyed the damage. Angry red welts crisscrossed the bottom of her foot, and Sparrow hissed in pain when he gently probed around the wounds.

"Sorry," he murmured.

"It's not as bad as it looks."

"No?" He glanced over at her. "Because it looks pretty bad. You won't be able to walk on those for a while." If the damage was bad enough, she could suffer permanent damage, she might never walk again, and even if she could it might be with a bad limp.

"If we have to walk, I'll walk," Sparrow said, her mouth set in a stubborn line, and he couldn't help but smile.

"I believe you, wisp." Setting her foot down, he grabbed the water they'd been given earlier. They hadn't wanted to drink it in case it had been tampered with, but he could use it to clean the wounds, and ensure they didn't get infected. Ripping at the bottom of his shirt, he pulled off a strip of material, then opened the bottle and poured a little of the water over it. Then he picked up one of Sparrow's feet again and proceeded to wash the welts as carefully as he could.

Although she didn't make a sound, he could feel by the tense way her foot rested in his hand that what he was doing was hurting her and he hated it.

"I'm sorry," he said helplessly.

"Not your fault."

"I'm hurting you."

"You're *helping* me," she corrected.

It didn't feel like it, but he picked up her other foot and similarly cleaned it. When he was finished, he ripped off another two strips of material from his shirt and used them to wrap around each of Sparrow's feet. "There we go, I wish I could do more."

"Thanks," she said, giving him a tired smile.

"Turn around," he instructed, waiting until she shuffled around until she was sitting with her back against the bars, just like she had last night. Then he slipped an arm between the bars, wrapping it around her chest, and pulled her back to rest against him.

She sighed softly and snuggled closer. "Are you okay? They hit you."

"I'm fine," he assured her. "Try to close your eyes and get some rest."

"Don't think I can relax enough to sleep."

He wanted her out of pain for at least a little while, and she needed rest to start healing. They had to assume the worst, which was that Omega would be back soon to inflict more pain on them. Sparrow would need her strength, and that meant getting some sleep.

Lifting a hand, he began to smooth her hair. It had been in a bun when they'd left for the hangar yesterday morning, but during the journey here it had come loose. Now it was hanging in soft, messy waves down her back. The strands were silky between his fingers, and he enjoyed the feel of them as he kept the motion gentle and repetitive, hoping to soothe her.

"That's nice," she murmured, and he could already hear in her voice that he was lulling her toward sleep.

"It used to help Sierra relax when she was sick and in pain."

"You were a good husband. I know how much you loved her, I understand why you can't let anyone else in," she said sleepily. "Sierra is already taking up all the space in your heart."

"Not all of it," he whispered, but Sparrow didn't hear him because she had already drifted off to sleep.

CHAPTER NINE

January 26th

2:44 A.M.

"I HAVE NEVER BEEN this hungry before in my life," Ethan grumbled, making her chuckle. She suspected that during his years in the military there had been times when he had gone longer than a couple of days without eating. She knew there had been times when she had.

"Stop being such a baby," Sparrow told him.

"My stomach is literally starting to eat itself," he whined. While she knew they were both hungry, she knew he was really just complaining to give them both something to think about other than where they were and what was going to happen to them.

He was doing a good job of it too. When they were

together some of the horrors of their situation faded away. He had been so sweet and gentle cleaning her feet when she'd been brought back to her cage, and again she was struck by what a good husband he had been. Sierra had been a lucky woman to have someone who had quit his job so that he could take care of her and be there for her. Sparrow hoped one day she would be that lucky to find a man who wouldn't hesitate to do anything for her, whether it be hold her hair back while she threw up, or attack armed guards just because they'd hurt her. Both of those things meant a lot to her, they were completely different ends of the spectrum, but she wanted someone who would do both. Someone who would put themselves between her and danger—even though she didn't need them to—and who would take care of her.

"See, my stomach is growling its displeasure," Ethan said, making her laugh.

"I didn't know you were such a whiner," she teased. "We haven't been here for more than a couple of days, suck it up, I've gone much longer without food before."

"You have?" Ethan asked, sounding curious now.

"Yep. I remember one year when I was nine when we had these horrible storms, huge hailstones the size of my fist. I remember at first, I thought it was so cool, they were so big, and it was fun watching them hit the ground and bounce. It wasn't until the storms cleared a few days later and I saw the damage done to our crops. I got it then. We lived a subsistence lifestyle, we grew what we ate, there was no store to pop to for extra food. That winter we hardly had enough food to get by, we went to bed hungry every night, and I remember there was a patch right at the end of winter where we went eight days straight with nothing at all to eat. That was a scary year. I think it was the first time I realized that maybe we weren't as safe on our farm as I'd always thought we were."

"Wow. I had no idea things had been so rough for you. I mean, it makes sense, but I guess I never thought about that side of how your lives must have been. It must have been so weird for you when you moved to Manhattan. Talk about two opposite ends of the spectrum."

"It was definitely weird. We were all grieving, we were all traumatized, Eagle was gone, Raven was recovering from her injuries, Falcon just shut down. For a while there I was the one holding the family together, and I was so scared I wasn't strong enough to do that." It was a lot of pressure for a twelve-year-old kid, but there had been no one else to step up so she'd taken on that responsibility.

"Hey," Ethan said, removing his arm, which had been resting against her stomach, and nudging her shoulder. "Look at me." When Sparrow turned around, she saw fire dancing in his blue eyes. "You are strong enough to do anything. And I mean *any*thing. You did keep your family together, I've never seen closer siblings, makes me wish I had brothers and sisters. And you thrived when you went to school, despite the way you'd been raised. You joined the Air Force, and not just that, you became an elite Nightstalker, you excel at everything you do, and I'm glad to call you my friend."

Something sizzled between them, she felt it, prayed he did too. More than that she prayed Ethan wouldn't run from it. If he would just give her a chance, he would find out that she didn't want to replace Sierra, no one could take his wife's place in his heart, but maybe he could just carve out a tiny space for her. She was small after all, and she wouldn't push for more than he could give, but she needed him to meet her halfway. No, not even halfway, all he had to do was take one step toward her—or even just hold up his hand for her to take—and she would show him that they could be happy together.

Ethan lifted a hand, slipped it between the bars, and palmed her cheek. His hand was calloused, exuding warmth and strength, and she tilted her head, soaking up more of that strength. She needed it, as hard as that was for her to admit. Her life had always required her to be strong, especially being as small as she was. She'd had to work harder to keep up with her brothers and big sister, and harder than anyone else when she'd joined the military. All her life she'd felt like she had to prove herself, prove her strength, her competence, her abilities, and it was exhausting.

With Ethan she felt like she could relax.

He always made her feel like an equal, and other than that one day when they'd first met, he'd never made her feel like she wasn't as good, or as smart, or as strong as anyone else.

Maybe that was why she'd thought about him often over the years. Even when he was married and all they had was friendship, he'd still felt like a safe place. While she'd thought he was hot, she'd never thought about him as more than a friend until after his wife had passed away. Now the only thing standing between them was Ethan's grief. Whether he gave them a chance or not was all up to him.

"Sparrow …"

"You, come," a voice ordered, and they both turned to the doors of their cages.

Sparrow was surprised to see the guards standing there—the same ones who Ethan had attacked earlier—she'd been so caught up in sharing a moment with Ethan that she hadn't even heard them coming.

This time they were opening Ethan's door, and Sparrow quickly lifted her hand to cover his, clinging to it, not wanting him to go because if he was taken away from her, he would be hurt, and she'd rather suffer a million times over than allow one hair on his head to be touched.

His gaze was tender when it landed on her. "It's okay, Sparrow. I'd rather it be me than you."

"Well, I'd rather it be *me* than *you*." She huffed.

Ethan grinned. His thumb swept across her cheek in a light caress, then he stood and walked toward the guards.

She wanted to beg him to stay but knew that it wouldn't do any good, so instead, she watched him be led away. The depth of her despair was heavy, heavy enough that tears pricked her eyes.

The pain of knowing Ethan would be hurt was so much worse than the lingering pain in her feet from the whipping they'd sustained. She would gladly endure that over and over again to spare him. It didn't even matter that he didn't feel the same way about her that she felt about him, she was falling harder and harder for Ethan Zimmerman, and she would do anything to save him.

Shuffling to the back corner of her cage, Sparrow rested her back against the stone wall, stretched her legs out so there was no pressure on her injured feet, and rested her bad arm in her lap. She felt exhausted, drained. She hadn't had a chance to even process the crash and the loss of the SEAL team yet because she'd been dodging bullets and missiles and hunting drug traffickers.

The worst was that even if she was rescued, or she and Ethan managed to somehow escape, she would have to go home without him.

Wasn't that a kicker?

Part of her would rather be trapped here because at least she was with Ethan while they were here.

She was unprepared for the sudden bright light that blinded her.

"Package found."

Sparrow startled at the voice. She had assumed the light

belonged to one of the guards, but that was her brother Falcon's voice.

"Can you get in there?" someone asked. She recognized the voice as Luca "Bear" Jackson, the leader of Prey's Alpha team.

"Did you really ask me that?" Falcon growled. "I can pick any lock, you know that."

Scrambling awkwardly onto her knees, she crawled toward the cage door. "Falcon?"

"I see time has changed nothing. I'm still bailing you out of messes," her brother said.

A joke.

Did Falcon just make a joke?

Her big brother hadn't made a joke since before their parents had been killed. Obviously falling in love had changed Falcon, and while she was happy for him, she felt a pang of regret for the brother she used to idolize who had cut her out of his life so easily.

"Pretty sure I bailed you out of trouble more times than you bailed me out," she said, but it didn't come out snarky as she had intended, it came out sounding somewhat sad and wistful. As kids they'd been inseparable and whenever they'd had time to play, they'd always gotten into mischief.

"You hurt?" Falcon asked.

"They whipped my feet."

"She's not mobile," Bear said into his comms.

"I can walk," she contradicted. She was fairly certain with socks and boots she could walk, it just wouldn't be fun.

"We'll see about that," Falcon said, and she got the feeling he didn't believe she had what it took to walk on her injured feet. As a kid, she'd thought her brother saw her as every bit as strong as he was, even if he teased her, but when he hadn't come to her for support when he'd needed her, and shut her out, she'd had doubts. Now she wondered if he'd ever thought she was anything but a small, weak woman who couldn't handle anything life threw at her.

"Ethan," she said, "we need to find Ethan. They took him, they'll be hurting him."

The door swung open, and Falcon stepped inside, crouching beside her. "We'll get him, but first let's take a look at you."

She brushed away her brother's hands. "I'm fine. We have to find Ethan," she insisted. That was the only thing that was important to her. They might not wind up together, but she wasn't letting him die here with rescue this close.

* * *

3:29 A.M.

ETHAN CONSIDERED TAKING out the two guards as they led him through a maze of corridors. He could easily knock them out, grab their weapons and the key to the cages, go back for Sparrow and bust her out. The problem was they had no idea where they were, how many people were here, where they would be, or how well armed they were. Without enough information it would be a suicide mission.

They had to have been missing for a couple of days by now. As soon as they hadn't turned up at Camp Lemonnier in time for Sparrow to catch her flight, someone would have noticed. When they were both found to have disappeared, people would start looking for them. Prey wasn't going to leave Sparrow behind, so they would go all out looking for the two of them.

But did he want to hang around and wait, hoping a rescue mission was being planned?

How long would it take for Prey to find them? And what condition would they be in by then?

Maybe relying on themselves was the way to go.

He could scope things out, then when he got back to his cell, he and Sparrow could compare notes. That way they would be prepared the next time the guards came for them.

It wasn't the best of plans, but it was better than just sitting here and waiting to be tortured over and over again until Omega got what he wanted out of them and had them killed.

He was taken up a flight of stairs and into a large study with a wooden table in the middle of the room. Ethan didn't even have to ask to know that this is where Sparrow was taken and whipped, and fury blinded him.

Ethan snapped.

No one hurt Sparrow and got away with it.

Without bothering to think about the consequences, he took a swing at the guard beside him. The same man he'd wrapped an arm around last night and started squeezing the life out of.

He'd wanted to do it too.

Nothing would have made him happier than ending the life of each and every one of these men.

Something slammed into his head. He growled and spun around, launching himself at this new threat.

Anger bubbled inside him until it had to come out.

With a menacing roar, he swung a fist which connected with a very satisfying crack against the man's jaw.

More men filled the room, and despite the fact that there were more of them than there were of him, he kept swinging, kept getting in hits. He took a few himself, but even those blows helped him to unleash years' worth of pent-up anger.

It wasn't just anger about Sparrow being hurt, it was the

unfairness of losing the woman he loved while they were both still young and in their twenties. When they should have had their whole lives ahead of them, it had been snatched away. They hadn't gotten to have kids, then grandkids, they hadn't gotten to grow old and enjoy the freedoms of retirement.

It wasn't fair.

Sometimes life sucked.

What sucked even more was that even after secluding himself away in the remote Goda Mountains, he'd still managed to find a woman who wanted him, who accepted him, who understood his loss and didn't try to diminish it by saying that time had passed and he should have moved on, and instead of embracing that second chance at happiness he'd run from it.

The only person to blame for not being with Sparrow was himself, and that made him angrier than anything these men had done.

He hadn't saved Sierra, and not only was he not saving Sparrow, but he'd been the one to cause her pain.

Two men managed to get hold of his arms. Ethan shook one free by curling his fingers into the man's groin and yanking hard.

With a howl the man released him, but another was there to take his place, and then two more, and he was dragged, kicking and screaming threats, to the wall where he was slammed against it and held in place.

Ethan was breathing hard, his body ached in so many places he couldn't even pinpoint where he was hurt or how badly. Blood trickled down his face so he knew at least he had a head wound of some sort, but he didn't know—or particularly care—what else.

Satisfaction settled inside him as he looked at the men surrounding him. They were all breathing as hard as he was, they were all sporting injuries, and it had taken half a dozen of them to subdue him.

"You're going to die slowly for that," the first man he'd attacked snarled as he leaned in close. Large hands circled Ethan's neck, squeezing, cutting off his air supply.

This was it.

He would die here and now.

Regret that he hadn't had a chance to tell Sparrow how much he cared for her, that he hadn't made the one night they'd spent together special, that he wouldn't get a chance now to figure out what his future held, filled him.

Death didn't scare him. In death he'd be reunited with his wife, but it did mean leaving Sparrow behind.

That wasn't something he could stomach doing.

Ethan was about to kick out at the man, but another of the guards shoved him away first.

"We need to know where the drugs are first," the guard reminded his colleague.

The first man sneered at Ethan, then slammed a fist into his face, breaking his nose. Blood dribbled down over his mouth, and he met the man's gaze calmly before spitting the blood onto the floor at his feet.

With a grunt of annoyance, the guard was ready to swing at him again when Omega appeared behind them.

"Stop it," Omega snapped, clearly annoyed with all of them. "You can beat him to death later, first he needs to tell us where the drugs are."

Omega looked at him expectantly, but he didn't have a clue.

"You found them, yes?" Omega asked.

Seeing no reason to lie, Ethan nodded. "Someone shot at my plane, the landing was pretty rough, the box broke open."

"Yes, that was my men getting a little overly excited," Omega said, throwing a glare at the soldiers holding Ethan in place. "When they saw the plane take off unexpectedly, they thought you had discovered the drugs and were taking them to the authorities. They decided shooting you out of the air would have solved the problem. They could get to the plane first, retrieve the merchandise, then leave your body there to be discovered, hoping the crash would be attributed to someone else." It was clear from the man's tone he hadn't been informed of this plan ahead of time and that someone had paid for it afterward.

"I don't have the drugs," Ethan informed him. "We left them on the plane where we found them." Evan must have gotten suspicious of Sparrow and decided to take the drugs and hide them. Chances were, they were somewhere on the compound, if they hadn't been destroyed in the missiles Omega's men had launched.

"Lying won't save you," Omega warned. "And it will result in pain for your lady friend."

Ethan knew he was being played, manipulated, and if he'd had any information on where the drugs were it might even have worked, because the idea of being the cause of more of Sparrow's pain made him feel ill. But he truly didn't know anything. You couldn't give someone what you didn't have. "I don't have the drugs."

Omega studied him for a long moment, then gave a single nod. "Then you're of no use to me."

When their boss turned and walked away the guards closed in around him. From the smirks on their faces, Ethan knew they'd been given permission to do with him whatever they wanted.

He wouldn't go down without a fight, and if he could he'd take out some of them with him. He'd do anything he could to get back to Sparrow, but the odds were not in his favor.

A fist slammed into his stomach, momentarily stealing his ability to breathe. When it was followed up by a blow to the head his ears began to ring, which was why he was caught off guard when the soldiers surrounding him suddenly started to drop.

Seconds later, he was the only one left standing, and without them to hold him up he slumped against the wall.

"Looks like you could use a little help," Asher "Mouse" Whitman said with a cheerful grin as he approached. Mouse was the second in command in Prey's Alpha team, Ethan had met the man and his young daughter once at a barbecue. If he was here, then the rest of his team was as well.

"Sparrow," he said, already pushing off the wall. Although he weaved a little on his feet, he remained standing and stumbled back toward the door that led to the stairs and the dungeon.

"We got her," Mouse told him, looking amused.

"Let's take a look at you," team medic Antonio "Arrow" Eden said, stepping forward.

"Later, we have to get to Sparrow," he said, brushing away the other man's well-meaning hands.

"She's saying the exact same thing to Falcon, Bear, and the others," Mouse said, tapping his ear where his comms unit was.

Of course she was. Sparrow had shown him over and over again that she cared, it was well past time that he did the same. While Ethan didn't know what the future held, he did know that he had a lot of self-examination to do if he ever wanted to be happy again.

* * *

4:11 A.M.

.   .   .

"WHO IS THAT?" Sparrow asked Bear when she saw his attention turn to focus on his comms. "Did they find Ethan?"

He threw her a quick glance and nodded.

She sagged against the wall in relief. Although she'd wanted to go straight to search for Ethan, Falcon had told her that Alpha team had split up, and Mouse, Arrow, and Christian "Surf" Bailey were looking for Ethan. He'd refused to let her up until her feet had been properly cleaned and bandaged.

The seconds had felt like hours ticking so slowly by she'd felt like she was about to lose her mind.

Now, she pressed against the wall and used it to lever herself to her feet. There was, of course, the expected sharp stabbing pain in her feet, like her boots had been filled with shards of broken glass, but she ignored it, concern over Ethan distracting her from the worst of it.

"Is he hurt?" she asked.

Neither Bear, Falcon, Caleb "Brick" Quinn, or Dominick "Domino" Tanner offered any response. Their lack of answers set her nerves—already frayed just about to the max —a hairsbreadth away from shattering entirely.

"Do you have a spare set of comms?" she asked Brick, who had been the one to bandage her feet and happened to be standing closest to her.

Instead of replying, he looked to her brother, which only pushed her closer to the edge.

"Don't look at Falcon. Do you have a spare set of comms?" she repeated, this time over-enunciating each word. They'd brought clothes—which thankfully she hadn't needed because Omega hadn't stripped theirs off them—and shoes for her. They should have brought a set of comms so she could help them get out.

"We don't have a spare," Falcon said, although she thought it was probably a lie.

"Is Ethan okay?" she demanded. The only reason she could think of for why they were all being weird was because they didn't want her to know that Ethan was hurt.

Or worse.

Had Omega killed him already?

They'd suspected that she was the primary target, especially after Omega had admitted that he knew who wanted her and that he had been willing to sell her to him unless she offered him a better deal. Maybe he had decided that Ethan was a liability, and it was better to get rid of him now before the two of them could figure out a way to get out.

"Domino, is Ethan dead?" Even Sparrow could hear the panic edging into her voice.

"No," he replied firmly.

"But he's hurt?"

"A little banged up," he admitted, earning him a glare from her brother.

Sparrow ignored Falcon and focused instead on the only person willing to tell her anything. She'd known of the four guys Domino was the biggest softie and the one who was most likely to be persuaded to give up information, and she hadn't been wrong. "I need to talk to him."

"We need to get moving," Falcon said. "Mouse and the others had to take out some of the soldiers. For sure they know we're here."

"I just need to hear his voice," she said, keeping her gaze on Domino, who hesitated and then gave a nod.

"Put Ethan on," he told the others. Then he removed his comms unit, wiped it on his sleeve, and slipped it on her, ignoring her brother's scowl.

"Ethan?" she demanded, uncaring that the desperation she felt bled into her tone.

"Right here, wisp."

It wasn't until she heard his voice that she took her first

full breath since he had been dragged away. "How badly are you hurt?"

"I'm fine."

His words didn't reassure her, she could hear the pain in his voice. "How bad? What did they do to you?"

"They just beat me up a little, wisp, but I really am okay," he assured her. "Just anxious to see you."

His admission almost made the pain of the whipping worth it. It was the first time he'd even come close to admitting that he cared about her. Maybe what they'd just been through had been enough to help him get some clarity about what he wanted out of the rest of his life. Having something with her didn't have to diminish what he'd shared with Sierra. She'd never try to come between them, she just wanted a chance for the two of them to see if they could be happy together too.

"I'm anxious to see you too," she told him. "Are we meeting up with the others now?" she asked Falcon.

"Soon. We're going to go back the way we came, clear the west side of the building, the others will clear the east side," her brother replied.

As much as she wanted to see Ethan right now, the others knew the layout of the building, and how many guards were there. She and Ethan didn't, so they had to do things their way even if getting eyes on Ethan was what was most important to her right now. "I guess I'll see you soon then," she said.

"Stay safe," Ethan said.

"You too." Reluctantly she handed the comms back to Domino. "Can I have a weapon?"

"You can't walk and handle a weapon," Falcon said.

"Falcon!" She glowered at her brother. Why was he suddenly treating her like she was made of spun glass? "I'm standing, aren't I? I can walk and handle a gun at the same time. Like you've never finished a mission injured before."

Why was he embarrassing her and putting her down in front of their employees? She might be in the Air Force, but she was still an equal part-owner of Prey with the rest of her siblings. Falcon was taking a more active role in running Prey these days, but that didn't give him the right to treat her like an employee, or worse, like a victim Prey was sent to rescue.

"It's not up for discussion," Falcon told her. "Your feet are in bad shape. I know you want to help, but right now, you'll be a liability more than a help." With that, he nodded to Domino who shot her an apologetic smile before bending and putting her over his shoulder.

Sparrow was so shocked by what her brother had said that she didn't even say anything as Domino picked her up and the guys started walking.

A liability?

Her?

So, she wasn't part of the elite Delta Force like Falcon had been before injuries had forced him out. Her job as a pilot was different than this, but she was still trained, she was still a perfect shot, she still knew how to kill with her bare hands, she could do everything he could do. She was no liability.

The guys seemed to have a plan because they moved seamlessly together, Falcon and Bear in front of Domino, and Brick watching their six. They didn't meet any of Omega's soldiers as they cleared the dungeon and headed up a different staircase than the one that led to the room where she had been whipped.

When they reached the top of the stairs the guys paused, and after a whispered discussion she couldn't hear from her perch on Domino's shoulders, they obviously devised a plan.

"Mouse said the shots they fired earlier have everyone swarming over to the east side of the building," Falcon told her as Domino carried her through the door and set her down in a corner of a large spacious living room. "We're going to leave you here, go in and help the others, they're pinned down. You need to stay here." He thrust a gun in her hand and gave her a look like he expected her to argue.

But she wasn't going to do that.

If Ethan was pinned down and in trouble, she wanted the guys to get there as quickly as they could, and while she wouldn't call herself a liability she was injured, and she would slow them down.

"Okay."

"That was easy." Falcon shot her a grin she didn't return, and he sobered. "We'll get Ethan out, don't worry."

She nodded. She did trust them, there was no one she trusted more than the men who worked for her family's company, but Ethan was in trouble, and this time she wasn't there to watch his back.

When the guys were gone, she sagged against the wall. She was tucked into the corner behind a large white leather sofa, she would be spotted if someone was looking for her, but she wasn't immediately noticeable when you entered the room.

For a couple of minutes everything was quiet. Wherever the others were, it was far enough away that she couldn't hear any weapons fire.

Cautiously, Sparrow inched forward. She had no idea what this place looked like because they'd been blindfolded when they were brought here, and it made her feel uneasy that she had no useful information.

Sparrow got to her feet as carefully as she could, wincing at the pain as her feet felt like they had been set alight. Limping as best as she could over to the nearby window, she glanced out. The house they were in was set into the hills. A long winding driveway was visible, winding its way through the trees back down to the road.

As she stood there, she saw three shadows slinking through the darkness.

Even from here she recognized the build and shape of the middle man.

It was Omega trying to slip away with a couple of his bodyguards.

That wasn't happening.

Sparrow didn't even hesitate. She quietly eased the window open and aimed her weapon.

She dropped the first bodyguard with one shot, but the second returned fire more quickly than she had been expecting. A bullet whizzed past her so close she felt its burn, but she didn't pull back. If she didn't get them now, the man who had kidnapped her and Ethan would get away. Omega was a dangerous man, one who tormented the communities around him, not only by trafficking drugs but by stealing their food and money, leaving them with less than they already had. He stole their young men to join his army, and their young women to service the needs of himself and his men.

He didn't deserve to live.

Her second shot took out the other bodyguard, leaving Omega vulnerable and alone. It was like their eyes met even though it was really too dark for her to be able to see his eyes with the distance between them.

She felt his acceptance of death and fired a third kill shot.

* * *

4:34 A.M.

ETHAN FELT his pain melt away at the sound of Sparrow's voice.

He was alive. She was alive. Half of Prey's Alpha team was here with him, the other half plus Falcon with Sparrow. He had no doubt that between the nine of them they would not only get out of here alive but also take down Omega.

"Don't worry, we'll get you back to your girl soon enough," Mouse said with a grin as he handed over some weapons.

"Sparrow isn't my girl," Ethan objected purely on instinct, but even as he said the words, he felt like somehow they were untrue. Sparrow might not be his, they weren't together, but because of her, happiness was starting to seep back into his soul.

"Sure she's not," Surf said with an eye roll.

"Brother, we've just watched this happen three times already in the last twelve months," Arrow added.

"The Oswald family is so organized and on top of things they even fall in love in order." Surf laughed. "Eagle first with Olivia, then Raven gets back with Max, then Falcon falls for Hope, and now Sparrow bags Ethan. Guess someone better call Hawk and tell him to be on the lookout for a Ms. Right to come barreling into his life. Poor Dove is going to hate being last, that girl loves her some attention."

The others all laughed, and even though Ethan was nowhere near ready to commit to anything with Sparrow beyond friendship, he found he didn't dislike the thought of them as a couple as much as he would have just a few days ago.

"We going to stand around here chatting like a bunch of girls or did we forget where we are?" he asked, more than ready to get back to Sparrow. She would freak when she saw the blood and bruises and torn clothes, but at least she'd know he was okay, and he'd be able to reassure himself that she was still in one piece. The Oswald family really did seem to have an uncanny knack for getting themselves into trouble.

Just like that, the guys snapped back to attention.

They spread out, checking out the two entries to the room. Ethan turned to Mouse and asked, "We were blindfolded when we were brought here. How big is this place? How many levels? How many soldiers?"

"Place is like a castle, and it's built into the side of the mountain, at least five levels plus the basement. We counted at least a couple of dozen guards as we were coming in."

"How did you find us so quickly?" Ethan asked.

"Olivia and Raven. Olivia had already been looking into the warlords, and once we got word Sparrow had gone missing, Raven came in to help. They tracked Omega to this area, and once we were here and got some drones up and flying, we thought this was as good a place as any to start looking for you guys. We hit the jackpot on the first go when we found you both here," Mouse said.

"Incoming," Surf announced from the door that led out into the house.

"We can't backtrack through the dungeon, we don't want to lead them back to Sparrow. We could get trapped down there as well if they come at us from the side the others are heading out," he added so it didn't sound like he was only worried about Sparrow. Even if it was true.

"Doesn't matter, they're coming at us from that way anyway," Arrow announced from the stairs.

"Falcon? Bear? You guys in trouble?" Ethan asked into the comms unit he'd been given.

"Negative. We're just about out of the basement. You guys need help?" Falcon asked.

"We're pinned down in the room at the top of the other flight of stairs," Mouse explained. "The gunshots have obviously been reported, and they're probably sending every guard they have to this location."

As if on cue, men began to come through both doors, firing at him and the others.

"We're on our way," Bear assured them.

While it was always good to know backup was on the way, he abhorred the idea of Sparrow coming toward danger instead of away from it. It was something he would have to get used to because he didn't think she was ready to leave the Air Force yet, and even if she did, it would probably mean she'd go to work with Prey. Sparrow enjoyed her job, and she was good at it. He would have to make sure he never made her feel like he couldn't cope with it because he knew she would never have done that to him.

Although they didn't have the numbers advantage, and they were pinned down, he and Alpha team were able to hold off the soldiers long enough for the other half of Alpha team to arrive, and what felt like hours but couldn't have been more than minutes later the room finally fell quiet.

"Did we get eyes on Omega?" Ethan asked.

"No," Bear replied.

"So, he has to still be here somewhere. He was here right before you guys came in, he thought I'd taken the drugs, but Evan must have hidden them before he left the compound. When he realized I had nothing to give him he ordered my death. The soldiers got in a few hits before you guys came in, guns blazing."

"He probably fled when he heard the shooting start," Falcon said.

"We can't leave him alive. Not only is he dangerous, but he knows who's after your family," Ethan told Falcon. "He told Sparrow that it's someone involved in weapons trafficking."

"As far as I know we don't have any family members involved in the weapons trade," Falcon said.

"If we can take him alive you might finally get your answers. Where's Sparrow?"

"We left her somewhere safe," Falcon assured him. "And left her with a gun. We figured all the guards would be heading here, and since she can't walk, I didn't want her anywhere near gunfire."

"This place is loaded with drugs," Mouse noted as the eight of them headed back through the house to retrieve Sparrow and get out.

"My vote is we blow the whole place before we leave," Surf said with a spark in his blue eyes. Despite the guy's laid-back and easy-going persona, he loved to blow stuff up.

"I second that," Brick agreed.

Everyone else voted for the blowing up the place plan, and Ethan didn't care what they did as long as Sparrow was all right. They were almost to the room where Falcon said they'd left her when they heard more gunshots.

Expecting the worst—to enter the room to find Sparrow dead in a pool of her blood, with Omega standing over her—when they did enter the room, he found Sparrow standing at the window, her gun in her hand and aimed at something outside.

"Sparrow?" he said as he limped toward her, his body beginning to protest the beating it had taken.

"He was going to get away," she said softly, not lowering her arms, which he could see were trembling.

"Who was, wisp?"

"Omega. I saw him and two bodyguards trying to escape." Her tone was dull, and while he knew she knew she'd done the right thing in stopping the man, he hurried to reassure her anyway.

"You didn't have a choice." Reaching her side, he gently

placed his hand over hers and extricated the gun from her white-knuckled grip. He handed it off to Falcon, turned Sparrow and pulled her into his arms.

She came willingly, and a little content sigh left her lips as she rested her head against his chest and wrapped her arms around his waist. "I know. Just never shot an unarmed man before."

"He might not have had a weapon on him when you shot him, but he was a dangerous man," he reminded her. Then he buried his face in her hair and just held her. For a while there he'd thought he would never get the chance to hold her again. When he had her like this, tucked tight against his body, it was hard to remember why it was he hadn't been willing to give her a chance. If only they could stay like this forever, then life would be so much easier. But they couldn't, and he would continue to doubt whether being with her was the right thing. Until he was sure he was ready to move on, he had no choice but to let her go.

Maybe not forever, but for now.

Reluctantly, he pulled back. Sparrow gave one last squeeze before she let him go and stepped away. As soon as she did, her eyes widened, and her mouth dropped open in shock.

"Ethan, you're ..."

"Fine," he said firmly.

"But you're bleeding, and your face ..." She reached up and her gentle fingertips whispered across his battered skin. "I knew you were hurt, but ..." Sparrow paused to drag in a breath. "I wasn't prepared to see you like this, all bloody and bruised, with your clothes torn. Are they all dead?"

"Yeah, wisp, they're all dead," he replied with an amused smile. The look on her face right now was as adorable as it was fierce.

"Too bad," she said.

"Hey, you got to take out the top dog," he reminded her.

This time she grinned up at him. "Yeah, I guess you're right. I would have liked to take out the men who did that to you, but I'm grateful to you guys for doing it." She looked over his shoulder at Alpha team who were gathered around them. "Thanks for coming for us and finding us so quickly."

Literally just in time, although Ethan wasn't going to tell her that. She didn't need to know that he had been minutes from death when Alpha team made their perfectly timed entrance. "Now it's time to get you off your feet, you have to be in agony."

"No worse than how you're feeling I'm guessing."

"You both need to be checked out," Falcon said. "Arrow and I will take you two back to the plane, and Surf can have his fun blowing this place up."

Ethan wrapped an arm around Sparrow's waist, helping to take her weight because he knew she wasn't going to allow herself to be carried out of here. He smiled when she immediately slipped her arm around his waist, trying to support him just as he was supporting her.

This woman made him smile when he'd thought there would never be anything in his life to smile about again. Now he was at a crossroads, he could continue down the same path he'd been on, spend the rest of his life alone, or he could give happiness a chance. Give Sparrow a chance.

The drama was over now, the drug traffickers taken care of, there were no excuses left. It was time for him to figure out what the next stage of his life looked like.

CHAPTER TEN

January 27th

2 :17 P.M.

"I'M NOT ASLEEP YOU KNOW," Sparrow told Ethan as he shifted carefully in his seat for the hundredth time. "You don't have to be so careful. You're in pain, I know that. Maybe if you'd taken Arrow up on his offer of morphine you wouldn't be feeling so awful."

"Hey, you didn't take any either." He huffed.

"But I didn't get beaten up," she reminded him as she opened her eyes and shifted in her seat, so she was propped up against the side of the plane. Yesterday, after Surf had had his fun blowing up Omega's house and the drugs inside, they'd started the long journey back home. They were drop-ping Ethan back off on the way, then they'd be going on to

New York. All she had left with Ethan was until the plane landed, it wasn't enough, but it was what it was. He was being more affectionate with her, but he hadn't said anything about the future, and she was too chicken to ask what he was thinking.

So, all she had was soaking up this last little bit of time with him.

"No, but you had your feet cut to shreds," he shot back, making her grin even though her feet were extremely painful and would be for several more days, probably the next few weeks. They were currently heavily bandaged and propped up with the seat's leg rest up.

"Yeah, I'm going to be stuck pretty much sitting down for days, but at least I'll get to boss my siblings around and make them wait on me hand and foot." She was actually looking forward to that. Not the bossing around her big brothers and sister, but just being able to hang out with them would be fun. She missed them being away most of the time, moving from base to base around the world, maybe she was finally ready to put down some roots of her own. Especially with Eagle getting married soon, and Raven and Max getting remarried, two new baby nieces or nephews on the way, and she'd like to be closer to home to be able to support Cleo as she continues to readjust to a normal life. As much as she loved her job the pros of being home more and closer to her family were starting to outweigh the cons of leaving.

"Sparrow, I ..."

"Shh." She reached out and took his hand. "It's okay. Really. I mean, I'm not going to pretend that I don't like you or that I don't wish things could have been different, but I truly understand that you're not trying to hurt me and you're not trying to jerk me around. You love Sierra, and in your mind she's still your wife."

"I thought I'd be spending the rest of my life with her."

"I know." As much as it sucked, she truly did understand where Ethan was coming from. In asking him to give her a chance she was basically doing the same thing as asking him to cheat on the wife he would always love. Because there was really nothing else to say, she just held onto his hand and turned to stare out the window.

They sat in silence for the remainder of the flight, and when they finally touched down, she had to force herself not to beg. If the two of them were going to stand any sort of chance, then Ethan had to be sure he had room in his heart for someone else. He had to come to terms with the fact that moving on wasn't betraying Sierra's memory. Until he got to that place, there was no hope for them.

When she went to stand, Ethan stopped her. "Don't get up. I don't want you to be hurting." He stood and looked down at her for a long moment before speaking again. "I'm sorry, Sparrow."

"You have nothing to apologize for," she assured him.

"I feel like I do."

"Well, you don't. You didn't make me any promises, and you're doing the right thing. We're just in two different places, and I've accepted the fact that you might never get to the same place I'm in. I hope if nothing else, we'll always be friends."

"Always." Ethan stooped and brushed a light kiss to her cheek, and then with a last wave, he turned and left the plane.

Tears pricked her eyes as she stared at the empty doorway. She knew Ethan was doing the right thing for both of them. It wouldn't be fair to try something he wasn't ready for, and she'd only wind up more hurt down the road if they started dating only for him to realize he couldn't commit to her.

"You okay?"

She blinked and finally looked away from the private jet's

door to see Falcon dropping into the seat Ethan had vacated. "Fine."

"You don't look fine. You need Arrow to give you something for the pain."

"Don't think they make anything to heal a broken heart," she murmured. It wasn't the pain in her feet that was bothering her, it was the pain of knowing she had fallen in love with a man who she feared wasn't capable of ever loving her back.

"If you want to talk, I'm here," Falcon offered.

Because the idea sounded so ridiculous, she couldn't help but scoff. "You? Here to talk?"

"It was only a couple of weeks ago that I left the woman I was falling for and walked away, thinking I wasn't good enough for her, that I couldn't give her what she deserved. But everything worked out for me and Hope. Maybe things will work out for you and Ethan as well."

The idea of her brother falling for a woman was so strange. Of all of them, she'd always thought that Falcon was the least likely to fall in love, and yet, apparently, she was wrong. There was a light in his eyes that she'd never seen before. He looked happy. Genuinely happy. He'd actually managed to find his other half while hers had just walked away.

It was pain that had her lashing out, although she wasn't proud of herself for it. "I don't want to talk about Ethan."

"If you change your mind ..."

"I won't."

"But if you do, then you know you can talk to me. I'm here for you."

Right. The brother who had abandoned her and their whole family when it suited him would be there for her. Somehow, she didn't think so. "I don't want to talk about this, not with anyone but especially not with you," she snapped.

Falcon's eyes narrowed. "Why especially not with me?"

"Because you left, you just shut me out of your life like I meant nothing to you. Me. The person you were closest to when we were kids. If you can shut me out then I can shut you out," she snapped, letting out the last three years' worth of anger at her brother just disappearing without a word. It wasn't fair, she knew that. She was taking out her sadness of Ethan leaving on Falcon, but her emotions had bubbled over, and she didn't know how to contain them right now.

Her brother made her feel worse because in true Falcon style, he didn't argue with her, didn't press her to talk, didn't even offer her an apology, just quietly stood and walked off to join the others, leaving her behind and making her feel like the worst sister ever.

Lashing out at Falcon didn't solve her problem with Ethan and only made her feel terrible. She should have left it at she didn't want to talk, there was no need to bring up the fact that she felt abandoned when Falcon had pulled his disappearing act.

Resting her head against the window, she ignored everything but wallowing in her own misery. This was the first time she'd ever had a broken heart. She'd never met anyone who made her feel the way Ethan did. She'd been sad when her previous relationships ended, but she'd known they were going to at some point. Ethan was the only one who had made her think about the future. She'd seen them having it all, a home, a family, a life they could have shared and grown old side by side.

But that future had died before it even got a chance to get off the ground.

The last few days and everything that had happened hit her all at once. She felt so alone, she didn't have anyone to turn to. Everyone else in her life was happy, excited about their future, moving on, finding love and happiness, planning weddings and baby showers.

Tears came in a flood, but she managed to hold in a sob. As if she needed to top things off with hysterics in front of men who worked for her. Who would never respect her again if they saw the weeping mess she was right now.

Curling in on herself as best as she could with her injured feet and broken collarbone, Sparrow had fallen so deeply down the rabbit hole of tears that she never even noticed that Falcon had never left. He'd just moved behind her where he could watch over her, which is exactly what he did.

CHAPTER ELEVEN

January 28th

 2:39 P.M.

HE'D GONE STRAIGHT to a hotel yesterday. Exhaustion had hit him hard, and other than taking a long, hot shower and ordering some room service all he'd done was sleep.

Partly because he truly had been exhausted and had needed the rest, but also because he wanted to put off coming here.

But Ethan knew he couldn't do that forever.

Besides, he'd come back here for this very purpose.

Climbing out of his rental, Ethan walked to the garden gate and stopped. Doing this was a whole lot harder than he'd thought it would be when he decided to visit the house he'd shared with Sierra.

They'd bought the little ranch house in a near-derelict state a couple of years after they got married. When he'd been home for a couple of weeks between deployments, the two of them had spent long days working on fixing it up. They'd be up before the sun, sanding, painting, laying floorboards, and tiling the bathrooms. It had been exhausting, but they'd laughed a lot, talked even more, and enjoyed each other's company. By the time he had left again the place had been habitable. But Ethan had wanted it to be special, so the next time he'd been home they'd made a huge wrap-around porch that circled all four sides of the house. He'd even built a wooden swing where they'd spent many a summer evening when he was home.

So many months he'd spent away though, leaving Sierra to tend to the house herself. She'd worked hard on the garden, planting a stunning array of flowerbeds that had something flowering all throughout the year. There was a huge grassy area in the back where they'd imagined playing with their kids, and a large oak tree in the front yard where he had been planning to build a treehouse.

So many dreams that had never had a chance to come to fruition.

At least not in the way he'd thought they would.

Lifting a hand, he opened the gate and stepped onto the property. After losing Sierra and deciding to move to Africa, Ethan had intended to put the house on the market, knowing he would never be able to live here, but Sierra's sister's husband had been in a bad accident putting them in dire financial straits. Rather than sell the place, he'd rented it to his in-laws for virtually nothing. The family were back on their feet now but still lived in the little house, now paying him more, but this was their home, and they hadn't wanted to leave.

Despite the snow that covered the ground a sled sat on

the ground by the tree, a couple of bikes leaned against the porch railings, and a snowman sat proudly around the side. The house looked lived in and loved, exactly how it would have if he and Sierra had raised their family there.

Ethan walked down the garden path and sat down on the porch swing. As much as it hurt to be here, he didn't get that same lost feeling anymore when he thought of Sierra. It still hurt, but the pain was dulled a little, and instead of feeling like he was lost in an endless sea of grief, now there was a life preserver beside him. Something to hold onto when the grief felt like it would drown him.

Sparrow was his life preserver.

He smiled as he thought of her. He'd done nothing but think about her. He'd thought of her when he was eating, pictured her in the shower with him, dreamed about making love to her when he climbed into bed.

The tiny wisp of a woman had gotten under his skin and stuck there.

"Ethan."

He looked up as the front door opened and Sierra's sister Sahara stepped out. It was like looking back in time. The two sisters were similar in looks. Sahara was a few years younger, but Sierra had been gone for four years now, and Sahara was just a year older than her sister when she died.

As weird as it was to feel like he was talking to his wife, Ethan stood and returned Sahara's hug.

"Long time no see," Sahara said, taking a step back to study him. She was so like her sister, from the way she tilted her head to the side, to the way she planted her hands on her hips, to the way she scrunched up one corner of her mouth. Even her voice when she spoke was the same as Sierra's. "You met someone."

"That's the first thing you say to me? Nothing about

this." He waved his hand around his face to indicate the brightly colored display of black, blue, purple, and red bruises.

"Okay," Sahara agreed, "you showing up with your handsome face covered in bruises is odd, but I just assumed it had something to do with a woman. Although I have to admit I have no idea how the two are related."

Since he couldn't mention being involved in taking down a drug trafficking warlord in Africa, and he wasn't ready to discuss Sparrow with Sierra's sister, he said, "Handsome face?"

"You know how good-looking you are." Sahara waved off his attempt at modesty. "In high school you used to love it that all the girls followed you around making puppy dog eyes at you."

"I never did anything with any of them." Ethan would hate Sahara to think that he had cheated on Sierra. Even back then he'd loved his would-be wife and would never have done anything to hurt her.

"I know." Sahara looked thoughtful again for a moment before indicating the swing. "Let's sit." Once they were both seated, she shifted so she could look up at him. "You know back then, our parents told Sierra she shouldn't fall for such a good-looking man. That men who look like you never remain faithful. They were wrong. You didn't just stand by Sierra when she was sick, you took care of her like she was the most precious thing in the world."

"She was," he whispered. Guilt over his developing feelings for Sparrow surged. Maybe his in-laws had been right about him. Here he was, Sierra had only been gone a few years, and already he had met a woman he could imagine sharing his life with.

"Don't do that. Please."

"Do what?"

"Think you're letting my sister down. You did meet a woman, right?"

"Yeah," he reluctantly admitted. But once he'd said it out loud, the first time he'd actually admitted to anyone that Sparrow was more than just a friend, he actually felt relieved. It was like a weight had been lifted off him and he could stop pretending that she meant nothing to him.

"And you're worried about betraying Sierra by moving on?"

"Yes. I promised to love her forever."

"And you will." Sahara reached for his hands, picking them up and squeezing. "You will love her forever, but you don't have to be alone to fulfill that promise to my sister. Sierra would be happy for you. She wouldn't want you to be mourning her the way you have been, all alone, cut off from your home and the people who care about you. She would want you to meet someone else, have the life you wanted with her with someone who would love you just as much as she did."

"You can't know that." While Sahara was telling him everything he wanted to hear, there was no way either of them could have known what Sierra would and wouldn't have wanted. Near the end, when they knew she wasn't going to recover, he hadn't wanted to talk about life after her. It had been too hard to think of going on without her, he'd just wanted to focus on the time they had left.

"I can know that," Sahara contradicted. "Because Sierra and I talked about it. She wanted you to find someone and move on. She didn't want you to spend the rest of your life focused only on your grief, she didn't want to be the cause of your pain. She knew it would take time, but she was hoping that one day there would be a special lady enter your life. When that happened, she hoped you wouldn't fight it. As much as she hated that you two wouldn't be able to make the dreams you'd had when you first got together happen, she still wanted you to have it all."

That sounded like his wife. Sierra had such a big heart. She was so kind, and warm, and generous in everything that she did. He'd been so focused on himself, on what he was feeling, on the grief, that he hadn't given much thought to what Sierra would have wanted him to do with the rest of his life.

"She wanted you to find someone who would love you with their whole heart," Sahara continued. "Someone who would make you smile, who could make you laugh, who could even make you forget—just for a little while—about your loss. Someone who would marry you and give you the children she couldn't, who would still be beside you when you were both old and gray. Who would take care of you like you took care of her, and who could make your life better just by being there. So, I guess there's only really one question I need to ask about this woman who has you all tied up in knots. Is she everything Sierra wanted for you?"

That was a question Ethan didn't even have to think about.

Yes.

Sparrow was everything that Sierra would have wanted for him.

Sahara smiled. "I can see your answer in the way your features just relaxed, and you got a little twinkle in your eyes. Ethan, if things had been reversed, if you were the one who was sick, the one who had died, what would you have wanted Sierra to do?"

"To live, to be happy, to find someone else who would love her just like I had loved her," he answered without hesitation.

"Then why would you think she wanted less for you?"

Ethan had never thought of it that way. He'd never

considered what Sierra might want him to do with the rest of his life, or what he would have wanted for her if things had been reversed. Now that he had, everything seemed so simple, so clear. The answers he had been searching for had finally been revealed.

CHAPTER TWELVE

January 29th

 :42 P.M.

Sparrow set down the cloth she used to scrub the kitchen counters when she heard the lift doors open. When she was home, she lived in a penthouse that Eagle had chosen for her, she hated this place. Well, maybe hate was too strong a word, she didn't hate it, it just wasn't her. Of all of her siblings, she was the one who had in that way adjusted the worst to their new lives after their parents' deaths. She didn't want a big pretentious penthouse that was accessed by a private lift with huge glass windows overlooking Manhattan. She liked small and cozy, warm woods, and beautifully crafted antiques.

Assuming it was one of her siblings or Olivia stopping by

with food, she picked back up the cloth. Even though the house had a cleaner who came in once a week, Sparrow kept busy so she didn't obsess over Ethan. He'd given her everything he had to give, and for that, she would always be grateful.

Didn't mean she wasn't missing him like crazy.

"Shouldn't you be keeping off your feet?"

She looked up, startled to see Falcon there. She hadn't seen him since they arrived in New York. She had met Falcon's girlfriend Hope, and she really liked the woman. They had gotten along great from the moment they met, and it only made her feel extra bad that she'd yelled at Falcon on the plane. She was happy for him, still hurt about what had gone down a few years back, but that didn't mean she didn't want him to be happy, he was her big brother after all.

"What are you doing here?" she asked. She was embarrassed about how she'd behaved on the plane, and while she wanted to apologize, she wasn't ready to discuss her feelings about it, or anything else right now. She felt ripped raw emotionally, in comparison the wounds on her feet were nothing.

Falcon held up a pizza box. "Brought you dinner."

Her eyes lit up at the sight of the pizza. Apparently, the rest of her siblings had decided that she needed to eat healthily and had been bringing her more vegetables than she'd eaten in a long time. "Pizza." She limped around the counter and reached for the box.

Just as she was about to grab it Falcon pulled it back, just out of reach. "It's not just pizza."

"It's not some sort of weird veggie pizza, is it?" Olivia had been talking about vegetable pizza yesterday since Sparrow had been complaining about too much healthy food, but as far as she was concerned pizza was supposed to be loaded with cheese and meats.

Falcon did one of his half-smiles. "I see Liv has been trying to sell the vegetable pizza to you too. No, this is real pizza, your favorite in fact," he added slyly. "But it's also a peace offering."

"A peace offering?" She was surprised that Falcon was here making the first move, her brother had really changed a lot since she'd last seen him.

"You're still mad at me and I don't like it. I want you to forgive me, but I can't apologize for doing what I thought was the only thing that would keep my family safe." Now Falcon was channeling his inner Eagle. Their older brother never apologized when he thought he was right, not even if whatever he'd done had hurt someone.

Sparrow turned and hobbled over to the table, dropping down into a chair. "You just left, Falcon. I mean completely. No warning, no heads up as to what you were going to do, you just left the hospital and disappeared. We had no idea what had happened to you, where you'd gone, if you were ever coming back, or if you were okay."

"If I was okay?" Falcon asked as he joined her at the table.

"You'd just been kicked out of Delta because you'd lost some sight and hearing, only two of your team survived the ambush that killed the others. I knew how much being in Delta meant to you and without it I was worried that ..."

"You were worried that what? That I would ... that I would kill myself?" Falcon looked aghast at the possibility, but she nodded because that was exactly what she'd feared.

"I kept thinking that you would call, or email, or even write a letter, anything to let us know—to let *me* know—that you were okay. I thought maybe you just needed time, but you were gone for almost two years, Falcon. *Two years.* That's a really long time to worry over someone. I kept wondering what I should have done differently when I saw you in the hospital. Should I have said something? Done something?

Something that would make sure you knew that I was there for you, whatever you needed, even if it was just to sit quietly beside you so you wouldn't be alone. I thought it was my fault. We were always the closest of our siblings, I thought I had failed you, that I hadn't done enough."

Falcon was just sitting there staring at her, so she shrugged. It was clear he didn't get it, but she'd spent nearly two years believing Falcon had ended his own life and that there must have been something she could have said or done to stop it from happening.

When she reached for the pizza box, Falcon grabbed her hands, squeezing them almost painfully tight. "I'm sorry."

"I thought you weren't here to apologize."

"I was wrong. I had no idea you thought that."

"Of course not, you never asked. You just came barreling back last year acting like you hadn't been gone for two years."

"I still think leaving was the only thing I could have done, but you're right, I should have done it a different way. You dropped everything to come and be by my side. I should have told you I had to disappear and leave it at that, I owed you that much. I'm sorry I hurt you."

That was exactly what she needed to hear her brother say. "I was hurt and angry with you, but I shouldn't have lashed out at you on the plane the way I did. It was uncalled for, and you didn't deserve it. I was upset about Ethan, and I took it out on you, that wasn't cool. I'm sorry, forgive me?"

"Are you forgiving me?"

She smiled, and her anger melted away. "Yeah, I think it would be mean not to, I mean, you *did* bring me pizza when none of the others would."

Falcon smiled back. "Hug it out?"

"Nah, that's okay, I know you don't like hugs."

Her big brother hesitated for a moment, allowing her a rare glimpse at the insecurities he hid so well. "I want to."

She stood, and Falcon did too. He wrapped his arms around her and lifted her feet off the floor. Sparrow wrapped her arms around his neck and hugged her brother hard. She couldn't even remember the last time they'd hugged. Falcon had never been big on contact like that, and then after their parents died, he had withdrawn even more.

"Now that you're talking to me again, tell me about Ethan," Falcon said as he set her in her chair and went to get them both sodas from her fridge. "Do Eagle and I need to go and beat him up? I'm sure Max would be happy to be in on it too."

Sparrow laughed as she opened the pizza box and pulled out a gooey, cheesy slice piled high with ham, bacon, and salami. "No, I do not need you guys to do that. I never did."

"I know, I remember when you were fifteen and that guy tried to pressure you to sleep with him. You kicked him right in the place where no guy wants to be hit," Falcon said as he sat down opposite her.

"He was trying to rip off my clothes even as I was telling him no," she said with a shrug. "Not that it mattered, you and Hawk still went after him anyway." She'd been furious both at the boy and her brothers, thinking they were implying that she couldn't take care of her own problems without them.

"We're your brothers, it was our job to look out for you."

"But I can do it myself."

"Doesn't matter, it's in the brother manual."

"*Ha ha*," she said sarcastically. "It made me feel like you guys thought I was weak."

"We never thought that, Sparrow, not once."

Since Falcon sounded sincere, she nodded. "Okay, but if Ethan needed beating up I could do it myself."

"Doesn't mean we won't be there to do it for you," Falcon said stubbornly.

"Well, it's not necessary. Ethan is a good guy, and I really like him, I could even see myself falling in love with him, but he's still grieving, he's not ready to move on. He might never be ready," she added. "If it was just a matter of time, I would wait but what if I wait and he's never ready, and then it's too late for me to meet someone else, fall in love, and have a family?"

"No one says you have to wait."

"I know. But when I think of my future, it's Ethan that I see beside me. It's so clear, you know? Like I'm watching our future play out on a screen, but then it goes fuzzy, and he fades away. I know he likes me, maybe even has some feelings for me, but he doesn't want to do anything about them, and I can't force him to."

"Advice?"

"Sure."

"Sometimes, when you're battling something internally, you just need a little patience. Hope was more patient with me than I deserved, and because of that, I had the space I needed to work things through in my head. Now I have the most amazing woman in my life, and I'm ... happy."

Her brother said it like he was surprised, and she was so happy for him. She hadn't even thought Falcon wanted to fall in love, but it was clear by the look in his eyes that he loved Hope. Maybe he'd only been able to fall in love because Hope was the right woman for him.

It made her hopeful for her situation was Ethan. Maybe if she was the right woman for him, he'd be able to find room for her in his heart and in his life.

And if she wasn't the right woman for Ethan then at least she would know.

CHAPTER THIRTEEN

January 30th

:50 A.M.

"Done," Ethan announced aloud, even though he was alone in the storage unit.

For the last day and a half, he'd been going through all the things from his life with Sierra. After her death, when he'd decided to move to Africa, he had thrown all of their belongings into boxes, unable to face dealing with them, and hired a storage unit where the boxes of belongings had been ever since.

But after talking to Sahara, Ethan realized he was ready.

Ready to finally let go of the grief and the anger of losing the woman he loved far too early.

It didn't mean he wouldn't miss Sierra every day for the

rest of his life, but it meant he was ready to be happy again. He couldn't quite call it moving on because the term made him feel like he was leaving Sierra behind, and he wasn't, she would always be carried and cherished safe in his heart. But he was ready to live in happiness rather than in grief, and that was a big step for him.

As much as he had been dreading doing this, and had being abducted and beaten by a drug trafficking warlord not forced his hand, he might never have actually done it, but looking through all of Sierra's things had ended up being cathartic. He'd laughed when he'd found some of the gag gifts she'd gotten him over the years. It was a tradition she'd started while they were still in high school and didn't have much money to spend on gifts for one another for Christmases and birthdays. Sierra had continued doing it even once they had jobs and it had never failed to make him laugh at the crazy things she managed to find.

Tears had been shed as well as he looked through photos of the two of them together, and sorted through her jewelry, and the almost hundred pairs of shoes she owned. Even just sorting her clothes had made him teary, especially when the smell of her perfume lingered on the material, tricking his brain into believing she was right there beside him.

And maybe she was.

Ethan had felt her spirit surrounding him. It felt like a warm embrace, like Sierra was happy for him, rooting for him to make things work with Sparrow. She wasn't a replacement for Sierra, nor did he expect her to live in his wife's shadow. Sparrow was her own person and what he felt for her was different than his love for Sierra had been, and for the first time he actually felt excited about the future.

It was time to focus on the future and not the past.

To that end, Ethan glanced down at his hand. It was time to take off his wedding ring. Sierra would always be his first wife, but maybe there was a spunky wisp of a woman with black wavy hair, big blue eyes, and a personality bigger than she was, who might become his second wife.

There was no way to know if he and Sparrow would work as a couple, but he was done letting his grief, his guilt at moving on, and his fear of losing another woman he cared about dictate how he lived his life.

Time.

It was definitely time.

Ethan carefully eased the ring off his finger, holding it for a moment in his palm. Despite the fact that the day was gray, and that the promise of snow was in the air, he could have sworn the gold band glittered as though caught in a ray of sunshine.

Sierra's blessing.

He was smiling as he pulled out his wallet and tucked the ring safely inside, that way he could still carry it with him each day but his hand—and his heart—were free for another woman to step in.

Closing the storage unit's door—Sahara would pick up all the boxes that were full of donatable items and take them to a local charity store. Anything not in good enough condition had already been tossed—Ethan picked up the final box of belongings he was keeping. He had just loaded it into the back of his rental truck when his phone rang.

The number was an unknown one, but still he answered it anyway. "Hello?"

"It's Falcon."

"What's wrong?" he demanded. The only reason he could think of for Sparrow's big brother to be calling was because something was wrong with her. They had both been checked out when they got back Stateside, and they'd both been lucky to have survived without serious injuries, but maybe Sparrow had developed an infection. Or anything else could have happened to her in the couple of days since he'd seen her. Accident, mugging, or maybe this person after her family had finally caught up with her.

"Nothing's wrong."

"Oh." Relief washed over him. Perhaps the scariest thing about moving on was allowing himself to love someone he could wind up losing. "Then why are you calling."

"Wanted to find out if I have to be preparing my sister to deal with a broken heart."

There was no anger in Falcon's tone, no accusation, not even any pressure. This wasn't just Falcon the big brother, this was Falcon a man that understood you could want something and be terrified of it at the same time. "You know I'm not trying to hurt her, and I'm not playing games with her. Sparrow knows that I still love Sierra, and that I always will."

"So, you're going back to Africa? You're not going to give her a chance?"

With a grin, Ethan climbed into the driver's seat. "Actually, I'm on my way to drop off some stuff at my sister-in-law's house, she's going to send it on to me, and then I'm on my way to the airport."

"International or domestic flight?"

"Domestic."

"You're coming here?"

"Yep. I don't know what the future holds for me and your sister, but I know she makes me happy, and I know that she's brave and loyal, and I know that I want to spend time with her and find out if things between us could work out."

"Good. Means Eagle, Max, and I don't have to beat you up."

Ethan laughed and turned on the engine. If he wanted to drop the boxes of stuff he was keeping off at Sahara's house then go to his hotel to shower and change and make his flight, he was going to have to hurry. "Somehow I don't think Sparrow will like it if you offer to beat me up for her."

"She wouldn't, she told me in no uncertain terms that if you needed beating up, she was more than capable of doing it herself."

"That she is," he agreed as he drove through the parking lot.

"She also said you didn't need any beating up, that she understood that you still loved and always would love Sierra, and that she didn't hold it against you that you weren't ready to be in a relationship again. She said she only wants the best for you but wishes things would work out. She really likes you, Ethan."

His heart swelled at how understanding Sparrow was being about the whole thing, especially given what a mess he'd made of things the night they'd had sex. "I really like her too, Falcon. And I'm coming to Manhattan to tell her that, and to give us a fair go, but it might take time. I might have to go slow, I can't promise your sister a ring tomorrow."

"She's not asking you to. None of us are. I just wanted to find out what your intentions were with my sister."

"You better hope your sister doesn't find out you called me," he said, only half-joking.

"I know, she'll think I called because I don't think she can fight her own battles, but she's working on realizing that people wanting to help her doesn't mean they think she's weak. I didn't call because Sparrow needs my help in this, or because I really would have beat you up if you weren't going to pursue anything with my sister, my family all understands your situation, but I let Sparrow down when I disappeared a few years back, and I won't make that mistake again. I'm going to be there for my sister whether she likes it or not."

"I'm glad to hear that. I know Sparrow was upset with you, but it sounds like you two cleared the air."

"We did."

"Good. Family is important. I'm glad that no matter how things work out between me and Sparrow that she has a family to have her back."

"Family is everything to us. We take care of our own. That includes Olivia, Max, Hope, and now you. You're one of us now, and that means if you ever need anything all you have to do is ask, and every resource we have at our disposal is yours. I'm happy for you, Ethan, and I know Sparrow is going to be thrilled to see you."

"Don't tell her I'm coming, okay? I want it to be a surprise." The first thing he needed to do was make up for their disastrous night together, and then he would take her out on a real date, which may or may not end with sex, but it was definitely going to end in a kiss. A kiss he knew he would be daydreaming about all the way to New York City.

* * *

8:15 A.M.

Sparrow stepped gingerly onto her feet as she stepped out of the shower and reached for a towel. She wrapped it around her long dark locks and gabbed another soft, fluffy pink towel to wrap around herself.

As she shuffled across the large bathroom, she paused in front of the mirror. The cut from the helicopter crash was healing well, and the doctor had removed the stitches after they got checked out back here in the States. The bruising was still noticeable but had morphed from dark blues and blacks to lighter greens and yellow. Her collarbone was feeling better too, although she had overworked it a bit the last few days with all the obsessive, keep-busy cleaning she'd been doing.

Still, she was feeling so much better, even her feet had improved, that she didn't want to be stuck in the house anymore.

She didn't want to be stuck in the city anymore.

There was only so long the distraction plan was going to work, and apparently it had reached its expiration date this morning.

As much as she didn't want to make Ethan feel pressured, she only wanted him to be with her if he felt he was ready, she missed him *so* much. It was like a physical ache, one for which there was only one cure. She could fly to Kansas, make it clear she was just there as his friend, and maybe they could hang out together until he went back to Djibouti, assuming that was his plan once his injuries healed.

If she got there and he wasn't pleased to see her, then she'd know for sure that things weren't going to happen between them, but at least she'd know. And if he was pleased to see her then the two of them could have some fun together until he returned to Africa.

Energized now she had decided to go and see Ethan, Sparrow quickly dried off, and threw on jeans and a sweater. The sweater was pink, what most people didn't know about her, and she hid it even though she wasn't embarrassed exactly, was that pink was actually her favorite color. Her room was pink, and most of her bedding, towels, and face washers too, but she thought the color was girly, and might undermine her efforts to show she was one of the guys, so she never let on to anyone outside her family that she liked it.

One thing she knew about Ethan was that he would never ever make fun of her for liking pink. She was confident in the way he saw her, felt strong and competent when she was around him, and never felt like she had to prove herself. Being around Ethan was comfortable, relaxing, and she was quickly coming to realize that she craved him and his presence. Even though she knew it wasn't a good idea to get her hopes up she couldn't seem to stop herself, she wanted it all with Ethan.

She wanted it so much she was already thinking about the future and what changes she would have to make. There was still another year left on her current deployment, but she wouldn't be re-upping after that. If Ethan wanted to stay in Africa, she'd move there too. She wanted to be closer to her family, but she was used to the distance between them and could make do. If Ethan decided to stay in the States, they could figure out what they wanted to do. They had plenty of time to figure it out, for now, they could take things slow and see where they went.

Excited, Sparrow headed into her bedroom and sat on the bed to gingerly slide on her socks and a pair of sneakers. She didn't want to waste time blow-drying her hair, she'd let it air dry and then she'd call and book a flight. No, she didn't need to book a commercial flight, she could take one of Prey's jets.

When she went searching for her cell phone it began to ring. It took her a moment, but she located it on the coffee table in the living room. She snatched it up just before it stopped ringing and saw the doorman's name on there.

"Hi, Steve," she said as she answered. Yesterday she'd combatted boredom by going on an internet shopping spree. She'd splurged on things for Cleo, and Eagle and Olivia's, and Raven and Max's babies. The fun thing about being an aunt was being able to spoil nieces and nephews and not worry about doing any of the hard stuff. Since she didn't know if Olivia and Raven were having boys or girls, she'd gone with things that worked for either, and was quite proud of some of her finds. She assumed the doorman was calling to tell her she had some packages that had been delivered.

"Good morning, Ms. Oswald. Sorry to disturb you so early, but there's a Ms. Esmerelda Takeda here to see you. She says she's a friend," Steve explained.

Esme was here?

She would not have called them friends, in fact in the few days she had spent with Ethan and his colleagues on the compound in Djibouti she thought she might have exchanged a total of two dozen words with the woman. If anything, Sparrow would have said that Esme disliked her for some reason, although she had no idea what that reason might be.

"Umm, okay, well send her up, I guess," she told Steve.

"Okay, Ms. Oswald, I'll do that."

Since the penthouse had to be accessed with a code if anyone other than her, her siblings who all had the code, and the maid wanted to come up, the doorman had to put in their unique code that would allow the person access to the top floor.

Not sure what possible reason Esme could have for dropping by, or even how the woman had found her address, Sparrow limped into the foyer so she could greet the woman as she got off the lift. She assumed this had to have something to do with what had gone down in Africa with Evan and the drug traffickers. Perhaps the woman was having trouble dealing with it and needed to talk. Or she wanted advice on whether or not she should go back to Africa. Or maybe she wanted to talk to Prey about whether they did security work, she might feel like they needed proper protection on the compound going forward.

A minute or two later the lift dinged, and a smiling Esme stepped out. In her hands she held a plate piled high with brightly frosted cupcakes.

"I'm so sorry to just drop by unannounced, but I wanted to thank you for what you did. If you hadn't been there then there's no telling what would have happened to Oliver, Ethan, and I," Esme gushed as she stepped forward, thrusting the plate into Sparrow's hands.

Guess that answered the question of why the other woman had shown up here. Still, Sparrow couldn't help but think it was odd. It had been clear Esme didn't like her, or at the very least wasn't pleased she had turned up there, but now the woman was grinning at her like they were best friends. "Umm, okay, you're welcome. It really was just a stroke of luck I ended up being there right when everything went down."

"Yeah, luck," Esme said, stepping closer.

Although something felt off, Sparrow couldn't figure out what. The other woman sounded genuinely grateful, and she had come with cupcakes, it was just the sudden change in demeanor. It was a complete one-eighty, and while it could be just that Esme had had a real scare when the compound was breached and had a change in attitude, it didn't feel real for some reason.

"You didn't have to come all the way over here to thank me."

"I wanted to," Esme said, stepping into Sparrow's personal space. "I haven't been able to stop thinking about you."

"About me?" Okay, something was definitely not right here. There was a gleam in Esme's dark eyes that said she wasn't quite all there. It wasn't something Sparrow remembered from her time in Djibouti. In Africa, the woman had seemed like a competent nurse, she just hadn't seemed very warm and friendly.

"Yes. You just showed up and everything changed."

A hint of resentment was edging into the other woman's

voice, and Sparrow decided it was time to put a stop to this. Once the woman was out of here, she'd have Olivia look into her again and see if there was a history of mental health issues. "Well thank you so much for the cupcakes, and I'm so glad that I was there when it counted, and Ethan and I were able to make sure nobody was hurt. I'm sorry about Evan though, I don't know if you two were friends or not but still losing him as you did had to have hurt."

She tried to take a step around Esme to get to the lift, indicating that it was time for the woman to leave, but Esme blocked her way, reaching into her purse and pulling out a gun. "I don't care about Evan, but you stole Ethan away from me, and for that you have to pay."

* * *

2:23 P.M.

ETHAN STEPPED out of the cab and looked up at the building before him.

Now he felt totally out of his league.

Of course he had known that Sparrow was worth billions, that she and her siblings had inherited an enormous sum of money upon their parents' deaths, and that Prey turned over several billions of dollars in profit every year, but since he'd only ever seen Sparrow the Nightstalker who was just one of the guys it was different being reminded of how wealthy she was.

This building was big and fancy, with fabulous views across Central Park, and he was now feeling like his small-town self wasn't good enough for Sparrow.

Determinedly, he shrugged off these new concerns. They sounded more like excuses than real reasons to be intimidated. Sparrow was rich, he wasn't, she was the one who had shown an interest in him first. If she was just after some rich billionaire, he was sure she could have her pick. But she'd made her choice, and it was him.

Of course he would be nervous about this. He was ready to move forward and excited about a possible future with Sparrow, but there were going to be moments when doubts overtook his mind, and he was plagued by guilt. All he had to do when those moments struck was talk himself through them and remind himself that if their roles were reversed, he'd want Sierra to find happiness and love again, and she wanted the same for him.

When he'd got off the plane, he'd texted Falcon to let him know he was in New York and asked if he needed a key or a code to get into Sparrow's penthouse. He had the code and Falcon had contacted Sparrow's doorman to let him know that Ethan was coming.

Curious hazel eyes watched him as he approached the door, and a man with a nametag that said Steve gave him a slow onceover. "You Sparrow's new man?"

The idea of Sparrow being with other men provoked a sudden surge of jealousy which Ethan had to tamp down. He'd been married, so it wasn't like he could think that Sparrow shouldn't have been with other men, but still, he didn't like thinking about it. "Yes, I'm Ethan Zimmerman." He paused then decided he may as well just ask, "Does Sparrow bring a lot of men back here?"

Steve smirked like he knew that Ethan was currently battling jealousy. "No, you're the first man I've seen come here to visit her."

That made him smile. "Falcon gave me the code to the penthouse so I can surprise her."

"She'll get an alert someone is on the way up," Steve warned him. "But her brothers and sister have been in and out the last few days, checking in on her and bringing her food, so chances are she'll think it's one of them. Good luck with your girl."

"Thanks," he said but prayed he wouldn't need it. Sparrow would be shocked to see him, but he hoped it would be a good kind of shock. She'd been clear about what she wanted, but also understanding of his hesitancy. It had only been a few days since they parted ways, it wasn't like she could have met someone else in that time, especially since she was recovering from her injuries and probably mostly housebound.

The lobby was impressive, and he made his way to the lift putting in the code Falcon had given him. Nervous butterflies took up residence in his stomach. It had been so long since he'd asked a girl out on a date that he was so out of practice it wasn't funny.

It wasn't like he thought Sparrow would turn him down, he wasn't going to have to twist her arm to get her to say yes when he asked her out, and yet still his hands were clammy, his pulse racing, and his heart was beating just a little too loudly.

Ethan clutched the gift he'd brought—an apology of sorts for giving her the run around—when the lift dinged and opened, revealing a spacious, although sparsely decorated, foyer.

The smile he'd had on his lips, anticipating seeing Sparrow waiting to see which of her siblings got off the lift died as he realized almost immediately that something was wrong.

There was a tray of broken and smashed cupcakes on the floor, and a puddle of blood nearby. A small antique table had been knocked over, shattering the crystal vase of flowers that must have been sitting on it, and a family portrait had been knocked off the wall.

Signs of a struggle.

Someone had been in here.

"Sparrow!" he screamed, dropping the bright pink box with the gift he'd bought for her inside and starting a frantic search of the penthouse. There was no time to notice or appreciate the stunning views or the impressive space, his entire focus was on looking for the woman he was quickly falling for.

When he was back in the foyer having come up empty in his search, Ethan was breathing hard, his pulse racing, heart hammering in his chest, hands sweaty, only this time for an entirely different reason.

"Someone took Sparrow," he said without preamble when he dug his phone from his pocket—his shaking hands almost dropping it more than once—and dialed Falcon's number.

"What?"

"I'm standing in her penthouse. She's not here, there's blood, cupcakes on the floor, and signs of a struggle," he relayed.

"Sparrow hates cupcakes," Falcon said as though that was the most important aspect of what Ethan had just said.

"Well obviously whoever brought them didn't know that," he snapped. Fear was like a living being inside him, tearing him apart, threatening to destroy him.

"Go down and talk to Steve. If someone got up to the penthouse, he had to have let them in. Eagle, Olivia, Raven, Max, Dove, Hope, and I all have the code for the lift, and Sparrow wouldn't allow someone she didn't know to come up, she would have gone down to see them, or sent them away. While you talk to Steve, I'll tell the others and see if I can get one of our cop contacts on the case."

Although Falcon's voice was calm, Ethan could feel the terror rolling off the other man. The Oswald family had been through so much and the threat of someone after them hanging over their heads—someone who might have finally got what he wanted and could right now have one of the siblings in his possession—had to be awful.

"All right, I'll call you back when I know who came up here. Falcon, tell your cop friend they can confirm I was on a flight and in a cab up until ten minutes ago, I don't want the cops wasting time looking into me as a suspect."

"I'll tell them. Find out what you can then come down to Prey. Once we know who was there, we can have Olivia and Raven start looking into them, see if we can figure out where they'd take her."

As Ethan hung up and rushed to the elevator, cursing the seconds it felt like he was wasting as he waited for it to get back down to the ground floor, he realized for the first time that he and Sierra had been lucky. They'd known she was sick, known she might not recover, and as much as the blow that she was terminal had hurt it had given them time. Time to do some of their favorite things one last time, time to do some of the things they had planned but put off, time for one last kiss, one last hold, one last goodbye. At the time, it had all been so painful it had been near impossible to see beyond that, but now he realized it had been a blessing.

It was better than this.

He'd been with Sierra when the end came. She'd been snuggled safely in his arms as she took her final breath. She hadn't been alone, she'd been with someone who loved her.

With Sparrow he might never have that.

She had no idea he had come here to ask her out, no idea he wanted to give them a chance. She was out there some-where, hurt, scared, facing an enemy on her own with no one at her back. He might not get her back, there would be no last kiss, no holding her at the end, she could die before they found her.

Finally, the lift opened, and he dodged past an elderly

couple who scowled at him as he ran toward Steve the doorman.

"Who was in Sparrow's place?" he demanded as soon as he threw open the door.

Steve's brow furrowed. "A friend of hers came by earlier with cupcakes."

"What friend?"

"I can't remember her name."

"Try," he begged. "Please, it's really important."

Sensing the urgency in him, Steve nodded. "She was medium height, medium build, dark hair, dark eyes, looked like she was part Asian. E something? Emmy? Ellie?"

"Esme?"

"Yes, that was it. Esme, her name was Esme Takeda."

* * *

3:34 P.M.

"Would you stop wriggling and squirming back there?"

Sparrow's eyes fluttered at the snapped words. Was she wriggling and squirming? The pounding in her head made it hard to focus on anything, which was bad news for her.

She'd been at a disadvantage back at her place because while Esme Takeda knew she'd come with kidnapping in mind, Sparrow had no idea. By the time she got that inkling that something was wrong, Esme had pulled out a weapon and slammed it into Sparrow's head.

Still, she'd fought as best as she could. Even managed to knock Esme down at one point but the other woman had pulled out a syringe and injected her with a sedative.

It was obvious the woman was unbalanced. Whether she always had been or if the trauma of the attack on the compound had pushed her over the edge, Sparrow had no idea. Nor did she particularly care. All she needed to do was keep herself alive because Esme hadn't gone about the abduction carefully.

Sooner or later—probably sooner rather than later—one of her siblings would show up at her place. There they would find blood and signs of a struggle and know immediately that something was wrong. Since you had to either have the code for the penthouse or be let up by the doorman, her siblings would know to go straight to Steve, and Esme had been stupid enough to give her real name so they would know right away who had taken her.

The problem would be finding her.

So, Sparrow had to do what she could to try to get away, or at the very least try to find a way to leave some clues.

Unfortunately, the second head injury in less than two weeks plus the drugs still coursing through her system made that rather difficult. She kept passing in and out of consciousness. When she was awake it was all she could do not to throw up, the motion of the car wasn't helping the nausea, and the world was too blurry for her to do more than make a weak attempt to sit up.

She had no idea how she got to be lying across the backseat of a car, covered head to toe in her own soft, fluffy pink blanket, but she willed herself to pull it together. Just because they would know who had taken her didn't mean that her siblings and Prey would be able to find her in time. And she had no idea how much time she had, it all depended on why Esme had taken her.

Which made finding out what Esme wanted with her the first task.

Wait.

Didn't she already know that?

Hazy memories began to fill her mind. Esme stepping off

the lift, passing her a plate of cupcakes which she had accepted even though she hated cupcakes, the woman acting weird, things feeling off, then Esme had said that Sparrow had stolen Ethan from her.

This was all about Ethan?

If Esme thought that she and Ethan were together then she was mistaken. Ethan wasn't ready to move on with anyone, not Esme and not Sparrow, so this whole kidnapping thing was completely pointless. It wasn't going to free up Ethan for Esme to swoop in and take because Ethan's heart already belonged to his wife and always would.

Was there a way to convince Esme of that?

With shaky arms, Sparrow pushed the blanket away and managed to push herself so she was sitting up. Her wrists were bound together but thankfully in front of her which meant she had some use of her hands. One of the seatbelts was wrapped around her hips, preventing her from slipping off the backseat, and Sparrow used it to help herself sit up.

"I thought I told you to stop wriggling around, lie back down," Esme ordered, her dark eyes glaring at Sparrow in the rear vision mirror.

Ignoring the other woman, Sparrow took the time to look out the windows. The landscape was rushing past making her stomach churn, but she breathed through the nausea and focused on looking for clues as to where they were.

The road they were on was quiet. She couldn't see or hear any other cars, trees lined both sides of the road, and there were no houses visible. Wherever they were it was somewhere remote which wasn't good news for her. They were driving too fast for her to open the door and jump— assuming the child locks weren't engaged—with her bound hands and a head injury, she wouldn't make it far before Esme would catch up to her.

Right now, it seemed like her best bet was to wait until they got wherever they were going and then make her move. She might be bound and woozy, but she had spent most of her life training to take down any opponent. She was used to most of those opponents being much bigger than her, but Esme was only a few inches taller and fairly slim. Sparrow believed that even with a concussion she could take the other woman.

While she didn't want to do anything that might make Esme decide to pull over and drug her unconscious again, she also wanted to get the woman talking, find out as much as she could about Esme's current mental state.

"I'm not with Ethan," Sparrow said, a little concerned by how weak and thready her voice sounded. It wasn't ideal to physically take on Esme, but there was always a chance that where they ended up there could be help she could get to nearby.

Esme tossed a glare over her shoulder. "Do you think I'm stupid?"

"No, of course not. I just think that you have your wires crossed. Ethan is back home in Kansas. He and I aren't together."

"He was different once you arrived, and I saw the way he looked at you. I'm not stupid you know."

Obviously being called stupid or someone implying that she was, triggered Esme. "I don't think you're stupid, I just wasn't sure if you knew about Ethan's wife who died."

"I know about Sierra," Esme screamed, slamming a fist into the steering wheel.

Sparrow winced, not because she was intimidated by the other woman, but because the loud shout seemed to cut right through her skull.

"I know that Ethan used to be married, he talked to me while we were there, okay? You're not the only one he talked to. We were growing close before *you* came along," Esme spat.

She knew that wasn't true. Ethan wasn't ready to move on with anyone, but she knew the kind of man he was and knew that if he was interested in Esme there was no way he would have slept with her. And when he'd been telling her about his colleagues, he hadn't mentioned anything special about the nurse, in fact, he hadn't mentioned much about her at all and Sparrow had known that Ethan had mostly kept to himself, and his closest friend there had been Evan, not Esme.

"If you hadn't come along, we would be together by now, but instead he came back here with you."

"He didn't come back with me," Sparrow insisted. "He came back because we were both abducted and he was hurt. He's here to recover and then he's going back." That was a lie, well it might be, she had no idea what Ethan's long-term plans were, they weren't any of her business.

"Stop lying," Esme screeched.

There was obviously nothing she could say to convince Esme that she and Ethan weren't together, even though it was the truth. If she couldn't convince the other woman of that then there was no way she would talk her way out of this.

"Ethan and I would have been happy together if you hadn't gotten in the way. You almost got us all killed. *You* brought in all that trouble, you got Ethan hurt, and because of that he left me. You're the problem. It's all you," the last was muttered under Esme's breath like she was speaking more to herself than Sparrow.

The trees blurred as they kept flying down the road, and her hopes of getting out alive were fading. Esme was delusional, she truly believed that if it wasn't for Sparrow, she and Ethan would be together. How did you combat that when it wasn't even vaguely based in reality?

"Ethan and I are just old friends," she said. The vicious throbbing in her head urged her to give in to the darkness and rest, and her ability to resist was weakening. "We were in the military together, but that's all there is. Ethan doesn't want to be with me, and he doesn't want to be with you, he's still in love with Sierra. I don't think he's ever going to have room in his heart for another woman." As much as she hated it, it was true. Ethan had found his soulmate and he didn't want another.

"That's where you're wrong. Once you're out of the picture I can step in, comfort him, help him grieve, and then he'll realize that we're meant to be. Ethan isn't the problem, and neither is Sierra. You are. You're the problem, but you're about to be eliminated. Permanently."

* * *

4:04 P.M.

"Please tell me you have something," Ethan begged as Olivia entered the conference room where he, Eagle, Raven, and Falcon were set up.

Raven was currently going through Esme's life with a fine-tooth comb, looking for something—anything—that might point to where the woman would take Sparrow, and why she would have gone after her in the first place.

Olivia had insisted she worked better in her office, so she'd been in there going through footage from thousands of CCTV cameras throughout the city hoping to get a lock on Esme's car. If they could follow which direction Esme was going, and track her progress, then maybe they could get ahead of her. Get to Sparrow before it was too late.

Ethan didn't have a good feeling about this.

There were too many unknowns. He had spent six months with Esme in Djibouti and while he hadn't really felt like he'd gotten to know her, what he did know was that she was smart, good at her job, and not afraid to come to a dangerous part of the world to make life better for people who had almost nothing. How had that dedicated nurse turned into a psychotic kidnapper?

"Actually, I do," Olivia said. The pretty blonde shot him a reassuring smile as Eagle pulled out a chair at the table for her. Her fiancé brushed a hand lightly across her small baby bump, and Ethan felt a pang in his chest.

He'd missed out on the opportunity to have kids with Sierra. Had he lost that same opportunity with Sparrow?

If he had, this time it would be his own fault.

Why had he pushed her away? Why had he told her he wasn't ready for a relationship when his heart was telling him the opposite? Why hadn't he dealt with the crushing grief earlier so he could have accepted and come to terms with the idea that Sierra wouldn't want her death to steal his happiness?

Talk about having major regrets.

"What did you find?" Eagle asked his fiancée as she opened up a laptop and set it before her.

"I found Esme's car," Olivia announced.

"Are they nearby?" he asked, hardly daring to hope she was still somewhere close.

"No, I'm sorry, Ethan. I was running a program to search for any signs of Esme's license plate. It's not as easy as it sounds because the cameras don't always pick that up. The angle can be wrong, there can be something like another car blocking the camera's view, weather conditions can make it harder to get a clear shot, and sometimes the camera quality is too poor to get a clear enough image. I can fiddle with an image, clear it up, but I have to have one to work with, that doesn't help me locate a car. It took longer than I would have liked, but I finally got a hit. It was from about an hour ago, and she's heading west toward Virginia," Olivia told them.

"On it," Raven said before he could tell her to look and see if Esme had any contacts or property either in that area or nearby.

"Did you get a good shot of the car?" he asked Olivia.

Correctly guessing that he was really asking if there had been any sign of Sparrow in the vehicle, Olivia shook her head. "No, I'm sorry. I got a clear shot of Esme in the driver's seat, but no signs of Sparrow."

"Why did she take her?" he roared to no one in particular, slamming his fist into the solid mahogany table just because he needed to feel something besides the soul-sapping fear. None of this made sense, and he needed answers.

"I might have an answer to that," Olivia said. There was something in her blue eyes that immediately had him on edge. It was like fingernails on a chalkboard kind of feeling, like something was scraping along his every nerve and he almost didn't want to ask.

"What?" he ground out.

"There was something I saw on her car," Olivia said almost apologetically. Since he knew that it wasn't Olivia's fault, and that she just knew whatever she was about to say was going to upset him, his nerves ramped up.

"Just say it," he growled.

"Watch your tone," Eagle warned. "I know you're not mad at Liv, and you're afraid for Sparrow, but no one talks to my fiancée like that."

Ethan raked his fingers through his hair. "Sorry, Olivia, I shouldn't take my fear out on you."

She reached across the table to squeeze his hand. "It's fine, I get it, totally. Eagle can just be a little overprotective sometimes." She rolled her eyes at her fiancé but then her gaze turned tender.

"What did you find?" he asked, calmer this time.

"There was a sticker on the rear window. It was a newly married one."

"Esme just got married?" She had never mentioned having a serious boyfriend in the six months they'd spent together in Africa, and she couldn't have met someone in the few days she'd been back. Could she? And what did that have to do with Sparrow?

"It says Mr. and Mrs. Zimmerman beneath it," Olivia said gently.

"Zimmerman?" he repeated, his brain not catching—not *wanting* to catch—the meaning of that.

"I think it means she wants to marry you," Olivia said. "I think that's why she took Sparrow. She must have figured out that there's something between you and Sparrow, and she wants to take out her competition."

Competition.

This was all because of him.

Esme had targeted Sparrow because she had been harboring some secret crush on him.

Sparrow was hurt, possibly already dead because of him.

Before he could fully process that, Raven's excited voice announced, "I found something. Esme has a great grandfather on her father's side who owned a property deep in the Appalachian Mountains close to a small town near the I-81 called Fallport."

Eagle's eyes lit up. "I know some guys who used to be in the military who all settled around there. They run Eagle Point Search and Rescue. One of them is actually also called Ethan."

"Call them," Ethan said immediately. The quicker they could get guys on the ground searching for Sparrow the better. "Does anyone live on this property?" he asked Raven.

She shook her head. "No, looks like it's been empty for a while too. Esme's father moved to Japan when he was in his early twenties, met her mother, and Esme was born soon after. When she was twelve her parents split, and she came here with her dad. They lived in Virginia Beach, her father managed a hotel there, not sure if she ever spent time at the great grandfather's place, but he lived there until he passed away at a hundred and six. Looks like the place was then handed down to her grandfather, and then her father, who didn't want it and passed it on to her a few years back."

An empty property, deep in the Appalachian Mountains, that left a lot of ground to be covered and a lot of places where you could hide a body.

Was Sparrow already dead?

If all Esme wanted was to eliminate the competition—not that there was any competition, Ethan wasn't interested in Esme at all whether Sparrow was in the picture or not—then it was likely she would kill Sparrow quickly and hide the body where it might never be found.

"Your guys better be good," he muttered to Eagle, who was speaking into his phone.

"Talk to them yourself," Eagle said.

"Hello?" he said into the phone when he took it.

"I'm going to assume you're the Ethan, Eagle just mentioned," a voice spoke. "I'm Ethan Watson, and we're already calling in the team so we can get out there and start looking for your girl. We're in contact with the local police department, they'll come with us to the property. If Sparrow is out here, we'll let you know. We won't stop searching till we find her."

The man's confident tone and take-charge attitude helped

settle his nerves a little. Esme had a major head start on them and was likely already at her great grandfather's place. Which meant Sparrow could already be dead and this would be a body recovery mission and not a search for a living victim.

As though sensing where his thoughts had gone, the other Ethan spoke, "Don't give up on her. I know what it's like. My girlfriend was right where your woman is now just a few months back. Taken by someone who thought it was okay to hurt others for their own purposes. I know the fear of knowing you might not get to her in time, that when we find her it might be too late, but I didn't give up hope, and we were lucky, we found Lilly in time. My team and I will do everything we can to make sure you get the same outcome."

Ethan appreciated the other Ethan's words, and he was glad that things had worked out for him and Lilly, but would Sparrow be that lucky? And if she wasn't, would he be able to live with the guilt of knowing she had lost her life because of him?

* * *

4:49 P.M.

THE SUN WAS SETTING QUICKLY, and the temperature was already starting to drop.

Sparrow could feel the chill in the air, and from the howling wind and dark clouds, she wouldn't be surprised if it started to snow soon. There was already a thin layer of snow on the ground, and she prayed that whatever was coming wasn't going to be heavy snowfall because she wasn't dressed to be out here.

If she had to guess, then out here was somewhere in the Appalachian Mountains. That was a really big area. Even if her siblings could track Esme to the mountains there was no way they could find her quickly. There was simply too much ground to cover.

Already they'd been walking for what felt like hours but was probably closer to thirty minutes or so. Sparrow's feet were burning with pain, her head ached with a blinding headache, and she was still dizzy which meant she kept losing her footing in the rough terrain and falling. Which wasn't helpful to her injured feet or the head injury.

It also didn't help that she wasn't dressed for hiking through the mountains in the middle of winter. She was dressed in jeans and a sweater, with sneakers on her feet, but she had kept hold of the blanket Esme must have taken from her bed before leaving her penthouse to cover her in the car. Sparrow had still been holding it when they'd finally stopped driving, and Esme hadn't told her to put it down, so she'd wrapped it around her shoulders and did her best to hold it in place with her bound hands while they walked.

And walked.

And walked.

Exhaustion was making the hike near impossible, and she was pretty close to reaching a brick wall. Once she did, she would crash and then she'd be helplessly at Esme's mercy, and she already knew the woman wasn't going to show her any.

"I can't go any further," Sparrow said with an exaggerated huff as she dropped down and rested against a tree. She *could* keep going a little longer, but she needed a distraction if she was going to have any hope of getting that gun away from Esme.

"We're not stopping here," Esme snapped with a dramatic sigh.

"We have to. Just hurry up and do it already. What are you waiting for?" Sparrow was pretty sure that Esme wasn't capable of outright shooting her unless it was her only option. If that was what the woman had planned, she would have done it already. They'd stopped driving deep in the woods. There hadn't been any houses around that Sparrow could see, so Esme could have shot her and buried her body right there, in some secluded spot where she would likely never be found. That they were walking deeper into the woods meant that Esme had something different in mind. Maybe the woman couldn't commit the murder herself so she intended to just leave Sparrow out here to let the elements do her dirty work.

"We're not there yet. Stop complaining, I haven't hurt you." Esme kicked her foot out, it connected with Sparrow's thigh making pain fly up her leg.

"You knocked me out," she reminded Esme.

Esme just shrugged. "I needed to get rid of you, you're in the way."

"Then do it," she goaded. "Get rid of me right now because I'm not getting up and walking any further. I can't. So, if you want me dead, shoot me now and be done with it."

"Don't taunt me," Esme growled. She lifted the weapon, pointed it right at Sparrow's head, but her arms were shaking, and Sparrow knew it wasn't because of the cold. Esme didn't have it in her to shoot someone, and that was something she could use to her advantage.

"You know there's one thing you should know about guns," Sparrow said as she coiled her muscles ready to spring. "You should only ever point one at someone if you're ready to use it. And you aren't."

With that she launched off the ground, latching her bound hands onto Esme's jacket and tackling her to the ground. They landed with a thud and the gun went flying off somewhere.

Sparrow knew she had to take advantage of this opportunity because she wasn't going to get another one. Ramming her hands up, she connected with Esme's chin, causing her head to snap back. She followed up by slamming a fist into Esme's nose.

While the other woman yelped in pain, Sparrow scrambled to her feet and took off. As much as she would love to search for the gun because she knew she could use it to get Esme under control, she was still the more injured of the two, and if she didn't find it quickly enough then Esme would be the one subduing her.

So instead she ran, hoping that the trees and the coming darkness would be enough to conceal her. She had no idea where they were, and while she could probably backtrack and find the car if given enough time it was unlikely that she would last that long.

The elements were a real concern out here. Hypothermia would come for her quickly, even quicker because she wasn't properly dressed.

Her head spun as she ran, and she made a lot more noise than she would have liked but at least she was moving and doing something to rescue herself. There was no use waiting and trying to rely on help that might never come. If she wanted to live, wanted a chance to convince Ethan to at least try with her, then she needed to get herself to safety.

The woods all looked the same, and she wished she had some idea of where they were so she could try to figure out what direction to go in. There was no real point in trying to get to the car first, Esme would likely be able to move quicker and might assume that was what Sparrow would do and wait for her there. Besides, Esme no doubt had the keys so at best the car would provide some shelter from the weather, but still wouldn't help anyone find her or help her get out of here.

So, Sparrow just kept running.

She was so focused on putting distance between herself and Esme, everything else had been blocked out, that she almost didn't see the hole in front of her until she was on it.

At the last second, she caught herself, managed to shift her center of gravity so she didn't fall down into the old mineshaft, or well, or whatever it was. Instead, she swayed backward, and landed hard on her bottom.

"Looks like you ended up right where I wanted you to anyway."

She looked over her shoulder to see Esme approaching. The woman looked smug, and she'd obviously found the gun because she was waving it in front of her like a trophy.

Sparrow's heart sank. She'd tried, but it hadn't done any good. Apparently, she had run straight to Esme's planned death trap all on her own. "You know this is never going to work. Even if you kill me, you won't get away with it and you won't get Ethan. They're going to know to go after you. My doorman knows your name."

Esme shrugged like that was irrelevant. "I'll use a scapegoat just like I did with Evan. Now no more talking. You go down there yourself or I'll throw you down."

Sparrow was still stuck on the Evan part of what Esme had just said. Was she saying that she had really been the one using Ethan's plane to smuggle drugs? That she'd set Evan up?

"Hurry up," Esme yelled. "I've had enough of you. Why won't you just hurry up and die? It's like you have nine lives."

She wished she did.

Because when Esme kicked out at her and she instinctively moved away from the blow, she found herself falling.

Sparrow landed with a thud that reverberated through every single part of her already aching and icy cold body.

The world began to spiral around her. She knew the risks, knew the cold would come for her soon. Her clothes were no match for the weather and stuck down here she wouldn't be able to work up enough body heat to hold off hypothermia for long, but she couldn't stop the blackness swooping around her from edging closer.

This was it.

How her life was going to end.

She had regrets. She wished she'd spent more time with her siblings and hadn't wasted a couple of days hanging around a penthouse she didn't even like and that didn't feel like home instead of going after Ethan right away.

Ethan felt like home.

As the darkness closed in around her, she clung to that thought, painting a bright picture of him in her mind and letting that soothe her. She might not ever wake up, and if she didn't, she wanted her last thoughts to be of the man she was falling in love with.

* * *

5:22 P.M.

As Esme watched, she could see Sparrow Oswald's eyes flutter closed.

Finally.

The woman was like a cat. How many times could she escape death?

Omega Chidubem was supposed to have taken care of her. Apparently, there was someone else's life the woman had messed up who was after her, and Omega was supposed to sell her on, but apparently the man had gotten greedy. Decided that keeping Sparrow was a better option, he'd actually believed that he could turn the woman, make more with her alive and working for him than if he'd sold her.

That greed had gotten him killed.

Since Omega had also decided to renege on the part of their deal that had her ending up with Ethan, she was glad that he was dead. He'd tried to double-cross her and have Ethan killed because he thought that Ethan was the one who had taken the drugs and hidden them, but he wasn't.

She was.

She was the one who had decided that she was tired of struggling to make ends meet as a nurse. Tired of having to listen to her father complain that she hadn't had what it took to make it as a doctor after flunking out of medical school and had to settle for being a nurse. She was tired of emptying bedpans and listening to complaining patients.

Esme had wanted more out of life.

It started out small. Swiping a few drugs from the storeroom at the hospital and selling them to a local drug dealer she'd found on the corner of the block where her apartment was located. That hadn't earned her much, and after getting annoyed that she was doing most of the work, but he was making most of the profits, she'd decided she needed to find a way to make more money.

That wasn't as easy as it sounded, but then one of the other nurses at the hospital mentioned that a friend of hers was retiring from a lifetime of work as a nurse with an aid agency in Africa, and they were looking for a replacement. She'd taken the job because she'd thought it would impress her father. It hadn't, but she had stumbled upon a drug deal while in the village one day.

And that, as people said, was history.

Now she had close to a million dollars' worth of product hidden away, Sparrow would soon be dead, and she intended to slip her way back into Ethan's life. When she'd started making good money helping Omega Chidubem traffic drugs across Africa, she'd realized that money was nice, but you needed someone to share it with.

Ethan was hot, sexy, smart, and she'd set her sights on him early on in her six-month stint in Djibouti. She had actually been making progress in winning his heart before Sparrow had come along and ruined everything.

With a last look down at the unconscious woman, Esme rubbed her cold hands together and turned away. She'd never taken a life before, and while it would have been so much easier to just shoot Sparrow Oswald and then bury her body out here where no one would ever find it, she couldn't make herself do it.

All that blood.

Esme shuddered at the thought.

So, this might not be the best way of eliminating her problem, but it was the best she could do. It was quiet out here, no one had lived on the property since her great grandfather died almost ten years ago so no one would find Sparrow, either before or after she died. If anyone did have questions for her, she'd simply say she brought Sparrow cupcakes then left, and someone else must have broken in after that.

Whatever, she wasn't worried about it. When Ethan found out the woman who had come between them had disappeared, she would be there to comfort him. She'd remind him of the heat that had simmered between them in Africa, of how close they had come, and of how good they would be together. Then she'd win his heart, and together they could conquer the drug trafficking world, and she'd have it all.

Money, respect, power, control, and love.

Never again would someone throw her away because she wasn't smart enough like her mother had done. Never again would they put her down because she didn't live up to their expectations like her father had. Never again would someone come between her and the man she loved like Sparrow Oswald had.

Esme was done being walked all over, done being second best, done with being shoved aside. From here on out she would be top dog.

After all, she'd earned it.

The walk back to her car was much quicker than the walk out here had been since this time she wasn't forced to walk at Sparrow's ridiculously slow pace. She hadn't been sure if the woman was faking being in pain or actually hurting from the blow to the head, but she hadn't really cared one way or the other, so she'd tried to hurry her along as best as she could.

It was completely dark by the time she finally climbed inside her car, and Esme was freezing. First thing she did was turn on the engine and get the heater blasting. It was after six now, too late to go calling Ethan, so maybe she'd wait until tomorrow to do that. Tonight, she'd head into the nearest town, a little place called Fallport, and find a hotel or bed and breakfast to spend the night.

As she drove, she daydreamed about what life with Ethan would be like.

They'd go back to Djibouti, she'd take over where Omega Chidubem had left off, and convince Ethan that they weren't really doing anything wrong. Drugs were here to stay, it wasn't like if they didn't traffic them then no one else would, so why shouldn't they be the ones to do it and profit from it? After all, they were only hurting losers like Evan anyway. Getting Evan hooked again had been the best decision she'd ever made and waiting till he made the trip to the village to score before having Omega's men attack the compound had been even better. Everyone had believed he was the smuggler, and no one had even blinked in her direction.

Take that, Dad, she cheered. She was so much smarter than he had ever given her credit for.

When she reached Fallport, Esme quickly located Whitney's B&B. The place looked nice and clean, and she thought it would be nicer than staying in some larger chain hotel, so she parked out the front, hoping there would be a spare room.

Hoping she didn't look too beaten-up, Esme hurried from her car to the front door. That stupid Sparrow could have ruined everything if she couldn't think up a convincing lie why her nose was all bloody and bruised.

"Good evening," a cheerful voice called out, and a pretty older lady with light brown hair and gray eyes appeared, wiping her hands on a tea towel. "Looking to check in?"

"Yes, please, if you have room," she said softly, stepping forward slowly and anxiously awaiting the woman's reaction.

"Yes of course. Is it just for you or ...?" the older woman trailed off as she obviously caught sight of Esme's face. Immediately concern covered her features. "Are you all right? Were you in an accident? Did someone hurt you? Do you want me to call the police?"

"Oh, no," Esme said quickly. "I'm ... I'm okay. I just needed some ... space tonight. Tomorrow I'll figure out what to do next." She hoped the woman thought she was fleeing an abusive boyfriend or husband, or had just been assaulted, or basically anything other than that she had been assaulted by someone she was trying to kill.

The woman hesitated, but then nodded slowly. "I'm Whitney Crawford, this is my place. How about I get you set up in a room so you can get some rest." She walked over to a computer and fiddled around for a moment. "Room six has a beautiful big bathroom with a lovely bathtub, just the place for relaxing."

"Sounds perfect," Esme said, relieved the woman wasn't going to push it. At least not tonight, although tomorrow morning was a completely different story. She'd have to be out of here early. She handed over a credit card and filled out her information, and then she was given a key and directions to her room.

Once she had the door locked behind her, she sagged against it and grinned. It had worked. She had successfully abducted and disposed of Sparrow Oswald. If the woman wasn't dead already, she would be soon with the cold weather and the storm blowing in.

Now nothing was standing between her and the man she loved.

A bath sounded like a pretty good idea, so Esme headed into the bathroom. She turned on the tap, added some bubble bath, and as she stripped out of her clothes, she imagined that it was Ethan undressing her. His large hands brushing against her sensitive nipples as he removed her bra. Then his knuckles would skim the soft skin of her inner thighs as he slid her panties down her legs.

His mouth would water at the sight of her naked body, and he wouldn't be able to resist palming one of her breasts as his other hand dipped between her legs. He would fondle her, tease her little nub as he slipped a finger inside her. Firm lips would find hers and his tongue would dual with hers as his long fingers stoked deep inside her and his thumb worked her into an ecstasy-fueled oblivion.

Esme climbed into the bath, shifting uncomfortably as her body begged for release, one of her hands moved between her legs. While it wasn't as good as having the real thing, she could still get herself off to daydreams of her perfect man.

* * *

6:39 P.M.

"Guys, you all need to hear this," other Ethan announced.

Although Ethan supposed since they weren't on the other man's turf, *he* was really the other Ethan. He'd met the rest of the search and rescue team, Ethan's twin brother Cohen or Rocky as he went by. Then there was Raiden, a former Coast Guard dog handler and his bloodhound Duke, Zeke who used to be a Green Beret and who now owned the town bar, On the Rocks, Brock who used to be in the US Customs and Border Patrol, Drew a former member of the Virginia State Police, and Talon who was from the UK and had been in the British Special Boat Service.

They were a tough-looking bunch of men, strong, dedicated, and smart, he knew they were good at what they did, and he couldn't hope for a better group of men to help him find Sparrow and bring her home alive.

"What do you have?" he asked hometown Ethan. While he, Eagle, and Falcon had hopped on Prey's private jet to fly to Virginia, Ethan and the search and rescue team had gone out to Esme's great grandfather's place, but they hadn't found Esme, her car, any signs of Sparrow, or anything to indicate that someone had recently been in the small cabin, the only building on the site. The search and rescue guys had come to meet up with them, but a couple of the local police had remained out there in case she showed up.

Esme either hadn't made it to the site yet, she knew about access roads into other parts of the substantial piece of property, or she had already been and gone before anyone got there.

None of those options boded well for Sparrow.

"I'm putting you on speaker," hometown Ethan said to whoever was on the line, then to the rest of them, "It's Whitney. She runs the local bed and breakfast," Ethan added for the benefit of him, Eagle, and Falcon. "Okay, Whitney, you're on speaker phone now. Tell the others what you just told me."

A woman's voice started speaking, "I had a woman come in just about ten minutes ago. She looked like she had a recently broken nose, and I thought she might be an abuse victim fleeing from her violent partner. I suggested calling the police, but she didn't want to, and I didn't want to push. Once I set her up in a room though I couldn't stop thinking about it. So, I called Simon and told him what had happened."

"Simon Hill is the police chief," hometown Ethan informed them.

Ethan knew that if this injured woman who had shown up at the bed and breakfast was Sparrow and she's managed to get away from Esme there was no way she would be hiding out in a B&B refusing to call in what had happened. Even if she'd had to kill Esme it would be a clear case of self-defense so there was no reason for her not to immediately contact her family. Which she hadn't done.

If the woman wasn't Sparrow and Whitney had called them then he had to assume it was Esme.

"When you told the police chief the woman's name, he knew who she was, right?" he asked.

"Yes," Whitney confirmed. "I told him the name she used to check-in—which matched the credit card she used—was Esmerelda Takeda, and he said there was an APB out on her. I gave him a description of the woman and it matched, so he told me to call and let you know she's here. She went up to her room, and she hasn't come down since."

Relief hit him hard. If Esme was nearby then Sparrow was too, but along with it was a surge of adrenalin that insisted he get moving, start doing something more than sitting around waiting for information, something that would bring his girl home.

"We need to get over there," he said, already pushing away from the table at hometown Ethan's house where they had gathered.

"We will," hometown Ethan soothed, "but first we need to get a bit more information from Whitney. Whitney, how did she arrive? Was she in a car?"

"Yes, I looked outside when she went up to her room wondering if she'd had to walk or even run here, but there was a car outside that hadn't been there before."

After confirming the make, model, and license plate matched what they knew Esme owned and had been driving, hometown Ethan asked, "How many other guests do you have there?"

"I have two couples and a young woman on her own," Whitney replied.

"Can you call them and tell them to lock themselves in their rooms and not to leave. Me and the guys are coming over, and I'm sure Simon will be sending a few of his men as well. You need to go somewhere safe too, wherever you can lock yourself in. Did it look like she had a weapon?"

"She didn't have a suitcase or overnight back or anything, just a purse, but it was big enough to hold a gun," Whitney told them.

"Thanks, Whitney, you trusting your gut means me might be able to find Sparrow Oswald in time," hometown Ethan said.

Ethan agreed.

If they hadn't gotten this tip, if the bed and breakfast owner had decided to wait until morning before doing anything about her strange guest, then they might have decided Esme hadn't come here after all and moved on. Leaving Sparrow to her fate.

"We need to get over there now," he said. Eagle and Falcon also stood, and he knew they were every bit as eager to get going, to get out there as he was.

"We'll work out a plan on the way," hometown Ethan agreed.

They piled into three trucks and kept in communication with each other so they could hash out what they were going to do once they got there. The ride didn't take long, but it still felt like an eternity to Ethan. Knowing that Sparrow could already be gone—probably *was* already gone—and that she'd died alone was killing him.

By the time they pulled up outside the B&B he was so edgy his hands were actually shaking. Steady hands were essential when you flew helicopters into enemy territory, usually while being shot at. With lives literally in your hands, you couldn't afford an attack of the shakes.

Now more than ever he needed to hold it together because Sparrow's life might depend on it.

"Whitney said Esme's room is around the back, she won't see us approaching," Zeke said.

"That's the car," Talon said, pointing to a white sedan. "We should check that first, make sure …" he trailed off and shot him, Eagle, and Falcon an apologetic look.

"Check my sister's body isn't in there," Eagle finished for him.

Talon nodded, and they all approached the vehicle.

"We don't have a warrant to check it," Drew reminded them.

Falcon merely shrugged. "I think I hear someone calling for help. Anyone else hear it?"

Of course they didn't, and if Sparrow was already dead, her body being carted around in there then they wouldn't hear pleas for help, but no one would disagree. If she was alive in there, they needed to know, and there was no way he was waiting for a warrant to do that.

"Yeah, I hear her," he said.

The others all voiced their agreement, and Falcon got the car unlocked and popped the trunk. Which was thankfully empty.

"I see blood on the backseat," Rocky pointed out.

"And the middle seatbelt is all twisted," Brock added.

"I think she had Sparrow on the back seat," Eagle noted.

"But she's not there now," Ethan said, and that was all he really cared about. "We need to get to Esme, make her tell us where she left Sparrow." Right now, there wasn't anything he wouldn't do to get that information. Even if Sparrow was dead, he would make sure her body was brought home.

"We don't need all of us to take down one woman. Ethan should go because she already knows him and apparently likes him," hometown Ethan said, jerking a thumb at the Mr. and Mrs. stickers on the back window of Esme's car. "I'll go with him, the rest of you can split up. Some of you stay inside in the hall, the others out here, just in case she tries to run."

Ethan didn't care who came with him, but he was definitely going to be the one to take Esme down.

Everyone quickly split up and he and hometown Ethan entered the bed and breakfast. Whitney had given them the room number for Esme's room, and hometown Ethan led him through the building until they were at the door.

Even though they hadn't worked together before, they both knew what they were doing, and using the key from Whitney he opened the door, and hometown Ethan covered his back as they stepped into the room. A purse sat on the bed, but the room was otherwise empty. After retrieving a weapon from the purse, he and hometown Ethan approached the bathroom. If her purse was here, then Esme was too, and that was the only place she could be.

Just as they were approaching the bathroom, its door opened and Esme stepped through it, wrapped in a fluffy white towel.

Her dark eyes widened when she saw them both standing there.

Instead of running—like he would have sworn she'd do—Esme burst into tears. "Ethan, I was so sorry to hear about Sparrow," she wept.

How would she even know about Sparrow unless she had been involved? It wasn't like they had plastered her disappearance all over the news. The only people who knew were him, Sparrow's family, Prey, the search and rescue guys, and police department here in Fallport, and a couple of cops back in Manhattan.

"What do you mean?" he asked, wanting to trip her up. If they couldn't find Sparrow alive then they didn't have any definitive proof at the moment that Esme was responsible. He wanted a confession, then he wanted the location of where she'd taken Sparrow.

Esme faltered. "I assumed you were looking for Sparrow because I heard she was missing."

"Yeah? How did you hear that?"

"I assumed. I went to give her some cupcakes as a thank you for all the help she gave us in Djibouti, and then when I was leaving, I saw cops in the building. I assumed something had happened to her," Esme said, tears still trickling down her cheeks.

"Why would you assume that? It's quite a leap. And why are you here? You said you thought I was here to look for Sparrow. Why would you think I was doing that here?" he demanded, his weapon trained unwaveringly on the woman.

"What are you doing?" she asked, nervously now as her gaze darted between him and hometown Ethan.

"I think you know." He lowered his weapon and stepped closer, getting into her personal space.

"Oh?" Esme dropped the towel and angled her body toward him as though he cared one iota about it and sex right now.

"Stop with the games, Esme. You took her, we're going to match her DNA to the blood in your car. You're not going to get away with this. The best you can hope for is that she's still alive, so you aren't charged with first-degree murder. Is she alive, Esme? Did you kill her already?" He towered over the woman and didn't bother to hide his anger and loathing.

Like a switch had been flipped the flirty, innocent persona dropped and in its place stood someone as close to pure evil, soulless, and devoid of morals as he'd ever seen.

"You'll never find her," Esme spat. "If she's not dead already she will be soon."

"Tell me where she is," he growled.

"Never."

"Don't do anything you'll regret," hometown Ethan warned. "She's not worth it. Sparrow is our focus, and we don't need her to find Sparrow. Guys checked out Esme's car's GPS system and have a location to where she was before she came here. Simon is here, let him take her, we'll go find your girl."

With a last look at Esme, he curled his lips into a smirk. "I'm glad she broke your nose."

When he turned his back on her she reached for him, trying to grab onto his hand. "Don't go, Ethan. Please. I did it for us, so we could be together. She was the one who got in the way. It's meant to be us, together," she cried.

Ethan ignored her as he walked away. Hometown Ethan

was right, Esme was nothing, she'd be spending the rest of her life in prison. Sparrow was all that mattered.

* * *

8:18 P.M.

WARMTH WASHED OVER HER.

Sparrow tried to move toward it, desperately seeking a respite from the oppressive cold, but the more she tried to grab hold of the warmth the further away it seemed to get.

Then it disappeared altogether, and she was back to shaking violently.

She was slowly freezing to death, she knew that, there was just nothing she could do to stop it from happening.

The only reason hypothermia hadn't claimed her yet was because of the blanket.

The silly, fluffy, pink blanket that her siblings had given her as a birthday gift a few years back because they knew she loved all things pink. It had sat on her bed ever since, she used it when the weather got really cold, but mostly it was too thick and too warm to sleep with.

Esme must have grabbed it to use to cover her in the backseat so it wasn't obvious she was hauling around a bound kidnap victim, but the blanket just might wind up saving her life.

If someone found her in time.

She had tried to climb her way out, but with her hands bound, the concussion, her injured feet, and the tightly packed dirt walls that didn't have finger or toe holds, the feat was impossible.

Which left her with zero options.

All she could do was huddle down here under her pink blanket and pray that someone found her in time.

Had Olivia and Raven been able to track Esme's car? Did they know where she was, or at least the general vicinity?

Did it even matter?

Unless they were close by, they weren't going to find her in time.

Because she couldn't just give up, it wasn't in the Oswald DNA, Sparrow somehow managed to get up and onto her feet, but promptly swayed and fell straight back down.

Her muscles were cramping badly from the constant shivering and her head hurt. She was so cold and numb she couldn't even tell if she'd hurt herself in the fall down here, but since she could move, she didn't think she'd added any other injuries to her tally.

Not that it was all that important, it was hypothermia that would claim her.

Feeling woozy and fuzzy, Sparrow rested her head back down against the hard, cold ground. She tucked the blanket completely over her, including her head, and curled in on herself, hoping she had enough body heat left to keep herself alive a little longer.

She wasn't ready to die.

A tear rolled down her cheek. The moisture in the icy air made it leave a burning trail in its wake.

Sparrow had no idea how long she lay there.

Sometimes she could have sworn the sun was shining brightly down upon her. She was back on the farm she'd grown up on. She and her siblings were splashing around in the lake on a hot summer's afternoon. Her parents were there too, and she threw her arms around her mother's neck.

"I missed you, Mama."

"I missed you too, my sweet girl."

As she snuggled into her mother's embrace, she felt

warmth spread through her. "I don't want to leave you, I want to stay here forever," she murmured.

"You can't, baby girl, it's not time yet."

"I don't want you to leave me again."

"I don't want to either."

Lips touched her forehead, and in an instant, the warmth was gone, and she was back to lying in the cold. Her body shook so badly it physically hurt. It was like every one of her muscles had been wound tight and was now being pulled until it was going to snap. Her jaw was clenched together in a mostly futile effort to stop it from chattering.

Now to top it all off she was hallucinating.

Her mother had been dead for eighteen going on nineteen years, and hadn't been here, but Sparrow wished she was.

She could feel her body slowing down. Everything about her felt sluggish, even her breathing had slowed way down. It was getting harder and harder to concentrate on anything other than how cold she was and how desperately she wanted to be warm again.

Drowsiness consumed her. There was no energy left to try to climb out, no energy left to get up and try to move around a little, generate her own heat, no energy left to do anything but lie here and wish things had turned out differently.

If only she had gone down to the lobby to meet Esme.

If only she had fought harder back at her place or here in the woods.

If only she weren't so tired, maybe she could figure out a way to get out of here, but she couldn't.

She faded away again. Images danced in her mind, happy times with her family and friends, most of them revolved around warm things.

The first time she and her siblings went to the beach. It

was while Eagle was home after his first deployment, he'd packed them all up and taken them on a beach vacation. Two weeks of nothing but sun, sand, and waves.

A vacation she'd taken with some friends to the Caribbean. They'd spent a month island hopping, and she'd loved every second of those long, lazy days lying on the sand and swimming in the ocean, and nights of partying.

Curled up in Ethan's arms when they'd been trapped together in Omega's basement. Even though she'd been scared, his steady presence and solid chest had warmed her in a way she hadn't experienced before.

Maybe that was the moment her feelings had changed, and she'd started falling in love with him.

How badly she wished he was here right now. Even if it was just for one moment, just long enough for her to tell him how much he meant to her. It was crazy to think that although she had thought of Ethan over the years, her feelings had grown so quickly in the short time they'd spent together.

"Sparrow!"

That sounded like Ethan yelling her name.

But that was crazy.

Sparrow pulled her blanket tighter around herself, noting with concern that she'd stopped shivering.

She wouldn't say she was warm exactly, but now she just felt numb.

No pain.

No cold.

Just numb.

"Sparrow, if you can hear me, call out."

That sounded like Ethan again.

Great.

Now she was hallucinating that Ethan was around.

Maybe she should take the opportunity to speak to him as if he was really here like she'd talked to her mom.

"Ethan, I know you don't love me back, but I just want you to know that I'm falling in love with you. I'm sorry if I made you feel pressured to do something you didn't want to do, and I'm sorry if what we did made you feel like you were betraying your wife, but I'm not sorry for what we shared, it meant everything to me."

Content now that she'd told Ethan how she felt, Sparrow let her eyes fall closed again.

Or maybe they had been closed all along.

She honestly had no idea.

"Did you hear something?"

That voice wasn't one she recognized. It seemed she was also hallucinating complete strangers now.

"Is it her?"

That was Ethan.

She thought.

Only she wasn't quite sure.

She didn't trust herself anymore.

"Duke's heading this way," another voice she didn't recognize spoke.

Duke?

Who was Duke?

Why was she hearing multiple voices?

Kind of over the hallucination thing, Sparrow shifted uncomfortably. All she wanted now was to go to sleep.

It was so tempting to let go, and it would be so easy. All she had to do was stop fighting it and unconsciousness would come for her, carrying her away to a peaceful place where there was no cold, no sadness, no anything.

The blanket must have shifted because she felt cold air against her skin and the blissful promise of rest that had been tantalizingly close now shimmered just out of reach.

"Down here, I see something pink, looks like a blanket."

She didn't know the voice, so she didn't bother to open her eyes, it was just some weird hallucination.

"Sparrow loves pink."

Ethan again.

Her hallucinations were even so confused that they couldn't keep one coherent theme going.

"Sparrow?"

She blinked.

Her eyes must be open after all.

She could have sworn that above her, in a bright shaft of light that hadn't been there before, was Ethan's face. His blue eyes seemed to glow, and she smiled, at least her hallucinations had finally gotten one thing right.

Now her final sight would be Ethan's handsome face.

A small smile curled her lips.

"Goodbye, Ethan," she murmured, and then the last of her strength faded away, taking her conscious mind along with it.

It was time to stop fighting against the inevitable, death came for everyone in the end, and it seemed like it was her time.

Ignoring the voices yammering above her, dismissing them as just the workings of her stressed-out mind that was on the brink of giving out, she metaphorically uncurled the fingers that had been clinging to life, and let go.

* * *

9:09 P.M.

"Goodbye, Ethan."

Sparrow's slurred words sparked a second of relief that

she was alive, conscious, alert enough to recognize him, that was too quickly followed by indescribable fear as her eyes promptly fluttered closed.

"Sparrow?" he demanded. Ethan was down on his hands and knees above what appeared to be an old mineshaft. They'd brought something of Sparrow's with them to use with a tracking dog, and once they'd gotten out of the car at the same spot where Esme had been parked earlier, Duke had immediately picked up a scent. They'd followed the trail, calling out to Sparrow, and each time they called her name and didn't get a response his hope had dipped.

Chances were, she was already gone.

There was no way she could survive long out here in the cold. Snow was forecast, and although it had so far held off, the feel of it was in the air, and with every second that passed without finding her his fear had grown.

Then they'd heard a voice mumbling something incoherently, and Duke had headed straight to this spot, where Raid had spotted the pink blanket.

Now Ethan was hovering just twenty feet or so above Sparrow, but she wasn't responding.

"I have to get down there," he said already swinging his legs over the side of the hole and judging the best place to land. There was enough space down there for probably three people, but Sparrow was unconscious, and he didn't want to accidentally land on her.

"Wait," hometown Ethan said. "I know how desperate you are to get to her, but if you hurt yourself on the way down then we have two people to carry out of here. That slows us down and increases the chances that hypothermia gets her."

As much as he wanted to deck the other man, tear down anything preventing him from getting to Sparrow in the next half a second, Ethan knew that the other Ethan was right. Sparrow's safety had to come first.

Obviously sensing that he was acquiescing, hometown Ethan said, "We'll lower you down to her, call the others and get them to bring a c collar and a backboard, and we'll get her out of there as quickly and safely as we can."

The fact that he knew hometown Ethan had searched these exact same mountains for the woman he loved so had firsthand knowledge of just how hard this was, made it easier for Ethan to nod his agreement.

While the guys prepared the ropes, he focused on Sparrow. "If you can hear me, you hold on, okay, wisp? You don't give up on me, not when I'm this close to you. You can do this, I know you can. I *need* you to," he added. "There's no way I can handle losing you as well. So, you fight for me, wisp. You fight with everything you have. You do your part, and I'll do mine and get you out of there."

"We're ready," hometown Ethan told him.

As quickly as he could, Ethan got himself hooked into the ropes, and then finally he was climbing down to Sparrow.

The second his feet hit the ground, he was on his knees beside her, ripping off his gloves so he could touch his fingertips to her neck.

"Thank you, God," he whispered when he felt a pulse, weak but there. "She's alive," he called up to the others.

"The guys will be here in five minutes tops," hometown Ethan assured him.

With how cold Sparrow felt he prayed that was fast enough.

For now, he'd do for her what he could. First thing he had to do was cut the bindings at her wrists. Bright red torn skin was beneath the plastic ties, and he gently smoothed along the skin beneath them, hating seeing her beautiful body marred.

Keeping the pink blanket wrapped around her—quite possibly the blanket was the only reason Sparrow was still alive—he pulled out the emergency blankets from his first aid kit and wrapped those around her too. With her cocooned as best as possible from the wind and icy air, Ethan grabbed some heat packs, cracked them, and then positioned them under her arms, around her neck, chest, and groin. Then he pulled off the knit beanie he was wearing and tugged it onto Sparrow's head.

Her breathing was way too slow and shallow, and she'd obviously been confused, perhaps hallucinating earlier when she'd said goodbye to him. The him she'd been talking to wasn't the real him it was an image in her mind.

It was Sparrow letting go.

Wanting to move her, to hold her, but unable to because he didn't know if she had neck or spinal injuries from the fall, he stretched out on the hard ground beside her, and pressed his body up against hers, willing his own body heat to warm her. He couldn't be this close to saving her only to lose her anyway.

"Come on, sweetheart," he urged, "don't you dare give up on me now. You got this, wisp, I know you do."

Ethan curled as much of his body around Sparrow's as he could and touched his lips to her too-cold cheek. She was still alive, breathing, her heart beating, he had to be grateful, had to be hopeful. Esme could have killed her outright then buried her body where it might never have been found, but she hadn't.

They still had a chance, a chance at getting her to the hospital in time, a chance for him to tell her how he felt about her, a chance to be happy together.

That was what he had to cling to right now.

"Ethan, I'm coming down with the c collar, we'll get that fitted then the guys will lower down the litter, and we'll get her loaded up," hometown Ethan informed him.

"All right," Ethan replied, reluctantly releasing Sparrow so he could sit up and be ready to get her loaded and out of here asap.

As he moved, Sparrow moaned, her body shifting weakly, and her lashes fluttered on her paper pale cheeks.

"Sparrow?" He leaned over her, took her face between his hands, and brushed his thumbs across her cold skin. "Are you with me, honey?"

Sparrow mumbled something he couldn't understand, and while her lashes fluttered against her cheeks again her eyes didn't open.

"Come on, sweetheart," he urged, "open your eyes for me."

Almost in slow motion her eyes opened, and she blinked, looking around her in confusion. "Ethan?"

"Right here," he assured her, a huge grin on his face.

"Said goodbye already," she whispered.

"No goodbyes for us," he told her firmly. "No goodbyes." If he had his way and it wasn't too late, then all he wanted for them was a lifetime of hellos. "Ethan and I are going to get you out of here, get you warmed up, and then we need to talk." There was so much he wanted to say but now wasn't the time. Now they had to get her out of here because although she was awake and talking to him, she wasn't out of the woods, literally or figuratively.

Her brow furrowed. "But you're Ethan."

"There are two Ethans now," hometown Ethan said with a grin of his own as he landed beside them and knelt on Sparrow's other side.

"So confused," she murmured.

"I know, honey, don't worry about it now, I'll explain everything once you're feeling better. For now, all you have to do is keep breathing and stay with me, okay? We're going to put a c collar around your neck in case you hurt it when you fell down here, then we're going to load you into a litter and get you out of here," he told her while hometown Ethan carefully fitted the collar.

"Tired." The word was more a breath of sound, and her eyes fluttered closed again.

"It's okay if you need to rest, honey, but you keep breathing for me, okay? I'm not going to lose you, you hear me? You're mine, and I'm not going to let you go, so you sleep if you have to, but you don't die on me," he warned.

He could have sworn one side of her mouth curled into a half-smile, and one of her hands got free from the blankets and reached for his. "Don't leave me, Ethan."

"That is something you don't have to worry about, I am not going anywhere. Ever," he added although her hand in his had gone limp and he knew she'd passed out again. There was dried blood on her head, and he guessed she probably had another concussion, likely part of the reason she was so tired and confused, but she was alive and that was all he cared about.

The other guys lowered the litter down and he and hometown Ethan got her loaded into it, covered with blankets, and with the heating packs still tucked against her clothes. As she was lifted out, and he and hometown Ethan climbed up, Ethan knew he was one lucky guy. If there had been any doubts left about his ability and willingness to move on, then almost losing Sparrow had eradicated them.

He was ready.

Ready to have the future he wanted with one of the two most incredible women he had ever met.

Now it seemed silly to have worried about whether there was enough room in his heart for another woman because Sparrow was already firmly lodged there and he felt no guilt, just joy and excitement for the future.

CHAPTER FOURTEEN

January 31st

 1:22 A.M.

WAKING UP WAS A SLOW PROCESS.

Sparrow felt like she was walking through a long dark tunnel. There was a pinprick of light way off in the distance, and although she felt like she was walking steadily toward it, it took a long time for it to grow bigger.

There was confusion and apprehension. She wasn't quite sure yet where she was or what was going on.

Bit by bit things began to trickle back in, but they were kind of jumbled.

Cupcakes.

A pink blanket.

Snow.

Two Ethans.

Two Ethans?

She had no idea what that even meant.

Wherever she was, Ethan wasn't here. Ethan was back home in Kansas. He was probably planning his return to Africa already, she doubted he'd want to just hang around in the States even if he should be taking it easy for a while after the beating he'd received.

As older memories continued to filter through the foggy darkness more recent memories joined them. Being attacked in her penthouse, the car ride, running through the woods, then falling into the old mineshaft.

Then she could have sworn that Ethan was there, but that was crazy, wasn't it?

The speck of light was growing bigger, and as it did, Sparrow began to become aware of her surroundings.

She wasn't cold anymore, that was the first thing that registered. The opposite in fact, she felt toasty warm. Comfortable too. Gone was the hard, rocky ground, in its place was something soft and fluffy, almost like a bed.

Hopeful now, she concentrated on the light, focused on making it bigger.

Sounds filtered in next. The whoosh of a door, hushed voices talking. Smell came after it, that antiseptic smell that could only be a hospital.

There was only one thing left to do, and that was to open her eyes.

It sounded so much easier than it turned out to be. There was still an ache in her head, although it had dulled, and cracking her eyes open only made it worse. Sparrow breathed through it, and slowly her blurry vision evened out.

Off-white walls, a whiteboard on the one in front of her, her name was written on it and some other words that were still a little fuzzy for her to make out. An IV pole was beside her along with a monitor.

"You're awake."

There was relief in those two words, but it wasn't that which made her head snap to the side it was that she recognized the voice. "Ethan?"

"Right here." He was grinning as he released his hold on her hand and smoothed a stray lock of hair off her cheek, tucking it behind her ear.

Sparrow frowned. "You're here." She wasn't sure if she meant it as a question, asking for an explanation on how and why he was sitting beside her hospital bed, or if she was making a statement, more to herself than to him as though attempting to convince herself that he was here.

"Where else would I be?" Although his tone was light, almost teasing, there was stark relief in his blue eyes. Her mind must not be working at one hundred percent yet because she had no idea why it was there. Or why he was here for that matter. It didn't make sense. They were friends, sure, but why had he come looking for her when Esme had abducted her?

"I ... I don't know," she stammered.

"Do you remember what happened?" Ethan shifted until he was perched on the edge of her bed, and he reached for her hands, cradling them in his much larger ones, careful to avoid the needle in the back of one. His hold was both gentle and firm, and his thumbs brushed soft circles on her palms.

For a moment, she couldn't even process his question because he was touching her, making her feel ridiculously schoolgirlish. Too bad this was one crush that wasn't ever going anywhere. "I remember Esme coming to my place with cupcakes. She pulled out a gun, and we fought, but she hit me then drugged me. I must have blacked out because things were hazy after that, but I remember her driving, and then we ended up in the mountains somewhere. I almost got away from her, but I fell into the mineshaft. After that, all I remember is being cold and getting sleepier and sleepier. I remember saying goodbye to you and then there were ... two Ethans."

Ethan grinned and chuckled. "Actually, there really were two of us." He nodded at a man with black hair and warm brown eyes that she hadn't even noticed. "This is the other Ethan. Although I guess since this is his hometown, I'm really the *other* Ethan. He's Ethan Watson, he's one of the guys in the Eagle Point Search and Rescue. They're the ones who helped me find you and get you to the hospital."

Still uncertain as to why exactly her Ethan had even known she was gone let alone come to help search for her, Sparrow shifted her attention to the other man. "Thank you. That doesn't feel like enough after you saved my life, but thank you, truly, from the bottom of my heart." Tears made the world blur again, and as much as she didn't want to cry in front of either of these guys, she also didn't want to pull her hands away from Ethan's, so she allowed a couple of tears to trickle free.

"You're welcome, no need for thanks," Ethan Watson told her, looking uncomfortable with her gratitude.

"You're going to be getting a whole lot of thanks," she said, already trying to figure out what an appropriate gift would be for the men who had literally saved her life.

"Absolutely," her Ethan echoed, reaching out to catch her tears with the pad of his thumb.

"I get why he's here," she said, nodding at the other Ethan, "but I still don't really understand why *you're* here," she said to her Ethan.

"I think I'll give you guys some privacy so you can talk," Ethan Watson said, slapping a hand on her Ethan's shoulder. "I'm glad you're going to be okay, Ms. Oswald."

"Sparrow," she corrected. "If you saved my life, you can certainly call me by my first name." Once the other Ethan was gone, she looked to her Ethan. "So, I'm going to be okay?"

"You have a concussion. Another one, that's not good and the doctors were worried at first, but your tests look good. Your body temperature is almost back to normal, and you should be released tomorrow morning."

None of that was a surprise, but she still didn't get what Ethan was doing here. "Why are you here? Wherever here is."

"Fallport, Virginia," Ethan supplied. "I'm here because you disappeared."

She nodded, still not really understanding. "Which one of my siblings found I was missing? I'm sorry they called you, they didn't need to drag you into this." It was hard for her to have him this close to her. She still wanted to be friends with him, but right now, when everything was raw and her emotions were all over the place, having him this close to her, touching her, comforting her, it was too much.

"I'm the one who found out you'd been kidnapped," Ethan said, his hands tightening almost convulsively around hers.

"I don't understand. How did you find that out?"

Ethan's smile turned tender, and he reached out to palm her cheek. As much as she wanted to turn into his caress she held back. She needed to know if anything had changed before she allowed herself to hope.

"I found out because I was at your place," Ethan told her.

"Why were you at my place?" It should be obvious, but she wasn't feeling completely herself yet, and she didn't want to read into it something that wasn't really there.

"I came to see you."

"Why?"

His grin turned wry. "Need to hear me spell it out, huh?"

"Yes."

"I came because I couldn't stay away from you. I couldn't let you and this chance slip through my fingers. I knew when we left Africa that I had a lot to think about. I knew I cared about you, I knew I wanted to be with you, but I also knew that I had to be sure I could give you all of me."

"But …"

"No, Sparrow. There aren't any buts. Not anymore. This is what Sierra would have wanted. She would have loved you, and she'd be happy for me. Once I accepted that I realized that I was the only one standing between myself and happiness. I'm ready to get out of my own way."

"What does that mean exactly?"

"It means I'm yours. It means I've never been so terrified as I was when I walked into your penthouse to surprise you and found signs of a struggle. These last twenty-four hours have been Hell on earth. I was so scared I would lose you, and you would never even know that I care about you." Ethan paused, drew in a long breath, then added, "I more than care about you, Sparrow. I'm falling in love with you."

That was everything she had longed to hear, and yet … "Is this real? Am I still hallucinating?"

Ethan leaned forward and rested his forehead against hers. "No, sweetheart. You're not hallucinating. I'm here and I want you, the only question is, do you still want me?"

There was actual doubt in his voice as he asked the question and she realized he was worried that she might say that she didn't. "Ethan, you were the last thing I saw before I passed out that last time. You were my last thoughts before I thought I was going to die. It would *never* be too late for us."

A breath shuddered out of him, his hands framed her face, and he pulled back so he could meet her gaze. "You don't know how glad I am to hear you say that."

"I do, because I was sure I was never going to hear you say you wanted me. Ethan?"

"Yeah, wisp?"

"You know there's something you're supposed to do now?"

He arched a blond brow. "Oh, there is, is there?"

"There is."

"And what exactly would that be?" he teased.

"You're supposed to kiss me." Sparrow lifted her hands to cover his, and when his lips finally found hers, it felt like her entire life clicked into place. This was where she was supposed to be.

CHAPTER FIFTEEN

February 1st

 :41 P.M.

"You feeling okay?" Ethan asked as he helped Sparrow out of the car that had picked them up at the airport and driven them back to her penthouse. Although all of her siblings had wanted to come back here with her, she had firmly thanked her brothers for coming looking for her but told them she was fine and just wanted some time alone with him.

No way he was arguing with that.

Alone time with Sparrow was what he wanted too.

While she was in the hospital, the search and rescue guys had been in and out, checking on Sparrow and keeping her entertained once she was awake and starting to feel bored stuck in bed. Eagle and Falcon had been hovering around her like the overprotective big brothers that they were. Other than that, one short time after she'd first woken up, they'd had no time just the two of them and he couldn't wait to have her all to himself.

"Fine, stop fussing," she said mildly. Although it was clear the constant fussing by him, her brothers, and the search and rescue guys, was annoying her, she hadn't complained as though she'd sensed that all of them—for varying reasons—needed to do a little coddling.

"Not sure I can do that, sweetheart," he warned. He was a fusser, it was what he did, how he showed he cared, and his way of trying to lighten the load.

Sparrow stopped short, right as they were going up the steps and he froze, looking down at her in a panic. Two concussions so close together were cause for concern, and while Sparrow had insisted that other than a headache and a lingering "fuzzy" feeling, she was doing fine, that could change way too quickly for his liking.

"What's wrong."

Her eyes were teary when she looked up at him, and his heart clenched. Tears in the eyes of the woman you were falling in love with were never a good thing. "Nothing is wrong. You called me sweetheart."

Ethan relaxed, his anxiety melting into a smile. "Of course I did."

Something flickered across her face, something that looked way too much like worry for his liking. "Let's go inside, we need to talk."

And the anxiety was back.

They greeted Steve, the doorman, who was very apologetic about allowing Esme up into Sparrow's penthouse, even though she reminded him several times that she was the one who had given the okay. The ride in the lift was silent, but Ethan kept a hold of Sparrow's hand as though that might be able to stop the sudden distance he felt between them from growing.

"This place is amazing," he said as they walked into the living room. Last time he'd been here there hadn't been time to take in the spectacular views because he'd been in a panic searching for Sparrow.

"It's nice enough I guess," Sparrow said as she came to stand beside him at the enormous windows that took up an entire wall of the large room.

"You don't like it here?"

"Just doesn't feel like home. Eagle picked it out for me and chose all the furnishings. Only thing I contributed were the things in my bedroom. This place is fine but it's too big, I like smaller and cozier."

That was what he preferred too. This place was stunning, but it felt more like a hotel than a home. He'd rather a smaller place on a nice-sized plot of land in the suburbs where his kids could ride their bikes in the street and play ball with the other kids. He wanted a home, and he wanted it with the woman standing beside him, but now he was doubting that was what she wanted.

"What's going on?" he asked as he guided her to a large overstuffed gray leather sofa.

Sparrow's blue eyes were troubled when she looked up at him. "Are you sure this is what you want? Us, I mean."

"I told you that it was."

"I know, and I want to believe you, but maybe it was just you getting caught up in the emotion of me being kidnapped. What if you have doubts later?"

"I won't."

"You know I would *never* ask you to stop loving Sierra. Ever. Not in a million years. I know you'll always cherish her and your memories of her. But I'm not going to be the same as her, I'm going to do things differently, like different things, have different expectations, different wants and needs. I don't want you to think that life with me would be the same as your life with her, and I don't want to live being constantly compared to your first love."

There was genuine concern in her words, and it made his heart ache, and his love and respect for her grow. "Sparrow, I don't want you to be Sierra. What I shared with her was different, it grew from young love into something real. What I feel for you isn't the same but it's just as strong. There hasn't been a single other woman in the last few years that I've even looked at, but you threw me off-balance right from the start. It has nothing to do with Esme abducting you, I was coming here to tell you I wanted to give us a try anyway. If I ever make you feel like I'm comparing you to Sierra, I want you to tell me immediately because I will never consciously do that to you."

He felt her relax at his words. "Okay, I just had to be sure, you know?"

"I know, I get it. If I was in your shoes, I would do the same thing. And if you still need further convincing that I want you in my future, while you were sleeping in the hospital I spoke to Eagle, Falcon, Raven, and Dove, about the possibility of making a search and rescue division of Prey Security. If it hadn't been for the other Ethan and those guys, we wouldn't have found you in time. I don't want to go back to Africa, but I still want to do something to help people, and something that allows me to put my flying skills to use. I know you still have a year left on your current deployment, but I'm hoping you won't reup after that, and you and I can set up and run Prey Search and Rescue together. It would mean you get to be a more active part of your family's company, get to fly, and we'd get to work together."

Sparrow grinned. "You trying to convince me?"

"Maybe."

"Well don't bother, I think it's a *fabulous* idea. I would love to be more active at Prey, but I wasn't sure where I fitted in, this solves that problem. It lets me keep doing what I love, and I'd get to spend all my time with my man."

"So, you're in?"

"All in." Sparrow threw her arms around his neck and hugged him hard, only wincing slightly at what he assumed was the pain in her healing broken collarbone. "I hope you're going to stay here so we can spend all the time I'm not away together, and when I leave next year, we can look for a place of our own that we both love. Then I want to marry you and have kids with you, give them all the things I didn't get as a kid, and grow old with you by my side. I think I'll still find you sexy when you're old and gray," she teased.

"You better because there isn't going to be a day that goes by that I'm not going to want to ravish your body." It would be hard to wait while Sparrow finished out her current contract with the Air Force, but it would give them plenty of time to get to know one another as boyfriend and girlfriend, and they could video call and email all the time. In the end, it would be worth it because when she came back home, they'd be able to start their lives together and he could give her everything her heart desired. "Speaking of things that you didn't get as a kid, I have a gift for you."

The gift had been left behind here, forgotten in his panic over Sparrow's disappearance. But when Raven and Olivia had come in to clean up the place and get it ready for Sparrow to come home, he'd asked them to find the brightly wrapped box and leave it in the living room. Now he reached out and picked it up, passing it to Sparrow.

"For me?" she asked.

"Yep. Something you said while we were in Djibouti made me think of it, and I knew I had to get it for you."

"I love the pink wrapping paper."

Ethan laughed. "I knew you would. I've never been a fan of pink myself but knowing that ridiculously bright pink blanket saved your life I think I've had a change of heart."

"You shouldn't say that until you see my bedroom," Sparrow snickered, her eyes twinkling.

"I've seen it." He grimaced as he remembered searching the room that had pink everything in it.

"Hey!" She swatted at his shoulder. "You just said you like pink now, so I thought you'd be happy to share my pink bedroom with me."

"Definitely not, babe. First thing we're doing is redecorating that room. I like pink, but I think I'd lose my masculinity if I had to live in there," he teased. To be honest, if it made Sparrow as happy as she looked right now he would live in an entirely pink house and wouldn't care about it. "Now, open your gift."

Sparrow tore off the wrapping paper and tossed it aside, then opened the box. She gasped when she saw what was inside, and her gaze flew to his. The mixture of joy, gratefulness, and adoration in those blue depths was something he would never forget.

Score one for him.

Ethan wanted to spend the rest of his life making his girl happy, and he was off to a good start.

* * *

2:12 P.M.

"It's a Cabbage Patch Kid," Sparrow whispered as she lifted the doll from the box. A memory flittered through her mind. The night the compound had been attacked Ethan had mentioned the code word for the others to let them into the bunker in the event the two of them were separated. The code word had been cabbage patch, and she'd mentioned that she'd liked the dolls but by the time she and her siblings had entered the conventional world she'd been twelve, in her mind way too old to play with dolls.

Ethan had remembered that throwaway comment.

Not just remembered it, he'd actually gone looking and bought her a Cabbage Patch Kid.

Any doubts she'd had melted away, and she clutched the doll in one arm and threw her other around Ethan's neck. "Thank you," she whispered. This was just another thing in a long line of amazing things this man had done for her. She was so thrilled he was willing to give them a chance and had already been planning out what their future looked like.

"You like it? I chose it because it looks like you. Blue eyes, black hair, she's even wearing a pink dress."

There was a tinge of anxiety in his tone, and that made him even more adorably attractive. Ethan actually cared about her, what she thought, and how she felt. It had been a long time since someone had been that concerned about her, and she loved it.

"I don't like it, Ethan, I love it. I love it because it's the single most thoughtful gift anyone has ever given me, and you remembered something so small and cared enough to make it a reality. I ..." Sparrow hesitated, it was too soon to say it, she knew it was, and yet it was in her heart, and she wanted him to know. Even if he didn't say it back. "I love you, Ethan."

His entire body went taut, and she was sure she had made a mistake telling him, but then he shuddered and buried his face against her neck. "I love you, too, wisp. I don't even know how it happened, but I do. I knew it when I had no idea where you were or if I would get you back. I love you."

Sparrow pulled back and grinned at him. "That means we're in love!"

She had never been in love, never known that it felt like this. A burning, all-consuming desire to be with him all the time, to touch him, kiss him, and hold him. To learn every single thing about him, no matter how small. To share all of herself, not holding anything back because there was freedom here, safety.

"You know," she said lazily, trailing a fingertip across Ethan's bottom lip. "There was one thing that I didn't get to do before we left Fallport."

Ethan's lips parted, and he sucked her finger into his mouth, his tongue flicking against it, and she squirmed as she couldn't not imagine his tongue on other, more sensitive body parts.

"I didn't get to take a proper shower. Care to join me for one now?" Sparrow asked.

"No, not this time," Ethan said, managing to stand and swing her into his arms in one smooth move. "This time we're doing it properly. I want to be able to watch your face, see every expression, and stare into your eyes. I want to be connected to you this time. This time we're making love not having sex."

How did this man manage to get better with every word that came out of his mouth?

"No arguments from me," she told him. Last time they'd had hot, sweaty sex, Ethan hadn't even been able to look at her while they did it. This time they were sharing something, going on a journey together.

"Didn't expect any." Ethan nipped at the side of her neck, then touched a soft kiss to the spot, his tongue swirling against her skin. "After we do it in a bed, I'm not opposed to the shower idea."

"Then we can christen every room of the house," she teased.

"Deal."

"Mmm," she moaned as he trailed more kisses down her neck. The more he did that the harder it was to think of anything but the sensations flaring like bright lights through her body.

But that was the way it was supposed to be, wasn't it?

Complete surrender. Joining their bodies and their souls. Connecting with another human being on a level unlike anything else.

By the time he stepped into her bedroom and set her on her feet before him, her body was already humming with need. She'd never felt this desperate to have a man's hands on her. It felt like if he didn't strip her naked in the next three seconds she would spontaneously combust.

She'd never thought that was possible, but now she absolutely felt like it was what would happen to her.

The heat in Ethan's eyes as he looked at her had her momentarily forgetting that she was only wearing sweats, no makeup, and her hair in a messy bun. He looked at her like he wanted to devour her, and she was more than ready to be devoured and to do a little devouring of her own.

Last time they hadn't undressed. This time Ethan stepped closer, took hold of the hem of her sweatshirt and pulled it over her head. She wasn't wearing a bra because with her healing broken collarbone it was easier without that pressure on her shoulder, and as soon as he had her bared to him, he knelt before her and took one of her nipples into his mouth.

First he sucked hard, then flicked at the hard little nub with his tongue before scraping his teeth lightly over the highly sensitive skin making her whole body shudder delightfully.

"You like that, wisp?" he asked as he blew on her wet skin then touched a featherlight kiss to her hardened nipple.

"Oh, yeah," she said breathlessly.

"Good, let's see if you like this better."

Ethan's fingers hooked into the waistband of her sweats and pulled them down her legs, lifting first one foot and then the other to remove her socks and shoes, and then the sweats, which he discarded on the floor where they were promptly forgotten.

Hooking his hands around her backside, he pulled her forward until he could bury his nose in the apex of her thighs. When he breathed deeply her legs began to tremble.

How was he doing this?

How was he making her body so turned on by barely doing anything?

The only guy she'd ever dated who had put his mouth on her there hadn't really liked it, and she had been too keenly aware of that to really enjoy anything he did. She hadn't gotten off and she hadn't bothered asking any other guy to do it.

But now she was already wet and aching for Ethan's mouth to be on her.

Nudging her legs apart, he ran a finger across her panties. "These are soaked," he said, a very smug smile on his face. "I've barely even touched you yet."

"What can I say, my expectations are pretty high."

"Then I have a lot to live up to."

"Doesn't matter if you don't, just means we need to practice," she said, shooting him a sultry smile.

Ethan gave a throaty laugh and then his fingers hooked into the waistband of her panties and eased them slowly down her legs. The pads of each finger trailed lines of tingling fire everywhere they touched, and she let out a soft moan.

"Baby, those moans are going to turn to screams in a moment," he said. His hands grasped her thighs, and he spread her legs wide and then his tongue darted out and swiped along her center. A groan rumbled through him, and his lips vibrated against her most intimate area making her insides clench in anticipation.

When his mouth closed around her little bundle of nerves and he sucked hard, Sparrow gasped, her head falling back, eyes closed, as she tried to soak up the myriad of sensations flying through her body. He suckled, and swiped at her with his tongue, and then he slid a finger inside her, curling it so it hit that special spot and she came apart.

Her legs trembled, threatening to buckle and she tried to absorb wave after wave of pleasure. Ethan didn't let up, continuing to spur her on with his fingers and his mouth, sending more ecstasy-fueled waves crashing over her.

"Ethan ... I ... I can't ..."

"Yeah, you can. Hold onto me, baby, and ride it."

Her hands clutched at Ethan's shoulders as she fixed her gaze on his blond head between her legs. She clung to him as he somehow managed to build more pleasure inside her before the last wave ebbed.

By the time it finally started to come down from her high, she was shaking so badly she sunk down to rest against Ethan's sturdy body.

"Don't even have words for that," she mumbled as after-shocks continued to rock her system.

"Too bad, guess that means we don't have to practice after all."

Sparrow swatted at his shoulder. "No way, buddy, we definitely need practice, and speaking of." She licked her lips as she looked at his long length straining against his jeans. "My turn to play."

Gently urging him to stand, she guided him to the bed,

where she unzipped his jeans and shoved them down his legs, his boxers went next, and he sprung free. Sparrow couldn't resist reaching out for a touch and grinned when it jerked at her soft caress.

Pressing on his shoulders, she sat him on the edge of the bed so she could pull his sweatshirt over his head, leaving him completely naked.

"You're so cut," she murmured as her fingers tried to touch all of him at once, tracing the lines of his impressive six-pack, and his totally sculpted pecs.

"You're pretty built yourself, babe," he said, reaching out to trace the lines of her own six-pack, which wasn't bad although not as impressive as his.

"Lie down," she ordered, and he shifted so he was stretched out on her pink bed. "All mine," she whispered as she took his length in his hand and began to stroke it.

"That's right, honey, all yours. I'm yours," he repeated, locking his gaze onto hers.

"And I'm yours."

Apparently not content to lie back and let her have her way with him, while she stroked him, slowly increasing her speed, he took her breasts in his hands and began to fondle them.

Every inch of her was hypersensitive, and her body went right back to feeling needy like she hadn't just had the best orgasm of her life a mere couple of minutes ago.

The more Ethan touched her, the closer she got to coming again.

The closer she got to coming, the harder and faster she stroked him.

The harder and faster she stroked him the more he fondled her, starting the cycle all over again.

"Need to be inside you, wisp," Ethan said. His breathing

was heavy, and he moved to reach for his clothes, she assumed to get a condom.

"Not this time," she said, grabbing his shoulders to stop him. "I'm clean, I get a contraceptive shot every few months, and it's still good. I don't want anything between us. Nothing, I want to feel every impressive inch of you."

She moved until she was positioned above him, more than ready to have him buried so deep inside her it was like their bodies had been fused together. Guiding him to her entrance, she sunk down on him faster than she'd intended, but as soon as the tip of him entered her body she had to have more.

And more.

And more.

Sparrow didn't think she would ever get enough of him.

Which was a good thing considering she wanted to spend the rest of her life with this man.

"Ethan," she moaned as he filled her, not just her body but every part of her.

"I know, sweetheart." From the look in his blue eyes, he was feeling the exact same thing she was.

Grabbing his hands, she laced their fingers together as their gazes stayed locked and their bodies moved.

It didn't take long before she reached the peak and was tumbling over it, rolling over and over again down the other side where nothing existed but pleasure and her and Ethan. He came just after she did. She could feel him empty himself inside her and knowing that there was absolutely nothing between them anymore made everything feel better, stronger.

As she came down from the high, she leaned down to kiss Ethan, then rested against him, his length still inside her, her head on his chest, his heart beating beneath her ear. Ethan's arms came around her, and she felt his lips press against her forehead and stay there. Without even realizing it she'd found perfection. Right here in the arms of the man she loved.

Hawk Oswald's one night stand is about to become so much more in the fifth book in the action packed and emotionally charged Prey Security series! Get it now: PROTECTING HAWK

ALSO BY JANE BLYTHE

SALVAGING MARIGOLD

TEN

Christmas Romantic Suspense Series

CHRISTMAS HOSTAGE

CHRISTMAS CAPTIVE

CHRISTMAS VICTIM

YULETIDE PROTECTOR

Conquering Fear Series

(Co-written with Amanda Siegrist)

DROWNING IN YOU

OUT OF THE DARKNESS

ABOUT THE AUTHOR

Jane Blythe is a USA Today bestselling author of romantic suspense and military romance full of sweet, smart, sexy heroes and strong heroines! When she's not weaving hard to unravel mysteries she loves to read, bake, go to the beach, build snowmen, and watch Disney movies. She has two adorable Dalmatians, is obsessed with Christmas, owns 200+ teddy bears, and loves to travel!

To connect and keep up to date please visit any of the following

Email – mailto:janeblytheauthor@gmail.com
Facebook – http://www.facebook.com/janeblytheauthor
Instagram – http://www.instagram.com/jane_blythe_author
Reader Group – http://www.facebook.com/
groups/janeskillersweethearts
Twitter – http://www.twitter.com/jblytheauthor
Website – http://www.janeblythe.com.au

There are many more books in this fan fiction world than listed here, for an up-to-date list go to www.AcesPress.com

You can also visit our Amazon page at:
http://www.amazon.com/author/operationalpha

Special Forces: Operation Alpha World
Christie Adams: Charity's Heart
Linzi Baxter: Unlocking Dreams
Misha Blake: Flash
Anna Blakely: Rescuing Gracelynn
Julia Bright: Saving Lorelei
Cara Carnes: Protecting Mari
Kendra Mei Chailyn: Beast
Melissa Kay Clarke: Rescuing Annabeth
Samantha A. Cole: Handling Haven
Lorelei Confer: Protecting Sara
KaLyn Cooper: Spring Unveiled
Janie Crouch: Storm
Jordan Dane: Redemption for Avery
Tarina Deaton: Found in the Lost
Riley Edwards: Protecting Olivia
Dorothy Ewels: Knight's Queen
Lila Ferrari: Protecting Joy
Nicole Flockton: Protecting Maria
Hope Ford: Rescuing Karina
Michele Gwynn: Rescuing Emma
Desiree Holt: Protecting Maddie
Kris Jacen, Be With Me
Jesse Jacobson: Protecting Honor
Rayne Lewis: Justice for Mary
Kristin Lynn: Worth the Risk
Callie Love & Ann Omasta: Hawaii Hottie

JM Madden: Rescuing Olivia
A.M. Mahler: Griffin
Ellie Masters: Sybil's Protector
Trish McCallan: Hero Under Fire
Rachel McNeely: The SEAL's Surprise Baby
KD Michaels: Saving Laura
Olivia Michaels: Protecting Harper
Annie Miller: Securing Willow
Keira Montclair: Wolf and the Wild Scots
MJ Nightingale: Protecting Beauty
Melinda Owens: Betraying Katie
Victoria Paige: Reclaiming Izabel
Danielle Pays: Defending Sarina
Lainey Reese: Protecting New York
KeKe Renée: Protecting Bria
TL Reeve and Michele Ryan: Extracting Mateo
Deanna L. Rowley: Saving Veronica
Angela Rush: Charlotte
Rose Smith: Saving Satin
Tyler Anne Snell: Cowboy Heat
Lynne St. James: SEAL's Spitfire
Sarah Stone: Shielding Grace
Jen Talty: Burning Desire
Reina Torres, Rescuing Hi'ilani
LJ Vickery: Circus Comes to Town
R. C. Wynne: Shadows Renewed

Delta Team Three Series
Lori Ryan: Nori's Delta
Becca Jameson: Destiny's Delta
Lynne St James, Gwen's Delta
Elle James: Ivy's Delta
Riley Edwards: Hope's Delta

Police and Fire: Operation Alpha World
Freya Barker: Burning for Autumn
B.P. Beth: Scott
Jane Blythe: Salvaging Marigold
Julia Bright, Justice for Amber
Hadley Finn: Exton
Emily Gray: Shelter for Allegra
Alexa Gregory: Backdraft
Deanndra Hall: Shelter for Sharla
Jenna Harte: Dead But Not Forgotten
India Kells: Shadow Killer
Amber Kuhlman: Protecting Paisley
Reina Torres: Justice for Sloane
Aubree Valentine, Justice for Danielle
Maddie Wade: Finding English
Laine Vess: Justice for Lauren

Tarpley VFD Series
Silver James, Fighting for Elena
Deanndra Hall, Fighting for Carly
Haven Rose, Fighting for Calliope
MJ Nightingale, Fighting for Jemma
TL Reeve, Fighting for Brittney
Nicole Flockton, Fighting for Nadia

As you know, this book included at least one character from Susan Stoker's books. To check out more, see below.

SEAL Team Hawaii Series
Finding Elodie
Finding Lexie
Finding Kenna
Finding Monica
Finding Carly (Oct 2022)
Finding Ashlyn (Feb 2023)
Finding Jodelle (July 2023)

Eagle Point Search & Rescue
Searching for Lilly
Searching for Elsie
Searching for Bristol (Nov 2022)
Searching for Caryn (April 2023)
Searching for Finley (TBA)
Searching for Heather (TBA)
Searching for Khloe (TBA)

The Refuge Series
Deserving Alaska
Deserving Henley (Jan 2023)
Deserving Reese (May 2023)
Deserving Cora (TBA)
Deserving Lara (TBA)
Deserving Maisy (TBA)
Deserving Ryleigh (TBA)

Delta Team Two Series
Shielding Gillian
Shielding Kinley

Shielding Aspen
Shielding Jayme (novella)
Shielding Riley
Shielding Devyn
Shielding Ember
Shielding Sierra

SEAL of Protection: Legacy Series

Securing Caite (FREE!)
Securing Brenae (novella)
Securing Sidney
Securing Piper
Securing Zoey
Securing Avery
Securing Kalee
Securing Jane

Delta Force Heroes Series

Rescuing Rayne (FREE!)
Rescuing Aimee (novella)
Rescuing Emily
Rescuing Harley
Marrying Emily (novella)
Rescuing Kassie
Rescuing Bryn
Rescuing Casey
Rescuing Sadie (novella)
Rescuing Wendy
Rescuing Mary
Rescuing Macie (novella)
Rescuing Annie

Badge of Honor: Texas Heroes Series

Justice for Mackenzie (FREE!)

Justice for Mickie
Justice for Corrie
Justice for Laine (novella)
Shelter for Elizabeth
Justice for Boone
Shelter for Adeline
Shelter for Sophie
Justice for Erin
Justice for Milena
Shelter for Blythe
Justice for Hope
Shelter for Quinn
Shelter for Koren
Shelter for Penelope

SEAL of Protection Series

Protecting Caroline (FREE!)
Protecting Alabama
Protecting Fiona
Marrying Caroline (novella)
Protecting Summer
Protecting Cheyenne
Protecting Jessyka
Protecting Julie (novella)
Protecting Melody
Protecting the Future
Protecting Kiera (novella)
Protecting Alabama's Kids (novella)
Protecting Dakota

New York Times, USA Today and *Wall Street Journal* Bestselling Author Susan Stoker has a heart as big as the state of Tennessee where she lives, but this all American girl has also spent the last fourteen years living in Missouri, California,

Colorado, Indiana, and Texas. She's married to a retired Army man who now gets to follow *her* around the country.

www.stokeraces.com
www.AcesPress.com
susan@stokeraces.com

Made in the USA
Coppell, TX
06 October 2022